Anthony Gilbert and The

⟩⟩⟩ This title is part of The Murder Room, our series dedicated to making available out-of-print or hard-to-find titles by classic crime writers.

Crime fiction has always held up a mirror to society. The Victorians were fascinated by sensational murder and the emerging science of detection; now we are obsessed with the forensic detail of violent death. And no other genre has so captivated and enthralled readers.

Vast troves of classic crime writing have for a long time been unavailable to all but the most dedicated frequenters of second-hand bookshops. The advent of digital publishing means that we are now able to bring you the backlists of a huge range of titles by classic and contemporary crime writers, some of which have been out of print for decades.

From the genteel amateur private eyes of the Golden Age and the femmes fatales of pulp fiction, to the morally ambiguous hard-boiled detectives of mid twentieth-century America and their descendants who walk our twenty-first century streets, The Murder Room has it all. **⟩⟩⟩**

The Murder Room
Where Criminal Minds Meet

themurderroom.com

Anthony Gilbert (1899–1973)

Anthony Gilbert was the pen name of Lucy Beatrice Malleson. Born in London, she spent all her life there, and her affection for the city is clear from the strong sense of character and place in evidence in her work. She published 69 crime novels, 51 of which featured her best known character, Arthur Crook, a vulgar London lawyer totally (and deliberately) unlike the aristocratic detectives, such as Lord Peter Wimsey, who dominated the mystery field at the time. She also wrote more than 25 radio plays, which were broadcast in Great Britain and overseas. Her thriller *The Woman in Red* (1941) was broadcast in the United States by CBS and made into a film in 1945 under the title *My Name is Julia Ross*. She was an early member of the British Detection Club, which, along with Dorothy L. Sayers, she prevented from disintegrating during World War II. Malleson published her autobiography, *Three-a-Penny*, in 1940, and wrote numerous short stories, which were published in several anthologies and in such periodicals as *Ellery Queen's Mystery Magazine* and *The Saint*. The short story 'You Can't Hang Twice' received a Queens award in 1946. She never married, and evidence of her feminism is elegantly expressed in much of her work.

By Anthony Gilbert

A Spy for Mr Crook

Anthony Gilbert

An Orion book

Copyright © Lucy Beatrice Malleson 1944

The right of Lucy Beatrice Malleson to be identified as the author of this work has been asserted in accordance with the Copyright, Designs and Patents Act 1988.

This edition published by
The Orion Publishing Group Ltd
Orion House
5 Upper St Martin's Lane
London WC2H 9EA

An Hachette UK company
A CIP catalogue record for this book is available from the British Library

ISBN 978 1 4719 0978 8

www.orionbooks.co.uk

Chapter I

THE LOBBY of the House of Commons was very full on the momentous afternoon that Miss Sarah Bennett, a composed and amused spinster, torn from her happy obscurity by an energetic and enterprising Minister of Labor, came from the Temporary Pass Office, up the stairs, through a corridor lined with effigies of the great. Through a door at the end, smartly pulled open by a policeman tugging on what looked like a giant's dressing-gown cord, she walked into a babel of humanity that halted her for a moment until, at a word from the friendly policeman on the door, she made her way to the policeman on the barrier, who gave her a green card to fill in.

"Mr. Stout? He's in the Chamber," said the policeman. "Just sit down a minute."

Miss Bennett sat on a green leather seat in the shadow of yet another effigy of England's greatness and surveyed the lively scene.

In one corner a deputation from the Ancient Company of Galoche Makers were so intent on trying out on one another the argument with which, in due course, they would smite the representative of the Rubber Control they had come to interview, hip and thigh, that they didn't even notice a quiet little man who stole up on rubber-soled shoes and walked round the compact vociferous body. He was like the last piglet of a litter, thought the unpoetic Miss Bennett, trying to butt his way in towards the dinner-pail. After a minute or so, the ranks remaining serried, the newcomer crept away again, and probably only the watcher realized that this was the unhappy official the deputation had come to tear to shreds.

A second deputation occupied another corner, from the Save The Spinsters Society this time, and these had, with the terrible singleness of purpose that makes the female so much more deadly than the male, cornered their Member, and were standing round him in a double semicircle, like a cordon of cows threatening a very frightened bull. You could see he wasn't sure what they mightn't do to him.

A conscientious Town Member was, inevitably, conducting a party of American officers round the House, under the impression that this is the kind of entertainment that American officers enjoy.

"But say," Miss Bennett heard one of them remark, "if you use the Lords' Chamber, how about the Lords?"

"They—er—meet in the Robing Room," explained the Member, who had been going to sweep his guests through the door with the dressing-gown cord attached and point out the exact place where the Speaker's Chair used to stand, and where impeachment trials used to be held.

The American nodded. "Peers not going so strong," he suggested. His voice said that all these old monuments were bound to crumble sooner or later because that's Nature's way.

When the party had disappeared Miss Bennett entertained herself watching constituents waiting for Members and Members waiting for constituents, and Members just being Members; they all looked so much alike she thought it was pretty clever of the policemen to know which were Members of Parliament and which just those common chaps, the electorate.

She was just reflecting that a good many M.P.'s must also be electors in their time and season, since not every Member resides in his own constituency, when the door was pulled open again, and a plump rather common-looking man in a regrettable brown suit, with a brown billycock apparently balanced on thick red eyebrows over eyes the color of a dog-fox, came swinging in. The policeman on the door appeared to know him. He stopped him and said a word. The new-comer nodded.

"I'll wait," he said and came to sit beside Miss Bennett.

They made a strange contrast. He looked, she thought, like a bookie's tout, and couldn't imagine why, for one moment, she had been reminded of Mr. Churchill. They weren't remotely alike.

Sarah was wearing her new 18-coupon gray pinstripe suit with a link button, a yellow blouse, one of those perfectly plain hats, gray with a yellow corded ribbon, that look as though they have been run up in about five minutes and ought to cost twelve shillings, eleven pence but for which in actual fact she had paid (with purchase tax) four pounds and fourpence. She wore tan stockings—silk, noticed Mr. Crook, who made a habit of never overlooking details—tan shoes, while on her knee lay a pair of tan leather gauntlets, the soft kind that wrinkle at the wrist, and a square brown leather bag that was obviously cleaned with a good quality boot polish every day of its life.

"She's come to give some poor devil hell," thought Mr. Crook sympathetically. "Less than the dust beneath her chariot wheel, that's what she thinks of them."

She looked like someone who has bought an expensive seat for a show and is now tranquilly getting her money's worth. And after all, Mr. Crook told himself honestly, show was about the word. After a minute he leaned towards her, saying confidentially, "You'd think they'd gone dredging under flat stones and robbing graveyards to find some of these. I bet you never saw anything like this crowd in your life before."

"You'd be wrong," said Sarah drily. "When I went to register with my age group I found the room packed with women and, believe me or not, I thought I'd got into a deputation for the Old Age Pension by mistake."

"Oh, I believe you," said Crook. "Every lady that's had to register with an age-group—over thirty, that is—has felt the same. Indignant they were, which is ridic'lous. Why, you should have gone home thanking your lucky stars you could put up a better show than the rest."

"Oh, I did," agreed Miss Bennett seriously, and her voice said it took something to make her feel thankful.

Crook saw with pleasure and a little surprise that she wasn't in the least put out by his remark. As indeed she was not. While not going so far as to believe that every creature of God is good,

3

she at least believed most of them are interesting, if only as curiosities, and seldom regretted a new experience.

"First offense?" continued Crook affably.

"First . . .?" For a moment even Miss Bennett was baffled. Then she understood. "Oh, I see what you mean. No, I've never been here before, though I daresay that presently I shall know this place as well as my home."

"Is it kind? Is it true? Is it necessary?" mourned Mr. Crook. "Even M.P.'s don't generally keep you that long."

"You don't understand," Sarah assured him. "I'm here professionally."

Crook cocked a suspicious eyebrow. "You mean, you're one of Nature's reformers?" He'd guessed it from the first.

"Nothing of the kind," returned Miss Bennett crisply. "One of Mr. Bevin's bloody sacrifices."

Crook grinned. "Smoked you out, did they? And you thought you'd get your own back by coming to work for one of the rats? Smart work."

Miss Bennett nodded towards the spinsters who were moving up to their Member with such dogged ferocity that presently they'd sweep over him like a wave and leave him flattened as a piece of seaweed when eventually they retreated.

"We've got a very enterprising Government," she said. "Ten years ago, when I might have been glad of a job, no one would have paid me three pounds a week, but now, just because I've had to register, they can find any number of holes to push me into. And all those women there are in the same boat. They could all get jobs tomorrow."

"Everything comes to him who waits," approved Crook, "even Home Secretaries." He stood up and went to meet a man who looked like a captive eagle, who had just entered the lobby from the Lords. Miss Bennett recognized him at once from his photographs.

"Mr. Crook?" said the Home Secretary, who, being a cut above the ordinary Member, didn't have to pretend to look pleased at the sight of a visitor. Besides, Crook wasn't a constituent of his.

"That chap, Jedburgh," began Mr. Crook.

"I've informed you already, I don't feel this is a case in which I can usefully intervene at the present time," said the Home Secretary stubbornly.

"It won't be much use intervenin' after Tuesday week, seeing the poor fellow's to be hanged that morning," Crook pointed out.

"It's impossible to consider reopening the case unless you can persuade me you have fresh evidence to offer."

"Evidence?" Mr. Crook looked like the dog in the fairy-tale who had eyes like mill wheels. "If that's all you want, that's easy."

"Evidence that will stand the test," added the Home Secretary in a stern voice. "The demands of justice. . . ."

"See here," implored Mr. Crook. "It ain't my job to look after justice. That's your pigeon. Mine's to get this chap off if I can. That's what he's paying me for. And if evidence is what you want and if evidence will save him, then I've got to have that evidence, if I have to sit up half the night manufacturing it. It's not a matter of choice, it's a matter of duty."

Sarah watched them fascinated. She couldn't help thinking it was a pity Mr. Crook wasn't the Member she had come to see. A man like that would give a secretary scope.

"You'd better get ready to make history by granting a free pardon in spite of all His Majesty's snuffy old gentlemen," Mr. Crook announced to the lobby at large. Even the Ancient Order of Galoche Makers stopped telling one another that these officials never have any sense of time and don't understand about other chaps being busy, to listen to him. "Because, as sure as my name's Arthur Crook of London Town, he ain't going to swing."

Tipping his brown bowler aggressively, he strode out of the lobby. The Home Secretary stared after him. So did Miss Bennett. So did the policeman on the barrier. In fact, general interest was so centered on him that Mr. Stout came through and turned towards the tea-room without anyone noticing him.

2.

Mr. Allen Wilkinson Stout, the Member for the Malvoison Division of Kent, was having tea with the Honorable Member for South Mould. Mr. Stout was a fine figure of a man, with a grand black mustache and a good obstinate jaw and hair as black as doom and a chin so long his mouth seemed to come halfway up his face. It was said of him by the Speaker that his family motto was "I was ever a fighter so one fight more . . ." and the Speaker was in a position to know.

They had been debating the question of War Pensions and already he had had a brush or two with the Minister of War Claims. Mr. Penberthy did his best to calm him down, but Mr. Stout was in no mood to be calmed.

"Don't be so damned tactful, Bill," he said. "This righteous indignation is good for my liver. As for Wilbur, I'd like him to live on a 100 per cent disability pension for six months and then come into the House and tell us it's adequate."

"I always forget what Party you belong to," murmured Mr. Penberthy, ordering tea and whatever-there-was.

"Independent," said Mr. Stout royally. "And don't ask me if I agree with X and Y and Z because I don't. I'm independent of the whole House of Commons."

"That" said the Honorable Member for South Mould soothingly, "makes the position perfectly clear." The tea arrived and he began to pour it out. The whatever-there-was looked like Ministry of Food experiments. "Do you remember," he continued wistfully, "the chocolate cake we used to get here before tht war?"

"Do you know," Mr. Stout countered in homesick tones, "there were things called oranges once? You had 'em in a salad with duck. Round things they were, like kid's balls. Well, anyway, you remember balls don't you, Bill? Before the Japs collared ninety per cent of the world's rubber supply you could buy them at Woolworth's. Do you know," his voice was reverent, "before the war even dogs had them—solid rubber with DOG printed on them?"

"Come, come," said Bill Penberthy, "you're thinking of drinking-bowls."

"It comes to the same thing," said Mr. Stout pessimistically. "They all belonged to the Golden Age that everyone's resolved shall never return." He poured himself out another cup of tea and announced that he couldn't stop as he was interviewing a prospective secretary. "The Ministry of Labor's taken mine," he added gloomily. "She'd committeed a crime, you see—at least her mother did."

"And the P.S. is afaid she'll follow in her mother's footsteps and perhaps go for you with a carving knife? I call that damned thoughtful of him. He doesn't give a damn if anyone knifes me."

"She got married two years too late," explained Mr. Stout rather obscurely. "So, of course, the girl was born two years too late. So Hugh's raked her in for the A.T.S. I went to see him about it, but he was hard as his own head and I can't say fairer than that. An older woman'll do for you, he told me. Where do I find one? I asked him, because you know as well as I do, Bill, that the Government collars the lot by *force majeure*. Not," he added recklessly, "because it really needs them, but one or two might slip through the net and go on doing something useful if he didn't have his eye on them. There's a very good O.A.P. club in my constituency, I told him. Perhaps you think I could find one there. Or, of course, there's the morgue."

"What did he say to that?" enquired Mr. Penberthy.

"That we all have to put up with substitutes in a war, margarine instead of butter, and dehydrated spinach instead of caviare, so surely I could put up with a corpse just for the duration."

Mr. Penberthy observed that a lot of the authorities were setting them a damn good example. Mr. Stout, however, was following up his own thoughts.

"You have to hand it to Hugh—he's solving the problem of the surplus women all right. Why, even the two glamour girls behind the bar in my special pub. are both over seventy, and one of them's got a wooden leg."

"Did she tell you?" enquired Mr. Penberthy in reverent tones. Women never told him things like that.

"Of course she told me," said Mr. Stout. "Aren't I her Member? She thought if I made representations in the right quarter I might get her a new one. She doesn't like the one she's got. Peeling or something."

"Which is the Ministry for peg-legs?" asked Bill. "Like Rosa Dartle, I only ask for information."

"There you are!" cried Mr. Stout in a voice that rang through the Members' tea-room like a tocsin. "My secretary would have known. The new one won't. I shall be expected to find out and tell her. It's ridiculous."

"I should think the Ministry of Health," speculated Bill.

Mr. Stout vetoed that. "Much too simple. You know Government Departments never work that way. If you want to get a man out of the Army, you can't just write to the War Office. He has to apply to his C.O., and show that he's got a vacancy waiting for him, scheduled under the Essential Works Act, and his prospective employers have got to put in for him to the appropriate Department, if they know which it is, and if they do they're a damn sight cleverer than I am, and the Ministry concerned approaches the War Office and by that time the fellow's probably been drafted overseas or written to his M.P. . . ."

"I have been in the House three years myself," Mr. Penberthy pointed out.

"So you see it's not likely to be the Ministry of Health. That would be too obvious. No, no, everything will depend on how she lost the leg. If she was a stewardess and got involved in a shipwreck, I suppose it would be the Admiralty. . . ." He drank some more tea. "And if she was a V.A.D. at Waterloo it would be the War Office," he wound up irrepressibly.

"Not Waterloo," objected Mr. Penberthy. "The War Office wasn't functioning in those days."

"No?" said Mr. Stout. "Then all I can say is we're a damn conservative country. Well, then, it's probably the Ministry of Supply."

"If it's a wooden leg," said Bill, "how about the Forestry Commission?"

"They're monopolized by M.A.P., aren't they? No, no, more likely to be Works and Planning. Works, you see."

"Is pulling beer-handles work within the meaning of the Act? What other Departments are there? I suppose it couldn't be the P.M.G.—unless her husband was a postman."

"She's not married," said Mr. Stout. "Oh, well, I must go and see my old girl. I saw one last night—but she couldn't do shorthand."

"Even if they can it doesn't make much difference, because they probably don't read it back—not what you thought you said anyhow—and if you argue with them, they say, 'Well, there's the shorthand outline,' knowing dam' well you won't know if it's right or wrong."

"This one," continued Mr. Stout musingly, "had always wanted to go into Parliament, but there was something wrong with her teeth."

"Does she suppose you go round biting fellow-Members?" demanded a mystified Mr. Penberthy.

"Oh, no," said Mr. Stout. "At least, I don't suppose so. She was waiting for them to grow or something. She had something wrong with her feet, too."

"She didn't write shorthand with them, did she? If so, she'd better go on the B.B.C. and tell the world how it's done."

At this juncture some intrusive official came up to enquire whether the two gentlemen were attending the Sub-Committee in Room 38 to discuss the Minister of Health's new scheme for Pig Insurance.

Mr. Penberthy, who didn't mind trying anything once, said he'd come, but Mr. Stout said hurriedly—and inaccurately—he knew nothing about pigs and that he must go and see his old girl.

The House rose early that day and policemen were shouting "Who goes home?" all over the lobby, and putting their heads into the library and the Plan Room and anywhere else where members might be congregating to warn them that the House was "up." Sarah hoped this meant Mr. Stout wouldn't be long.

She had some time ago ceased to be entertained by the spectacle of Members walking in and out of swing doors, bursting in and out of telephone booths, creeping or bouncing into the Post Office, dictating letters round the pedestals of statues, or just standing about and talking to themselves, presumably because they liked to hear a clever chap talk and a clever chap reply. When Mr. Stout appeared, not from the Chamber, but from the corridor leading to the tea-room, she saw a gleam of relief on the face of the policeman on the door and realized that her moment had come.

"I'm afraid I've kept you waiting," apologized Mr. Stout politely, his heart full of misgiving. "The fact is we've been having a very intricate debate—rights and privileges of Government Departments—I came away in the middle of it as it was," he added, feeling it was absurd he should have to make all these explanations and she accept them like a lady patroness taking a bunch of flowers from a child at a charity show.

"What exactly was it this time?" asked Miss Bennett kindly. He thought she had probably been a trained child's nurse when she was younger—or it might have been performing seals. Either way she'd be sure to feel at home in the House of Commons.

Mr. Stout drew a deep breath. "Post-war planning," he said. Well, in a way it was true. The Peace would certainly be on before poor old Maisie got her new pin. Why, you had to get priority even to build a fence these days, let alone make a leg, and by the time that had passed through the various Departments the country would probably be thinking about its next war—and certainly Maisie would have passed into that sphere where, it is understood, wooden pins will be redundant.

"Damn!" said Mr. Stout aloud. "One even thinks in official terms. Can you do shorthand?"

Miss Bennett said she could.

Mr. Stout explained the difficulty as viewed by Mr. Penberthy and himself.

"And he's right," he said, "half the time it isn't what you've said."

"Perhaps your friend's secretary had a reforming tendency," suggested Sarah.

10

"She hadn't got a husband, that was the trouble," was Mr. Stout's startling reply. "Wives work off their good intentions at home; spinsters take it out of their employers, most of whom are married anyhow, so they get a double dose. By the way, I ought to warn you this isn't a reserved occupation. They called up my last. . . ."

"How old was she?" enquired Miss Bennett uncompromisingly.

"Twenty-three. But. . . ."

"You'll find it'll be reserved to me," Sarah assured him. "I'm forty-two and proud of it. Thousands of women will never achieve as much. It seems to me that to have survived the Great War, the World Depression and the London Blitz for forty-two years and still not be a mental or physical paralytic is something to be proud of."

"Yes," said Mr. Stout helplessly, thinking with actual longing of the lady who didn't write shorthand with her feet. Miss Bennett, for all her prim appearance, made him feel as though he'd got into the Zoo at feeding-time when all the cage doors were open and the keepers were late.

"Are you free now?" he enquired.

"Perfectly free," said Sarah.

"You're sure your present employer. . . ."

"I haven't a present employer. I'm a conscript."

Mr. Stout was having a lot of shocks this afternoon. He remembered the last war in which he had played the usual inconspicuous part of the ordinary man who enlisted in 1914 and came out at the Armistice. He didn't get any medals, of course. Ordinary people hardly ever do. He remembered how they'd viewed conscripts then. Bloody gentlemen, they'd said, he and his friends, seeing the new drafts come out towards the end of 1917. Some of them had minded, but if you said that to Miss Bennett she wouldn't mind. She wouldn't give a damn what anyone thought of her. Really, he reflected, seeing how much braver women are than men it's staggering they don't send them into the front line. There were women he knew who'd actually been thrilled by the bombing of London. He didn't know any men who had. Sensitive sex my Aunt Fanny, he thought.

"Before the war I was a poster artist," Miss Bennett explained. "You've probably seen my work in tube stations."

"You ought to be in the camouflage department of the M.O.I.," suggested Mr. Stout.

"I thought of that, too, but the M.O.I. decided it would be even better camouflage if I became a filing clerk at the War Office."

Mr. Stout gave that up. "Have you any political views?" he asked, still seeking like a harried fox for some earth in which to go to ground.

"My sympathies are with the conservatives," said Sarah. "The other parties can talk of the beauty of labor, but only conservatives can afford the even greater beauty of bone-idleness when the mood takes them."

Mr. Stout saw a loophole and leaped for it. "I ought to warn you I work extremely hard," he said.

"Oh, I knew you weren't a conservative," Miss Bennett assured him.

Mr. Stout felt absurdly pleased. It was nice to think that anyone knew enough about him to know that.

"You—er—had heard of me then?"

"I looked you up in Dod's Parliamentary Guide," explained his companion. "Well, naturally I wanted to know something about you. . . ."

"Did you"—Mr. Stout's tone was elaborately courteous—"think I might be engaged in the white slave traffic?"

"I didn't suppose Dod would tell me if you were. And in any case," the lady matched courtesy for courtesy, "I take it I'm only doing your political work."

Mr. Stout let that pass. He was getting the worst of it anyway. Besides, he had just thought of something he had always wanted to know.

"Do they," he enquired, "ask you very obscene questions at the Ministry of Labor?"

"Nothing the Government is responsible for is obscene," returned Miss Bennett firmly. "They simply take a paternal interest in you and your affairs. For instance, they asked me who paid the rent of my flat."

"Did you tell them?" asked Mr. Stout, secretly filled with admiration for any official who had dared ask the formidable Miss Bennett so searching a question.

"Unfortunately, I did. I said I paid it myself. If I'd had the wit to say that a succession of gentlemen paid it for me they wouldn't have touched me with a barge-pole. It's practically the only reserved occupation left for single women," she added.

"I didn't know that," murmured Mr. Stout, wondering how it is that in practical matters secretaries nearly always seem to be better informed than Members.

"Nor did I, at the time. I supposed the Government wanted to make sure I was sufficiently Galahad-minded to be worthy of a job at one of their Ministries."

Mr. Stout supposed—but not aloud—that they'd decided she wasn't to be so regarded. He envied Government Departments who know all the answers; he'd already realized that if Miss Bennett made up her mind to come to him come she would.

"You didn't get a Government job," he murmured wistfully.

"I said I couldn't live on the pay of a T.G.S., and they said that didn't matter because I could do my own work in my spare time."

"So that in a way you'd be better off for being called up. Do you know, there are times when I think we deserve to win this war. So much strategy in the country that they can afford to pour it out like wine at the Ministry of Labor. How about sleep? Did they mention that?"

"I did, but they said we must all be prepared to make sacrifices in war-time for our fighting men."

"One of the things that might have been more happily put," agreed Mr. Stout, his mercurial point of view changing again. One touch of nature and so forth, and he'd had brushes with the Ministry of Labor himself. "Tell me one more thing. If you had to get a replacement of a wooden leg for a constituent, which Ministry would you approach?"

"Assuming you wanted her to get the leg, I should leave the Ministries out of it and get in touch with her Approved Society," Sarah told him.

"What's that?" For Mr. Stout had taken a little blue card out of his pocket and was writing on it.

"Card of admission to the Plan Room. That's where Members' secretaries work. I'll show you on your way out. But first of all come and have a drink."

Sarah decided a few minutes later she had done well. Mr. Stout clearly knew something about some of the things that matter.

Chapter II

THE PLAN ROOM in the House of Commons opens off Westminster Hall, down eight stairs and through a door that promises more than the room performs. Since the House was damaged by blitz, M.P.'s secretaries are allowed as a favor to work there. The room is long and has a number of small, romantic-looking windows looking out onto some grass. It is not, however, very easy to see the grass because there is a good deal of black-out down there, also owing to the blitz, and in any case the windows are never opened. Those who work under them complain bitterly if they are, with the result that the room cannot be ventilated and by four o'clock is like the tortoise house on Bank Holiday. There are always half a dozen typewriters clicking for dear life and a telephone that rings all day. Anything from four to fourteen Members are generally dictating against the background of this din, and their secretaries are women of such caliber that most of the time they contrive to dish up something remarkably like the original speech of the parliamentarians. The furniture of the room consists of lockers, not available to the secretaries, long trestle tables and leather-seated chairs that are just too low for the typists to use them with any comfort. There are also a good many waste-paper baskets, on the whole scorned by the Members who prefer the floor, of the kind that make runs in war-time stockings.

Sarah sat at the end of one of the long tables, on one of the only two chairs high enough to be conveniently used, and split open Mr. Stout's morning mail. The life of a Member's secretary is not entirely without its entertaining side. The post this morning was rather like a pre-war Woolworth counter. You might find anything there.

Regrets, of course, were predominant. The War Office regretted it couldn't grant a compassionate posting; the Minister of Pensions regretted he couldn't agree that a pension was due to the widow of one Tom Robinson, since the said man had been on leave when his fatal accident occurred; the Ministry of Food regretted that it couldn't as yet divulge its autumn savoy program (for security reasons). Also, presumably for security reasons, it didn't explain why knowledge of this program should materially help the Germans to win the war, but of course idle talk costs lives and idle letter-writing possibly even more.

When the official letters had been docketed Sarah dealt with what she called the intercessions. There is no limit to the subjects on which enthusiastic constituents will address their Member. They cover income tax relief, thieving neighbors who pick your best flowers while you're rolling bandages at the Red Cross, the inadequacy of fish, milk, cheese, cake and biscuit supplies; the infamy of the Rent Restrictions Act. . . . This morning a doggy woman wanted to know what the authorities intended to do about the supply of meat for dogs (God's creatures as much as we, who do not deserve to suffer for the sins of men), a clergyman was seriously perturbed about the waste of bread crumbs and bacon rinds on sparrows and gulls (in view, Sir, of the widespread starvation in Europe), a fond mother asked if her husband could be brought back from North Africa (because Sonny Boy does so want a little sister).

She was busily typing replies to all the letters Mr. Stout wouldn't want to answer himself when he burst in like a cyclone. Several people clutched their letters as in an earlier age they'd have clutched their hats. Miss Bennett didn't mind the noise. She (fashionably) regretted the passing of the age of great men, big stalwart creatures with solid faces and forthright manners who couldn't go in and out unnoticed; this generation of men with neat features and mealy-mouthed speech made her wish she had been born a century earlier. She mightn't have been Miss Bennett then; she'd have found some man of her own size to wed.

"Anything special this morning?" demanded Allen Wilkinson Stout, attacking his letters like a terrier enlarging a rabbit-hole.

"One personal letter," said Miss Bennett handing it over, "one grateful acknowledgment from Mrs. Green for getting her a War Service Grant and saying you may use this in any way you please—two or three people writing to you as a last resort. . . ."

"If humility is the rock foundation of the virtues, then Members of Parliament stand a chance of getting pretty high hereafter," remarked Mr. Stout, disemboweling his mail. "The motto of constituents seems to be, try everyone else and if they all fail take a million-to-one shot and tackle your M.P. By the way," he slit the envelope of the personal letter, "I see the Home Secretary's given that fellow, Jedburgh, a pardon on new evidence. Bit of a shock, that."

"Not to me," Sarah was surprised to hear herself say. For until this minute she had not known she had this confidence in Mr. Crook.

"Don't overdo it, Miss Bennett," Mr. Stout advised her. "I can believe a lot but not that you thought Pertwee would reprieve that fellow. Why, all the evidence was dead against him."

"Not the new evidence," explained Miss Bennett, "the evidence Mr. Crook sat up all night manufacturing."

"Crook?"

Sarah explained.

"Did you get his telephone number?" demanded Mr. Stout. "My God, what sort of a secretary are you? Why, a chap like that might be invaluable. If you could convince me that there's a fellow living who could prove you hadn't committed a murder you knew you had—then, put a hatchet in my hand and I'll create history in the House of Common this day."

"I wasn't your secretary then," said Sarah equably.

"But you meant to be, or you wouldn't have bothered to come to the House. Oh, Lord, here's Bunch."

A tall fair young man crossed the floor of the Plan Room looking like the understudy for the Angel Gabriel in a morality play, and said there was going to be a meeting of the All England Democrats in one of the Committee Rooms that afternoon and was Mr. Stout coming. Mr. Stout thought not. The Angel Gabriel said they needed support; though the war was more than four years old there were still people who believed in class distinctions. Mr. Stout said Yes, he did, and he was sure he wasn't in the Democrats' class. Bunch, his real name was Smythe and he was an Honorable, said the Democrats embraced all classes. . . .

"Nothing too high, nothing too low," scowled Mr. Stout. "Well, but I'm more particular. Anyone," he added as the young man faded away with an offended expression, "would know that Bunch was a Duke's son. He wears Burke's peerage like his dress. No commoner would dare be so democratic." He took up another letter. "Hell!" he said. "Wilbur's turned down Mrs. Robinson for a pension."

"Why not?" asked Miss Bennett cordially.

"Why not? Because I knew Tom Robinson. He was a damn good fellow and it's an infernal shame his wife shouldn't have a pension."

"He was on compassionate leave when he was killed. It was a road accident. . . ."

"Oh, was it?" snorted Mr. Stout. "How do they know? They found Tom unconscious by the side of the road with his motorcycle in the ditch and he died before he could speak. Isn't that just as likely to be murder as accident?"

"What motive?" asked Sarah, who had been brought up by a logical grandmother.

"That's for the authorities to find out. But I knew Tom. His father was my father's gamekeeper. He wasn't a bit the sort of chap that gets himself run down by some drunken civilian in a war, with our man-power position what it is at the moment. No, there's more in this than meets the eye, and its a dam' shame of Wilbur. . . ."

"It's no use blaming the Minister," said Sarah drily. "He didn't know Tom Robinson. If you want him to be sympathetic you must rouse his interest. I'm not surprised so many pension cases get turned down; what does surprise me is that any of them get through. How can you expect the Minister to take an interest when they're hardly so much as names to him, and the Members do nothing to give them individuality?"

"The personal touch?" suggested Mr. Stout.

"If you can fire his imagination, make him see himself in the other man's place. . . ."

"That's asking too much," protested Mr. Stout. "Remember, these are chaps who have to earn their own living. You can't ask a Minister to try and see himself through their eyes."

"Then appeal to his self-interest," suggested Sarah unscrupulously. "Point out that if he continues to refuse to allot pensions with this routine monotony he can't hope to get re-elected after the war."

"Will they have a Minister of Pensions after the war?"

"Of course they will. Someone's got to reject claims, and what right has he to throw himself on the rates of a more or less bankrupt country, which is what it will come to if he's not more tactful? Someone ought to point that out to him. . . ."

"I don't suppose being Pensions Minister leaves him any time for reading his own letters," said Mr. Stout. "But I don't mind having a shot since you're so keen. After all, Maggie Robinson ought to have a pension."

"And it's up to you to make the Minister understand that," added Sarah. "At least, you can write him something that will stand out of the ordinary ruck of letters."

Mr. Stout sighed gustily. "You're so ambitious," he complained. "By that sin fell the angels." He put out his hand and took a bit of paper.

"Not that one," said Sarah kindly, taking it away from him as a watchful nurse stops a baby putting the wrong toy into its mouth. "That's one of the letters you're going to sign." She gave him a packet of notices that had just arrived from the Ministry of Public Welfare. This Ministry really does want to keep Members informed of the little day-to-day incidents that will keep up public morale. Encouragement is its watch-word, and it goes in for snappy headlines. Championship Results, it says, and then in small tidy print, "In the epic fight between Thrift and Squanderbug last week, Thrift won a closely-

19

matched tussle on points." The Ministry hopes—in print—that Ministers and parliamentarians generally make use of its broadsheets. Ministers certainly do. So do secretaries. Scrap paper is short just now. Mr. Stout, having accepted the material offered him, took out a bitten red pencil and began to cogitate. After a minute he looked up and said, "Have you got my pension file handy?" Sarah obligingly produced it. Mr. Stout abandoned himself to mathematical calculations. He rustled a lot of papers, dropped several cases on the floor, put down some figures, did some adding and subtracting, waited till Miss Bennett had succeeded in contacting the Parliamentary Secretary's secretary at the Ministry of Plain Speaking, and said, "Take this down, will you, and we'll see what it looks like when it's done."

His thick brows drew together; his mustache bristled; he looked the sort of man female Victorian audiences would have died to satisfy.

"I think I'll write him an informal letter, nothing official," he announced. "Something he can keep off the record if he likes."

"You're going to write it by hand?" said Sarah, but without much hope.

"Oh, no," said Mr. Stout. "You know what Ministers are—he's a busy man—and my handwriting's been described as very good when you're used to it. But naturally I've always had my letters typewritten, so he hasn't had a chance of getting used to it."

"I see," said Sarah.

Mr. Stout got down to it.

" 'My dear Wilbur,' I'll write that in, Miss Bennett. (Members generally do this when writing to Ministers; it gives the impression of being on terms of intimacy with the great.) 'This is a friendly letter.' New paragraph.

" 'I am concerned at the present situation as regards Pensions. I see that out of the last forty cases I have submitted to you only two havt received favorable consideration. That, Wilbur, I consider a defeatist total. I am not, of course, questioning the rightness of your judgment. Ministers, par excellence, are always right. The point I wish to make is this. Are there not occasions when it is better for public morale in general for the Minister to have the courage—to say nothing of the tact—to be wrong? If this point has not occurred to you I do suggest that it may conceivably be better from time to time to be wrong and make a number of people happy than be right and deprive them of hope.' New paragraph.

" 'With special reference to my constituent, Tom Robinson. Fill in the military identification, Miss Bennett.' In rejecting his widow's pension claim you raise two points, both of which I intend to contest. You say, first, that my constituent is not entled to a widow's service pension because her husband was on compassionate leave at the time of his death; and secondly, you rtgret your decision, which you state is based on statutory regulations, which cannot be altered. I will take these points in order.' New paragraph.

" 'One. Can you offer any proof that Robinson was not on active service on the night of his death? Compasisonate leave—I quote from a letter received this morning from a letter from the Under-Secretary to the War Department—is not lightly given during the present emergency. Very special circumstances must be demonstrated. These circumstances are entirely absent in Robinson's case. It has never been suggested that he might be more useful in his civilian capacity and no appeal was ever made by any other Ministry to the Air Ministry for his temporary release. Nor would his domestic circumstances warrant any such compassionate leave.' You'd better mark that paragraph (a) Miss Bennett. Then a new sub-paragraph inset." (Mr. Stout was a monster for details.)

" '(b) There is another point which appears to have escaped your notice. At the time of his death Tom Robinson was riding a motor-cycle.' Underline motorcycle, will you? I want to draw Wilbur's attention to it. 'Motor-cycles, as you may know, are run on petrol. Petrol is one of the weapons of war. It is doled out as miserly,' " Mr. Stout paused. "Miserly," he repeated in tentative tones, "miserly. . . ." He looked at Sarah.

"I don't think so," said Sarah.

"Start again from war," ordered Mr. Stout. " 'Under the

impartial management of the Secretary of State for Motor Spirit, petrol supplies are most vigorously controlled. Even Members of Parliament cannot get all they need; there is literally no surplus at all for joy-riding. And yet when he was run down by an anonymous car Tom Robinson was on a motor-cycle. That, Wilbur, strikes me as extremely suggestive, and I should be glad if your Department would make further investigations.' Fullstop. New paragraph.

" 'Two. You say your decisions are governed by statutory regulations that cannot be altered. Here again I see traces of the defeatist spirit. I am no Cabinet Minister, and from what I have seen of Cabinet Ministers I am never likely to qualify for such exalted office. I am only a poor, benighted M.P. I live'— inset, Miss Bennett—

> " 'For the cause that lacks assistance,
> For the wrong that needs resistance,
> For the future in the distance,
> And the good that I can do.

And yet even I don't consider myself bound by statutory regulations. What man has done that man can undo—and I look forward to undoing a good deal in my time.' New Paragraph.

" 'It is obvious to me and, I should imagine, to the majority of the House of Commons that the present regulations of your Department were not drawn up by a widow. Before they are amended I would like to propose that you get in touch with a bunch of typical widows and get their views. No man liveth to himself alone and no man dieth to himself alone, and serving men least of all, because they leave their widows virtually in your hands. Be of good heart, Wilbur, take your courage in your hands along with the widows and refuse to be shackled by the statutory regulations that make you reject 38 out of 40 claims in my constituency alone. Think of the future when you and I are dust, think of the generations of happy pensioners forever freed from want and the exigencies of the means test, think of those wild wintry evenings'—inset, Miss Bennett—

" 'When young and old in circle
Around the firebrands close;
When the girls are weaving baskets,
And the lads are shaping bows;
When the goodman mends his armour,
And trims his helmet's plume;
When the goodwife's shuttle merrily
Goes flashing through the loom;
With weeping and with laughter
Still will the tale be told
Of Wilbur on the Widows' Front
In the brave days of old.'

I'll stop there, I think. Anything else will be anticlimax. What do you think Wilbur will make of it?"

He asked the question quite humbly. He knew that if it's difficult for a man to be a hero to his valet it's practically impossible for him to impress his lady-secretary. But he was a trier, was A. W. Stout. Even the people who didn't like him had to admit that. Miss Bennett would have worn down a less resolute man weeks ago.

"He'll be enormously impressed," said Sarah with absolute sincerity. She was impressed herself.

"I didn't want to put all my cards on the table at the start," said Mr. Stout eagerly. "Of course, I can offer him something else in the way of bribes. I might point out that if he gets the pensions raised and the scope enlarged the Mothers' Union would probably put up a plaque at the local Headquarters."

"Are you going to write to him again on the subject?" asked Sarah a little dazed.

It was Mr. Stout's turn to look surprised. It's obvious you haven't been in the House of Commons long. You never do anything with one letter, not when you're dealing with a Ministry. That," he nodded towards her pages of neat short-hand notes, "is what's called the Opening Gambit. There'll be quite a file before we're through." He picked up a typical Plan Room pen and began rapidly to sign the letters Sarah put before him. He glanced through them for form's sake, but he wouldn't have dared alter them with Sarah looking on.

"You might send that out when it's finished," he added pushing back his chair.

And he strode out as impressively as he had romped in.

Chapter III

ALLEN WILKINSON STOUT was accustomed to spend his week-ends at Bramham Manor, which belonged to him in name and to his mother in everything else. She was one of those small fragile-looking women, a Lady in her own right, made of whipcord and with about as much scruple as you could hide under a threepenny bit. Such women, by reason of their delicate appearance and excellent capacity for self-exploitation, always have men like Allen, who was large and hearty, at a disadvantage. However, he didn't see a great deal of her, believing with St. Paul that whatsoever thy hand findeth to do that do with all thy might, and most of his week-ends were spent going round the constituency or interviewing the tenants on his modest estate.

"Allen is like a dog that never understands it's not supposed to get on the table and take the breakfast bacon," Lady Catherine used to say. "It doesn't matter how much you smack it, it gets up again next morning. Allen must have had his eyes blacked by every Minister living, and every Monday evening he travels back to London thirsting for more."

"That's a boy that should have been a girl," was another favorite remark of hers, "so fond he is of poking his nose into everything."

"It's what a Member of Parliament has a nose for," Allen would protest, stroking his own nose that was large, handsome and unforgettable.

"I should hope even a Member of Parliament can remember he's a gentleman," Lady Catherine would retort, "and gentlemen don't go where they're not wanted. If I'd been a Member of Parliament. . . ."

"You'd have been in the Cabinet long ago," prophesied her son gloomily. "You wouldn't have been able to help yourself."

"Then it's a pity you take after your father," retorted she, quick as lightning. Like most people, she had a pretty poor opinion of Members of Parliament. Neither fish, flesh nor fowl, she used to say. Neither honest commercial gentry who make fortunes, nor elegant ne'er-do-weels who decorate society.

"You and my Miss Bennett would have a lot in common," observed Allen pulling on his coat, "and never forget that, for all your chemises may be stamped with coats of arms, you married a Stout."

"I suppose we'll not be seeing you the rest of the day," commented Lady Catherine in withering tones. "If I'd known how little satisfaction I was going to get out of it, I'd not have had you at all."

Mr. Stout remembered the fifth commandment and suppressed the obvious retort. In apologetic tones he said he was going to see Maggie Robinson.

"Are you sure she wants to see you?" his mother enquired.

"The Minister's turned down her pension claim. I must see her and explain. . . ."

"You mean, you're going to apologize for a fellow-Member," demanded Lady Catherine, scorn lighting her eye like an incandescent mantle. "I'm ashamed of you, Allen. Is this all you learned at Eton?"

"You know perfectly well, my dear mother, one doesn't go to Eton to learn anything, but just so that you can say you've been there when you're applying for a job. And since we're on the verge of delivering—with instruments, I grant you, but delivering all the same—the new democratic world, even that won't have any value in the future."

"It'll have its true value," said Catherine Stout, grimly.

"That's what I meant." Anxious for once to have the last word he caught up his hat and left the house.

As he set out across the fields, he was thankful he'd been born in the bad old world where men weren't regimented for their own good and where an Englishman's home was his castle and no one thought the social ideal a flat and a communal kitchen. As he went across the fields he whistled softly and noticed the state of the crops. He was full of theories about agricultural development and had almost plagued the life out of the appropriate Department with suggestions for post-war planning. The harassed Minister suggested we had to win the war first, but Mr. Stout regarded that (in writing) as a cowardly evasion, and he said he hadn't forgotten the aftermath of 1918, even if the Minister had.

He came through pasture-land, and a field waiting for the plow where he walked through tall flowering grasses until he reached a gap in the hedge and squeezed through into a narrow lane. He dropped down over a bank so high that it blotted out all sign of Bramham Manor, and now the only building in sight was Maggie Robinson's cottage. This had a remote quality like a Lovat Fraser drawing, standing back from the road, and only those with a seeing eye noticed its existence. It was a low building washed a dull cream-color, much the same tint as the tall pale reeds that grew up in front of it, marching rank by rank to the pond, whose waters were black even in sunlight.

As he drew near the cottage, it occurred to Allen for the first time that there was something awe-inspiring about the place. It wasn't precisely sinister, but he had a feeling that even the leaves on the trees could see him coming. Everything was alert, watchful, deathly still. He paused, his hand on the gate. As usual, the three drakes, Shadrach, Meshach and Abednego, were clustered under a tree, their grave heads together like elders at a conference. The day was so windless that the reeds never stirred; sometimes, when the weather was more stormy, they clashed together and the cypress at the corner of the fields creaked in a manner to chill even sane country blood. There were wild-flowers out on the bank, and bluebells in the field beyond, but no one ever saw them, since they'd built the by-pass beyond the Pikle.

It was like a bit of Nowhere, and as at last he opened the gate Allen thought how odd it was for a man like Tom Robinson to have lived here in such content. For Tom hadn't been the slow, quiet countryman they knew best hereabouts, he wasn't the whimsical poet beloved of novelists and the London stage, nor was there anything of the Churdles Ash romanticism about him. He had been a man of great vitality, and the reputation in his youth of being a dashing reckless creature with plenty of scalps at his saddle-bow. But he hadn't married any of the young women who had made themselves conspicuous in his company.

He had come back one summer from the North with a quiet woman with foreign blood in her—some said Belgian, some Flemish—several years his senior—a foreigner in every sense of the word. There had been a good deal of gossip and speculation and more lively curiosity, but Maggie Robinson (she had been christened Marguerite but all the village called her Maggie) satisfied none of it. Her little house was her kingdom, and she was like Solomon's virtuous woman. She baked and washed and polished and sewed; she seldom went out and then only with her husband; she never joined in the village gossip and seemed unaware that she might herself give rise to any of it. People wondered sometimes why Tom had made this extraordinary marriage, and if there was anything behind it. But Tom was as close on the subject as she. He didn't seem to have changed much by virtue of becoming a husband; look for the ringleader in any new venture and you found Tom Robinson, but he was like a man who has built a new room on to his house and spends a good deal of his time there, with the door shut.

Maggie was the new room. They had been married six years when he was run down in the black-out, as was supposed, by a driver who hadn't stopped, and people wondered what she's do now. Maggie did precisely what might have been expected of her. She remained in Tom's house, the same calm, enigmatic figure. Even at the funeral she had not unbent. She had followed the coffin, dressed in deepest black, and she had ignored the local custom of asking the neighbors to baked funeral meats. Anyway, by 1943 baked meats were scarce. Still, most people would have spread tea and cakes. But Maggie simply walked back from the cemetery—he hadn't been buried from the aerodrome—through the little gate, up the garden and into the still house. And the walls closed round her and hid her from everyone.

When Allen rang the bell she came to the door at once. Her expression told him nothing. It might conceal uncontrollable grief, stocism, resentment, despair. He couldn't guess. She was a woman of about fifty, with a sensible quiet face, dark hair drawn back, patient purposeful eyes. Yet for all that sense of purpose, she was capable of great repose. When she stood and spoke she was really still; all those little fretful unconscious movements most people make as they talk were missing here. Perhaps, he thought, it was that sense of security that had attracted Tom.

And yet, is she really secure? he asked himself as, leaving his hat in the hall, he walked into the sitting-room. Everything here had a static perfection; tables and chairs were polished, ornaments precisely symmetrical. The curtains hung straight by the gleaming windows; a plant stood on a small table. Allen began to experience an extraordinary sense of unease. It was too quiet, too controlled. There was here none of the emptiness of death, but a deep pulsing life too far beneath the surface for its movements to be visible.

"Pull yourself together, man. You're a politician not a poet," he adjured himself. All the same, he wondered how much Tom had known of the foreign woman he had married, if perhaps that hadn't been her particular attraction for him, that she represented the mystery that is woman's great charm for men, a secret the women of today either didn't believe in or had forgotten or didn't care about.

"Hullo!" he exclaimed, looking around and breaking suddenly into impulsive speech. "Since when have you been on the telephone?"

"Tom had that put in about three months back," returned Maggie in her still voice. "He said that I should not be too much alone when he was away. He spoke of having another woman to live here, but that would be too much. I said I would have the telephone."

"What an efficient chap Tom was!" said Allen sincerely.

"You could say the litany three times over on your knees to the P.M.G. if you were a Londoner and you'd not get an instrument. Yet he managed it."

"Tom always had what he wanted," said Maggie and he received the impression that the words covered far more than he could realize. He felt a tremor of fear.

"Do you use it much?" he murmured to cover his momentary sense of being at a disadvantage.

She shook her head. "Oh, no, Mr. Allen. For myself I don't care for it. It seems unnatural."

"Not more so then the wireless."

"You can turn off the wireless. But no one can stop that bell ringing and a strange voice perhaps speaking to you. . . . I have always been able to shut the door against anyone I did not want in my house, but with a telephone . . ." She drew a deep breath, "they come right inside and you are helpless."

"You can always hang up," protested Allen.

"No sense in that. They only come again. Or, if they do not, you sit all the evening waiting. It is a terrible thing, that waiting in a quiet house for an invisible man to speak to you." She made it sound like a nightmare; he wondered whom she meant by "they." Someone special? He looked at her sharply, but again her face told you nothing.

"It's got its other side," he murmured. "Your friends can contact you."

"You can open the door to your friends. There is no need for a thing like that to be in touch with them. But it will not be there much longer," she added resolutely. "I have told them to take it way. I shall be less lonely when it has gone."

"Are you going to stay on here?" Mr. Stout enquired.

"It was Tom's home. If you will let me stay, Mr. Allen. . . . But perhaps you need the cottage. . . ." Her face clouded with sudden apprehension.

"Of course I don't want it," said Allen, rather roughly. "It's enough that Tom should have given his life. By the way, he was on compassionate leave, wasn't he?"

"He told me so," replied Maggie in an expressionless voice.

"That's why there's all this trouble about the pension.

Normally, of course, you'd be entitled without question. But we're plugging away. They always refuse the first time. It's the correct thing."

"I would not have asked," said Maggie. "I don't know that Tom would have wished for it. He never cared for charity. . . ."

"Charity be damned!" exploded Mr. Stout. "It's your right."

"Perhaps," agreed Maggie, and she said it in such a way that her Member was arrested in his headlong flight down the hill of disapprobation. "Already they have asked me questions, questions I did not want to answer, but they said I must. For myself I would have asked for nothing, but one does not wish to seem—odd."

"The whole thing seems pretty odd to me," commented Allen candidly. "You haven't told me yet why he had compassionate leave."

"I don't know," said Maggie simply. "He told me so little. Oh, I might guess, I suppose, but what proof had I that I was guessing right? It is better to leave things alone."

"But you're pretty sure there was something—fishy. . . . ?"

"Mr. Allen!" For the first time he saw human emotion in that still face. "You know how it is. If you turn over a perfectly innocent-looking stone you cannot tell what you may disturb. And Tom was never quite like other men."

"And he never told you anything?"

"He told me nothing and I asked nothing. Wise wives do not ask. They wait and if they are not told then they stay quiet in the dark."

Allen felt his flesh creep at the strength of purpose words and tone revealed.

"I knew there was more in this than meets the eye," he commented. "Compassionate leave, my Aunt Fanny. I'd like to know, all the same, what Tom was really up to."

"You won't let them go round ferreting things out, will you, sir?" Maggie pleaded. "If I that was his wife am willing to let things be, that should be good enough for the others."

"You're a wise woman, Maggie," commented Mr. Stout. "You know things aren't always as simple as they look. That," he nodded towards the telephone, "was just camouflage, wasn't it?"

"I don't know exactly what you mean," the woman murmured, "but Tom wouldn't have had that thing put in when he knew I didn't like it, not if he hadn't felt he had to. Besides, it was always him that used it. No one I know would have spoken to me over a wire."

He found himself thinking, "Ah, but you didn't really know anyone—except perhaps Tom—and who's to say that anyone really knew him?" It was a lonely thing, the human soul. He shivered a little. Presumably that was one of the chief reasons why people got married, so that they shouldn't feel so solitary. The tragedy was that so often the spell didn't work. You couldn't escape the human destiny that way.

"Did Tom use it a lot?" he asked, coming suddenly out of his momentary reverie.

"It was more the ones that wanted him."

"And you don't know who they were? No, of course you don't. You never asked questions."

"No, sir. When you marry a man you take him the way he is."

"That's the trouble with most wives. They don't. They start the reforming process right away. My mother reformed my father into his grave within ten years."

"I never knew a lot about Tom, and I don't want to start gossip among the neighbors. There was enough of that when we were married. I know how folks whispered. They laughed a bit in their sleeves, thought me a fool, I know, taking up with a handsome fellow like that, ten years younger than me. Mostly they thought I had a bit laid by and that was the reason. But," she shook her head, "it wasn't none of that. The truth is Tom didn't need any woman's money. He had plenty of his own."

"Tom had?" Mr. Stout looked as if he couldn't believe his ears. He'd known Tom longer than Maggie had, and he'd never known a time when Tom wasn't broke to the wide. He was as reckless about money as he was about everything else—a gambler every way.

"Yes, sir." She was a quiet woman but she didn't miss much.

"That's another thing I didn't understand. But I didn't ask questions. What a man doesn't tell you he doesn't want to be asked about. And if you do badger him, well, he's like brock, he goes underground. But sometimes Tom was so flush I'd wonder. I know what a sergeant-pilot in the R.A.F. draws. Not enough to go buying the sort of presents he gave me. Diamond earrings even. . . ."

"Diamonds? Oh, but not. . . ."

"Yes, sir. Real diamonds. I could show you. . . ." She opened a drawer and produced a little box.

"They're real all right," agreed Mr. Stout. They weren't showy, but they were worth quite a lot of money. And Maggie was right. You don't buy diamond earrings on a sergeant-pilot's pay. "Of course, you knew from the start this wasn't an ordinary accident?" he went on.

"Well, sir," Maggie sounded as respectful as ever. "Men don't mostly go out of their own natures, and it wasn't like Tom to be mixed up in an acident, not a silly sort of accident like this one. He was careful in a way for all his recklessness. And he was interested in living. Some men don't seem to care. Tom was never like that. And in a way he lived more than most men, because he lived in two worlds. One world I didn't know anything about; that was the world he was in when he was killed. And he married me because I belonged to the other world, the world where he was safe, where in his heart I believe he wanted to be. I daresay it all sounds nonsense to you, Mr. Allen. . . ."

"On the contrary," said Mr. Stout, "it sounds more sensible than anything I've heard for months. Though you have to remember I spend most of my time in the House of Commons. Maggie, is there nothing I can do?"

"What could there be? Tom's dead. You can't bring him back. I suppose really I always knew he'd end somehow like this. Tom's sort don't die in their beds."

He was reminded of the tragic mother in *Riders to the Sea*. In a sense, he thought, it was a relief to her that the suspense and the dread were over, all the waiting and wondering, the days of silence and the nights of fear. He wanted to ask her what she suspected, but could not. Did she know what Tom had been up to? Was she inwardly glad it had ended as it had begun, in the dark? He didn't suppose anyone would ever know.

"About the pension," he said rather awkwardly.

"Don't give another thought to that," said Magige. "I'll be all right. I've my strength and I can work. Tom didn't wish it when he was here but it's different now. I'd not have put in for the pension if he hadn't told me, and said it was queer if I didn't."

"He?"

"One of the officers at the airfield. He came to see me after he heard about Tom. A little dark man. He asked if I was all right for the time and told me about the pension. Well, you don't want to seem different from anyone else. . . ."

Poor courageous Maggie! he thought. That was her grief. She'd wanted to be simple and straightforward in her dealings with her husband and with life, and all these years she'd been living a second existence under the surface, an existence no one had known anything about. Not even my mother, reflected Allen with a start. Lady Catherine wasn't easily deceived, yet Maggie had hidden the truth from her also.

"They were very kind," Maggie added. "I went up to see them when I got the letter from the Ministry. I asked for Mr. Winter—that was the one I saw the first time. He wasn't in. I had to wait, and then it was the O.C., Mr. Lindsay—a Wing-Commander he is. He said they'd all admired Tom, they'd like to help—but I told him there wasn't anything he could do. He couldn't bring Tom back to life again, could he?"

"No," agreed Allen painfully. "No." He looked round. He hadn't thought of the conversation turning out quite like this. Desperately he put out his hand and touched a finely-carved old chair standing against the wall.

"That'll be in a museum one of these days," he said.

Maggie smiled—a derisive smile he thought it. "That's what the Vicar said when he came. I'm not educated, I know. I don't understand about putting things behind glass that were made for ordinary wear. It would make Tom laugh to think of his old chair in a museum."

"What can you do with a woman like that?" Allen asked

himself despairingly as she let him out of the cottage and he walked down between the tall reeds shaking a little now in a wind that had sprung up from nowhere. Shadrach, Meshach and Abednego watched him with bright mocking eyes.

As he walked back, more slowly and thoughtfully than any of his colleagues in Parliament had ever seen him move, he thought what a solitary woman she was! He realized that they none of them knew anything about her. There had been a seed of aloofness in her from the first. Most women wouldn't have been satisfied with a little cottage with no modern conveniences—lamps, pumped water, outdoor sanitation. They'd have wanted company, entertainment, a bus-service nearer than two miles away. But she hadn't seemed to care.

How much did she know? he asked himself again, as he unlatched the shabby blue-painted door that led to the wooden plank spanning the ditch that separated the long garden of the Manor from the adjoining fields. He couldn't answer his own question.

He found Lady Catherine in the drawing-room; it was odd to think that so fragile a creature had given birth to the great burly man he had become. He always felt clumsy, inept, in her presence, like a water-spaniel in a spinster's villa.

His mother was arranging flowers in vases and bowls of clouded glass, narcissi with orange hearts in a blue pot, pink and white hyacinths in a china jar.

"Well?" she said as he pushed his way through the French windows. "What did you learn?"

"Learn? Oh, nothing really. I went to tell her about the pension. That's all."

"And what did she say?"

"That she didn't want any more trouble about it. Not that it would make much difference if she did so far as Wilbur's concerned. But mostly they want you to fight for it to the last ditch."

"Maggie Robinson's not like most women," said his mother drily. "Most women wouldn't have been able to keep it to themselves."

Allen Wilkinson Stout looked staggered. "Keep what?"

"The truth about Tom Robinson. Didn't you realize that no one has ever known that but Maggie, and probably she doesn't know much. Still, she knows more than anyone else."

(So his mother had guessed after all.)

"Whatever she knows," said Mr. Stout slowly, "she'll never pass on. We shall never know anything at all. The matter will stop here."

But in saying that he reckoned without the Minister of Pensions (War Claims Department).

Chapter IV

THE OFFICE of Minister of Pensions (War Claims Department) had been created when the war was no longer young in order to obviate the inevitable confusion arising from the fact that all the Departments have their own pensions arrangements and consequently are pestered with claims that should have been sent elsewhere. The Service Departments, Health and Pensions all deal with these claims and there was, in short, so much friction that it was resolved to create a central clearing house which could deal with the hopeless cases on its own responsibility and distribute the rest to the appropriate Departments.

The Rt. Hon. Sir Wilbur Wilberforce, J.P., M.B.E., M.P., looked, as Mr. Stout had once remarked, exceedingly like a goldfish, standing on its tail and also bore a striking resemblance to a well-known Anglican divine. Caution and Conscience were the great twin brethren in his book of life, and the two warred perpetually the one against the other, so that there were premature lines round his eyes, and his mouth never dared smile for fear it gave birth to hopes that would not later be realized. He had, like so many parliamentarians, eaten his dinners in the Inner Temple as a young man and his legal training had stood him in good stead when he was elevated to his present responsible position. He had evolved a program of replies that occupied the least possible time, and his Ministry was, in fact, a model of rationalization and good sense. Believing that if you must refuse a man no amount of flowery speech will soften the blow, he employed a curt formula that broke the news and slew hope in three lines. Neither he nor his satellites wasted time—in fact, he had a printed motto over his desk—Time won is a battle won—and no one, not even people who disliked goldfish in general and Ministers in particular—ever suggested he was less than efficient.

He had one printed form he used a great deal and that unquestionably saved his typists a great deal of work. It said: The Minister of War Pensions (Claims Department) has the honor to acknowledge your letter which has been passed to the appropriate Department for attention. He found that disposed of about sixty per cent of his correspondents. Another thirty per cent was dealt with by a similar formula, though this time it was typewritten and not printed. It said: Your claim for a pension has been most carefully considered but it is regretted that the evidence available is insufficient to show that your disability can be attributed to your war service.

Most people gave up hope after that, but now and again a sturdy rebel against red tape went hither and thither and found some fresh medical evidence and triumphed in spite of all official discouragement. A letter like that from Mrs. Robinson seemed at first sight an easy matter. The man had been on leave when death occurred; therefore the authorities had no responsibility. The most obstinate and importunate widow could hardly, thought Sir Wilbur, fly in the face of so obvious a truism. Mr. Stout's letter, therefore, came to him as a considerable and most unpleasant shock. He saw in it the fulsome triumph of a man who knows he holds the ace of trumps. And the Minister's trouble was that he couldn't be certain what trumps were.

Hurriedly he sent for his secretary, an eager conscientious man who believed his duty to God and his neighbor was to lift as much responsibility as possible off his chief's shoulders. For this cause was I born and to this end came I into the world, Enoch Dowsett would whisper when some more than usually tiresome case presented itself, and Conscience being his middle name also he and the Minister rubbed along very well.

"What do you make of that?" Sir Wilbur enquired.

Mr. Dowsett read the letter carefully. The place where

his eyebrows would have been, had he possessed any, rose as he passed from paragraph to paragraph.

"Is it possible," he ventured, laying the letter aside (Touch not, taste not, handle not the unclean thing, whispered Conscience), "that the Member was—er—under the influence at the time?"

"It is possible," agreed the Minister, "but his secretary would not be. And surely she would have noticed the phraseology and suggested to the Member that it was a trifle—unconventional—as addressed to a Minister, that is."

"A trifle unconventional!" repeated the secretary. "The British genius for understatement. Unconventional." He hugged himself in a kind of respectful ecstasy.

"Bring me the Robinson file," commanded the Minister sternly.

The secretary ran with a rabbit's agility and produced it. He stood, ears and nostrils twitching for the next command. The Robinson file was a meager affair, being composed of the usual forms and acknowledgments. No inspiration there at all, you'd have said.

The Minister sighed. Mr. Dowsett looked intelligently receptive.

"A quite ordinary case, is it not?" he ventured.

The Minister annihilated him with a glance. "It is perfectly clear that it is anything but ordinary," he replied. "This man, Stout, knows something. That is perfectly obvious. Otherwise he would never have sent me this." And he tapped the letter lying on the desk before him. There was a long pause; Mr. Dowsett controlled his ears and nostrils. Now he was like an automatic figure waiting for someone to put a penny in the slot, when he would begin to jig obediently once more.

The Minister put the tips of his fingers together. "There is that point about the petrol," he said at last. "It merits consideration." He considered. "Stout is unquestionably right," he announced. "Petrol is not given on demand, and if this man, Robinson, was in possession of petrol it follows that he had some special claim to it. As a private individual there is clearly no ground for a case for the Petroleum Board." He stopped again.

The secretary said respectfully, "I believe there is a black market in petrol."

The Minister's eyes glared. "That would be a matter for Mr. Lorimer. As you should know, Mr. Dowsett, it is not etiquette for one Minister to poach on another Minister's preserves."

"Naturally not," agreed Mr. Dowsett humbly.

The Minister continued to sit like a medium at a seance when the spirit control is proving troublesome. At last he lowered his eyes.

"Have there been any other pension claims in connection with this airfield?" he enquired.

"They'd also come through Mr. Stout, of course," ruminated Mr. Dowsett. "He sends in a large proportion of our claims, but I hardly remember. . . ."

"I entirely fail to follow your reasoning," said the Minister in a cold voice. "Why you assume Mr. Stout would sponsor any case from the Whipley Cross aerodrome. . . ."

"It's in his constituency," explained the secretary.

"Pension claims not infrequently are received from the dependents of men killed on active service." The Minister was elaborately polite. "Such dependents may live in any part of the country. The fact that a man is temporarily stationed in a particular Parliamentary Division has, so far as I can see, no bearing on the case."

Mr. Dowsett looked genuinely frightened. "Are you asking me to go through all the pension cases over a period of time to ascertain whether any others came from Whipley R.A.F. Station?"

"There was one, I remember," reflected Sir Wilbur, "the case of a boy called Burr, whose parents claimed a pension—unjustifiably, of course. The boy was only twenty at the time of the accident that cost him his life, but it could scarcely be suggested that his parents were in any way dependent upon him. But—it was an unpleasant case. I wasn't altogether satisfied about the accident."

"You think it might have been—suicide?" breathed Mr. Dowsett.

"I think it more probable it might have been sabotage. There is a great deal more of that kind of thing going on than the public or most Government Departments are aware."

"How un-British!" deplored Mr. Dowsett. "But, of course, it probably isn't our people who're responsible. All these aliens. . . ."

"It is always our people who are responsible for these things," contradicted the Minister, coldly. Mr. Dowsett was certainly getting the rough side of his tongue today. "The man in authority assumes responsibility for all his juniors." His penetrating glance reminded the unhappy secretary of every slip he had ever made in a letter, a telephone message, an interview. He had the feeling that the Minister was weighed down by the burden of his underling's misdemeanors.

"I should like the files examined during—say—the past six months and a note made of any other cases of accidental death, with subsequent pension claims, emanating from this Station."

"Yes, Sir Wilbur," whispered Mr. Dowsett. "I'll have to take some of the clerks off their usual work."

"If it means restricting the weekly output of jumpers and babies' socks I am, naturally, sorry," said the Minister in his most courteous voice, "but I'm afraid the demands of the country come before even such domestic considerations."

Mr. Dowsett wilted.

"And get the Secretary of State for Air on the 'phone. I want to talk to him."

Sir Wilbur never put anything on paper that could be used against him afterwards. He'd have broken Scotland Yard's heart.

The Secretary of State for Air said he would be pleased to see the Minister of War Claims (as he was colloquially styled) at any time, and Sir Wilbur therefore left Great John Street for Little Peter Street that same afternoon.

"I've got a rather disturbing case," he admitted in his dry legal way. "You might be able to throw a little light on it."

"Have a cigarette," said the Secretary of State for Air.

"I don't smoke," said the War Claims Minister. "Tell me—in confidence, naturally—have you had any trouble recently at Whipley Airfield?"

The Secretary for Air said, "In the interests of security," to which Sir Wilbur said, "Bah! You're not on a platform or the floor of the House now, you know. All I want to know is whether you're aware of what's going on there. If not, perhaps a brother Minister might give you a little enlightenment."

As he had anticipated, this put the Secretary for Air (Sir Ortolan Hawke, M.C.) on his metal. Just as wives don't like being told about their husbands by other women, so Cabinet Ministers in charge of Departments don't want to hear about intimate departmental scandals from other Ministers. So now Sir Ortolan drew himself up, thrust out his nose as though presenting a petition, and said, "I am naturally aware of a number of unfortunate occurrences that have taken place recently at the aerodrome you mention. Every precaution is being taken, but you are aware that one must be governed by certain accepted premises. . . ."

"And in the meantime men are being killed, men we can't afford to lose," interrupted Sir Wilbur, who knew the truth of the maxim—Hit first, hit hard and keep on hitting. "It's not good enough, Hawke. This fellow, Robinson—oh, there's been a nice bit of camouflage about that. . . ."

Sir Ortolan looked up sharply. "So there is a leakage," he bayed. "Yet we have been most careful. . . ."

"Common sense put the member on the track," said Sir Wilbur, bluntly.

"Ah yes. The Member is . . . ?"

"That fellow, Stout. You might as well try to muzzle him as stop a runaway train single-handed. He knows there's something fishy going on."

"He may suspect," corrected Sir Ortolan in forbidding tones. "He cannot possibly know."

"You don't know Stout very well. Anything he wants to know he finds out. That's why I'm asking you."

The Secretary for Air looked uncomfortable, "In the national interest," he began, but was astounded to fetl his arm held in the traditional grip of iron.

"I'll tell you something, Hawke, that you may not know. I have a son. He's twenty—and he's not stationed at Whipley. But he took up a machine nine months ago. At 5000 feet it went into a spin. At 500 feet he pulled it out of the spin. At 400 feet it went into a second spin. By sheer genius he managed to land it on its side, and by a miracle the petrol tank didn't explode. He was in bed for six months; now on a good day he can get round the room on crutches. In another six months he may be able to tackle stairs."

Sir Ortolan looked horribly embarrassed, also shocked. Englishmen don't talk like that. "I'm very sorry," he muttered.

"Eventually the doctors tell me he's going to be ninety-five per cent fit," continued Sir Wilbur, paying not the slightest attention to his companion's obvious ill-ease. "But—he was the leader of three and there weren't any survivors from the other machines. When they came to examine Teddy's they found it was deliberate sabotage—the airlooms cut half-way through so they'd be bound to give way at a height. What happened at his aerodrome may easily happen at others. We're surrounded by spies and strangers; as a race we're slow to suspect treachery. Stout is convinced there's been dirty work, and I'm convinced, too."

"What do you expect me to do about it?" demanded Sir Ortolan.

"Put your cards on the table. This fellow, Tom Robinson, for instance. How did he die?"

"He—there was a coroner's verdict. Death by misadventure."

"And has anyone explained how it was that the deceased had sufficient petrol to be—er—joy-riding at that hour of the evening?"

"We have no evidence that it was joy-riding," said the Secretary for Air sharply.

Quick as light, Sir Wilbur pounced. His legal training had made him an adept at this sort of thing.

"Am I to suppose that you admit you have evidence to the contrary, that he was, in fact, proceeding on official business?"

Sir Ortolan couldn't put up much of a show against this sort of thing.

"I didn't say. . . ."

"The man was either using petrol for an illegal purpose or he was engaged on national reconnaissance. Since his widow has applied for a pension, presumably on the ground that he was actually in the service of his country at the time of his death, we may assume that he was, in fact, doing work of a secret nature in connection with his wartime duties."

"I don't know what the Ministry of Security's about," grumbled Sir Ortolan. "When a matter like this is common knowledge. . . ."

"The matter, so far as I am aware, is known to you, to myself and to one Member of Parliament," pointed out Sir Wilbur frigidly. "You can scarcely suggest that constitutes COMMON knowledge."

Mournfully Sir Ortolan gave way once more. He felt he could sympathize now with the feelings of the little British force being slowly driven backwards into the sea. Only, for him, he reflected, remembering Wilbur Wilberforce's reputation, there'd be no Dunkirk. He'd be like the German forces in Tunisia—defeated utterly. (Subsequently he wrote a poem on 'The Victory of Defeat' which appeared in a Sunday paper, and he caused a lot of trouble by framing the check instead of cashing it.)

"If the man was not, in fact, on compassionate leave but was still a member of the Service to which he was attached—a working member that is—his widow is entitled to a service pension," continued Sir Wilbur stolidly.

"I suppose she would be," said Sir Ortolan. "All right."

"Stout scores again," said Sir Wilbur simply.

And went out.

The following week-end Mr. Stout himself took the news to Maggie Robinson. For all the outward change he could perceive, time might have stood still in this secluded corner; the three drakes were still clustered gravely under the big tree, the shadow still lay over the reeds, the black water glimmered somberly. Allen walked quietly up the path and rapped on the door. Maggie opened it at once and he stepped inside.

"I've brought you news," he said.

"Yes, Mr. Allen?"

"It's about the pension. They've decided you are entitled to it, after all."

He saw a small shiver pass through her, and then she was very quiet; she was, he thought, the quietest woman he had even seen. He watched an expression pass over her face as the shadow passed over the reeds. He said nothing more because there was nothing to be said. After that minute she seemed slowly to come to life again.

"Will you take a cup of tea, Mr. Allen?" she asked. "The kettle's on the boil."

"No, no," said Mr. Stout. "My mother's expecting me."

"Lady Catherine's been very kind," said Maggie. "She came to see I had everything I might want. It was good of her."

"Why, you're one of us," said Mr. Stout before he could stop himself.

She looked at him steadfastly out of those deep inscrutable eyes. "You mean, I was Tom's wife," she said.

And he thought, "That's true. That's how we've always thought of her. Never as a person. Why, I don't even know what her unmarried name was! She was Mrs. Tom Robinson from the start," and he said abruptly, "You're not going to try and refuse the pension or anything ridiculous now, are you?"

For once he seemed to have surprised her. "Oh, no, Mr. Allen," she said. "I suppose if anyone's got a right to the pension I have. I always knew it wasn't an accident, and I think Tom expected it."

"You mean, he said something?"

"No—not exactly. But he gave me a message that evening. 'Ring up the aerodrome,' he said, 'and say I'm coming. Say it's Hargreaves. And I'll be at the Bird In Hand at nine.' Then he stopped a minute, as if he wasn't sure he'd say anything else. And then he turned and put his hand on mine and said, 'And

45

tell him, if I'm not there by half-past, I'll not be coming. I'll have been prevented. See? I'll have been prevented.' Oh, I didn't ask questions, what was the use? But he knew he might never get there, and that was his way of telling me. When he didn't come back that night I told myself, this is what you've been waiting for. Well, it's all over now."

Allen shook his head. "Tom's share is over, perhaps—that's all. The rest of us go on. We haven't any choice."

She said nothing to that. He felt suddenly as though he were talking to darkness, to emptiness.

"If there's anything you know," he blundered on, "you ought to tell us. It's your duty, and it's what Tom would have wished. It wasn't only his life—it's other people's, and they're still in jeopardy. You know what he was doing, don't you?"

"I think so," said Maggie. "There was trouble up at the aerodrome. I don't know any more than that. But I do know Tom didn't die by accident."

"He died for England as much as any man who falls in battle," Allen heard himself say, quite unbelievably because he wasn't much good at platform oratory. "Isn't that some comfort?"

"If it was your son or your wife, Mr. Allen, you wouldn't say that. It's as if just losing them is so much it takes all your mind. Like being caught in a fog; the sun may be somewhere, only it doesn't matter to you, because you can't see it."

"I'll find the chap who's responsible, I promise you that," said Allen, grimly. But he saw from her face that his vow brought her no satisfaction. Indeed, she looked more troubled than before.

"I hope I've done right telling you," she murmured. "There was one more thing. That evening, quite late, the telephone rang, and a voice said, Is Hargreaves there? I said No. And the voice said, Who's speaking? I told him Mrs. Robinson. He said, Is your husband in? I said No, and he said, When do you expect him? and when did he go out? I told him, and he said, When he comes in tell him I'm waiting, and rang off."

"No telephone number?"

"I supposed Tom knew that. Anyway, what was the good?

46

I—knew Tom wasn't coming back. In the morning, just before six, there came a knock on the door and it was a policeman. He told me there had been an accident, and I was wanted at the mortuary."

"And you never said a word to anyone?"

She shook her head. "I hadn't any proof. Besides, I didn't know enough. I didn't know what Tom was doing. I didn't know who it was safe to talk to. I didn't know anything."

That, reflected Mr. Stout, might be all right for Maggie but it left him in something of a quandary. For he was not only a citizen with a strong sense of duty that told him his job was to assist the police at every turn and that to conceal what might prove to be vital information was to be an accessory after the fact, but he was also a Member of Parliament, and as such stood in a very particular relation to the public at large and his constituents in particular. He had every reason to suppose that a particularly horrible crime had been committed in what he chose to regard as his terrain, and though he realized he had nothing but Maggie's intuition coupled with his own, to go on, he didn't feel comfortable about leaving the matter where it was. He thought of the police and dismissed them; he thought of going up to the aerodrome, but reflected that he didn't know anyone there and they didn't know him and might send him away with a flea in his ear, so he compromised and got in touch with the Secretary of State for Air, who should take an interest in matters of this kind.

When his secretary told him that Mr. Stout wanted to speak to him on the telephone, Sir Ortolan Hawke began to think there was something to be said for being a desert hermit. You lived in happy seclusion, and if you became lonely there always seemed to be a friendly lion or dragon to give you innocent companionship; if you wanted to cross a river, assuming that there were rivers in the desert, you whistled up a crocodile with more ease than nowadays you can find a London taxicab, and rode triumphantly on its back. He wasn't a particularly brave man, but he had thought—like several other Ministers in charge of War Service Departments—he'd sooner face a crocodile than Mr. Stout out on the warpath and rarin' to go.

47

To his dismay he found Allen Wilkinson Stout following closely in the footprints of Sir Wilbur Wilberforce—like King Wenceslaus's page, following his master through the snow. But he maintained a bold not to say jaunty front.

He said he wasn't answerable for any action taken by the Minister for War Pensions (Claims Department): when Mr. Stout pressed for an explanation of the period of compassionate leave granted to the dead man, he said he had received a very strong recommendation from the C.O. in whom he had every confidence, and had decided that the case was an exceptional one.

"We'll hope so," agreed Mr. Stout grimly, and not in the least satisfied and feeling that Bruce's spider had nothing on him, he went to see Sir Wilbur. As soon as he mentioned Tom Robinson's name, with the rider that he'd just come from the Secretary for Air, the Minister said, "I know what you're going to say—that it looks fishy. And you're right. It looks fishy, it smells fishy, it is fishy. But I'm going to quote your own letter to you. There are times when it's better for the sake of public morale to let ill alone. That's only a rough paraphrase," he added, "but I think it was your point."

But Mr. Stout continued to look belligerently unhappy. "I don't like it," he said.

"No one likes it," pleaded Sir Wilbur. "Ortolan doesn't like it, any more than you or I."

"And so for security reasons we do nothing? Security's like charity, it covers a multitude of sins, but—it won't do, Wilbur. The skeleton's bones are sticking out in every direction."

"Even if they are," said Sir Wilbur desperately, "do you have to call attention to them? I've seen the Air Ministry. They've got the matter in hand. They don't want anyone butting in. . . ."

"I'm sure they don't," Mr. Stout agreed. "But—I have a conscience, too, you know. It's damned awkward, but there it is."

"And what," inquired Sir Wilbur stonily, "do you intend to do?"

"Don't get me wrong," said Mr. Stout in earnest tones. "I'm

not stirring up mud because I like making pies. But—if this trouble goes on at the airfield I'll have to do something."

"But nothing precipitate," urged Sir Wilbur. "You'll only be playing into the hands of whoever it is if you do. Besides, it's not exactly your Department."

"Am I my brother's keeper?" demanded Mr. Stout. "All right, have it your own way. As you say, I can't bring Tom back, and I'm not the police, and my job was to get Maggie the pension and I've got it for her."

"And there is the matter of etiquette," said Sir Wilbur earnestly.

Mr. Stout was too broken in spirit to argue the point. "A triumph for the bureaucrats," he said to Sarah whom he found drafting his weekly article.

"I wouldn't say that," demurred Sarah. "You've got the pension. That's what you were asked to do. Besides, this isn't the end of the story. Only the first chapter."

"You think there'll be a second?" Mr. Stout looked apprehensive.

"We must hope for the best," soothed Miss Bennett. "There's always the chance there won't be. Quite a lot of manuscripts never get beyond chapter one. I know. I've tried to write a book more than once myself."

Chapter V

FATE, HOWEVER, was more persevering than Miss Bennett. It played Mr. Stout as an experienced angler plays a salmon. At first he was on the *qui vive* all the time, looking askance at sealed envelopes, making his weekly journey to Whipley Cross in a state of apprehension, prepared for anonymous letters, murder threats and even attempts against his own life. But when none of these materialized and when the voice at the other end of the telephone didn't mutter vengeance at him, when, moreover, it seemed that the trouble at the airfield had passed over and the accidents ceased occurring, he resumed his normal optimistic outlook. His speeches in the House became as lively as ever. He practically invited the assassin's knife on more than one occasion. He fought a quite impossible case with the Ministry of Food and triumphed; Maggie drew her pension, Sir Ortolan Hawke, finding him in the bar, bought him a drink and talked of nothing more compromising than the chess problem in the Expert Chessplayer, and it seemed to Allen that he had done well to let sleeping dogs lie. And then, when everything seemed calm, the dog awoke and barked with a vengeance, setting up an echo that rang all round the country, and was even reported in the more distinguished provincial papers outside Mr. Stout's own area.

It was Lady Catherine who, so to speak, knocked on the kennel door. She had speedily uncovered the fact that Maggie Robinson had got the pension in spite of departmental declarations.

"This Wilberforce person can't be as alarming as they say

if you can best him," she informed her son. "A sleepy lot, I call them."

"Well, don't call them that in public," Allen begged her. "The less said about all this the better. You won't find Maggie will talk and nor shall I."

"Why you both have to behave as though there were something shady about the whole affair is more than I can understand," announced her ladyship candidly. "We were proud of doing our duty when I was a young woman."

"Had they ever heard of discretion when you were a young woman?" demanded the goaded Mr. Stout.

But though he could be discreet when occasion demanded, and Maggie Robinson was discreet by nature and training, no one would ever persuade that spoiled darling of the peerage, Lady Catherine Stout, that discretion was anything but what her own cook would have called "creeping." As well command a lamb to stop bounding in a meadow as expect her volatile self-willed ladyship to hold her tongue. It was soon all over the village that Maggie Robinson had got the pension in spite of "them" at Blackpool, and all because Mr. Allen had spoken for her. And it was less than a month after this that the dog began to bark.

The first sign of the beast's existence was a letter, apparently like a host of others, carefully if somewhat illegibly written by a constituent of the name of Sally Routh.

This lady had recently become a widow, owing to the inconsiderate behavior of a horse on her husband's farm. He, poor man, had appealed for leave in order to make the necessary arrangements for carrying on his business during his period of Army service, and before the two months granted him were over the horse kicked out, struck him on the head and he died without recovering consciousness. Mrs. Routh applied for a pension as a matter of course and after a decent interval the Ministry turned down the claim.

"If only some of these wives would read army regulations," said the sorely-tried official at Lytham-St.-Anne's, whither all such claims were referred. "This one would know that her husband was temporarily a civilian and therefore no responsibility of ours."

Mrs. Routh, however, was not one to lie down under such treatment. She stormed round to the offices of Mr. Ferguson, Mr. Stout's agent, flourishing the Ministry's letter and insisting on seeing the Member.

"Where is he?" she demanded furiously, looking round her as though she thought he might be hiding behind the wallpaper.

Mr. Ferguson, feeling you couldn't blame him if he were, said where would he be on a Thursday but in Westminster.

Mrs. Routh, like practically everyone else in the country, had no notion which days of the week Parliament sat, and said belligerently that he needn't think he could get out of it by skulking in London, and when was he coming to Whipley?

Mr. Ferguson said he was having a constituent's day on Saturday afternoon.

"Come along then and you can talk it over with him, but I'm afraid under statutory regulations you haven't a case."

"Haven't a case?" shrilled Mrs. Routh. "What about Maggie Robinson. Wasn't her husband on compassionate leave the same as mine?"

"Perhaps there were special circumstances," hazarded Mr. Ferguson.

"And Maggie Robinson's a foreigner, what's more," exclaimed Mrs. Routh. "Kissing goes by favor in this village, that's easy to see. You tell Mr. Stout I'm coming on Saturday."

She tramped home and, getting out a penny bottle of ink, purchased in the days before the war and seldom uncorked, and a pen never used for any social purposes, she proceeded to put her case on paper.

When Mr. Stout saw the letter he said, "Hell! We might have expected this."

"Didn't you?" asked Miss Bennett.

"What the devil do we do now?" inquired Mr. Stout. He read the letter again. " 'Seeing as Joe and I was among them as put you where you are today we have our rights like others, to say nothing of foreigners. I am a widow the same as that

Maggie Robinson and can show you my lines any time.' Well, well, well. What next?"

"I can tell you," said Sarah. "You take up the case with Sir Wilbur, he sends you a printed acknowledgment, Mrs. Routh writes to know why she hasn't got the pension, you write to say the matter's still under consideration, I ring up Sir Wilbur's secretary, he says he can't remember the case offhand, but he'll look it up and ring me back and never does. Eventually Sir Wilbur writes that he has reviewed the matter most sympathetically, but regrets that in the circumstances and owing to a statutory regulation over which he has no control, no pension can be awarded in this case; you send on the top copy to Mrs. Routh and I file the duplicate (for all Government Departments thoughtfully send two copies of letters of this kind, so that the constituent may be convinced he or she is not being fobbed off by the Member)."

"And Mrs. Routh goes round to raise hell with Ferguson and then comes and raises more hell with me, and when that doesn't bring her any satisfaction she starts a bit of gossip about Maggie Robinson and enough cats come out of bags to do a circus act. What are you smiling at?"

"I was thinking of the rhyme my grandmother used to teach us: 'Oh, what a tangled web we weave when first we practice to deceive.' "

"Hell!" said Mr. Stout indignantly. "I believe you're enjoying this. He thought it might be a good idea to turn Miss Bennett on to Mrs. Routh should that infuriated lady actually beard him in the House of Commons, but more mature deliberation reminded him that women always hang together, and if he found it took all he had to stand up to Miss Bennett, a combination of Miss Bennett and Mrs. Routh was enough to make the Prime Minister shake in his shoes.

Everything fell out precisely as Sarah had prophesied.

"I'm not goin' to be passed over like this," declared Sally Routh.

"But you aren't actually entitled to the pension," protested Mr. Stout.

"That's got nothing to do with it," retorted his constituent.

"If others can have it, so can I. Being entitled hasn't got nothing to do with it."

Mrs. Routh, when her Member failed her in this cowardly and deplorable fashion, carried the affair to the court of appeal, that is to say, she called at Bramham Manor and asked for Lady Catherine. Allen's mother was popular in the constituency, which wouldn't have had the smallest use for the Hon. Mr. Smythe's Universal Democrats. Whipley Cross didn't need to be told that what politicians call the proletariat was as good as the aristocracy. Nature had told them that long ago, and they liked Lady Catherine, because she knew her place and didn't try to edge out of it and occupy a lowlier one, thus ousting the real holder of it. These self-righteous females who went round asking questions and trying to find out what a chap earned and what rent he paid and how much he gave his wife, all in the name of democracy—if that was typical of the new order, said the sturdy inhabitants of Whipley Cross, give them the bad old ways. It was a pity, they declared, if the Government hadn't something better to do than mess about with what didn't concern them. If they wanted a rise of pay or improvement in conditions of work, what were the Unions for? A chap didn't pay his dues for some la-di-dah fellow from Westminster to come down and make rambling speeches about the world after the war. Let 'em do that in the House of Commons where they'd been sent by their constituents in the hope that they'd stay there.

Lady Catherine had been born on Guy Fawkes Day and never let anyone forget it. When Mrs. Routh, sulky, independent and aware, she said, of her rights, came to complain about the treatment she was receiving from a country that had no compunction about taking a woman's husband and, having killed him, was ready to let his widow starve, she said briskly, "It's very bad luck, Mrs. Routh, and I'm very sorry for you, but you can't hold the country responsible. Your husband was killed at his work, and as he was his own employer there's no question of Workmen's Compensation either. I suppose you got the insurance for the funeral?"

Mrs. Routh said sullenly that she had, but that had gone on black for herself and Leila.

"Leila?" repeated Lady Catherine, momentarily stumped.

"Our girl," said Mrs. Routh, more rebelliously than ever.

Lady Catherine recalled a pudding-face atrocity whom she'd always classed as M.D.

"I can't think how you had the coupons," she remarked. "You'll get the widow's pension, I suppose?"

Mrs. Routh said that, seeing as Joe was his own master and not a slave like some she could name, he hadn't never been insured, so she wouldn't even get that.

"You've got some sort of insurance, though, I suppose," frowned Lady Catherine, who was led up the path far less often than her impetuous son. She wasn't afraid of Mrs. Routh starving. She had the small holding and the livestock, and she was pretty in a lumpish sort of way, and there'd been talk of a small farmer at Barston, so it wouldn't be surprising if the banns were up again within the year.

"It's all wrong," flared Mrs. Routh. "There's that foreign woman, Maggie Robinson, got the pension that Mr. Allen made them give her, and Tom Robinson was no more serving his country when he died than my Joe."

"Of course he was," exclaimed Lady Catherine, exasperation outrunning wisdom. "Tom was engaged on secret service work for the Government and that's why he died. Maggie had every right to the pension or my son wouldn't have got it for her."

"Secret Service?" Mrs. Routh looked incredulous. "That's the first I've heard of it."

"I told you it was secret," retorted Lady Catherine. "Of course you hadn't heard."

Mrs. Routh's mind was slowly exploring this new fact like an insect exploring the pollen supply of a new kind of flower. After a minute she looked up and said, "I suppose you mean Tom Robinson was murdered."

"Murdered!" It was exactly what Lady Catherine had meant, but you couldn't have a vicious ninny like Mrs. Routh spreading that story round Whipley Cross. "What a ridiculous idea! Of course not."

"If he'd died of an accident," persisted the stubborn Mrs. Routh, "I don't see why Maggie should have the pension. Nor she wouldn't, neither. No, that's the way of it. He was murdered and Mr. Allen knows it, and that's why he got Maggie the pension. Oh, well that makes everything all right, doesn't it?"

"I don't know what you mean by that addle-pated remark," observed Lady Catherine more acidly than ever. "If you really think murder is all right. . . ."

"What I want to know is—if it's murder why haven't we been told? Mortal lot of use the police are in these parts. Now in London . . ." For Mrs. Routh was—deplorably from the point of view of her neighbors—a townswoman and a Londoner at that . . . "in London you can depend on it we'd have heard plenty about it. Stands to reason. . . ."

"Reason," interrupted the goaded Lady Catherine, "seems to be the last thing that has anything to do with it."

"They know something. And it's not right. Why, the murdering villain might be waiting to run me and Leila down this very night!"

Lady Catherine reflected that villains rarely prove so obliging or so sensible.

"If they give Maggie Robinson the pension you can count on it there's something up . . ." continued Sally Routh in the flat, nasal voice that was beginning to make Lady Catherine feel that if there was sympathy in the world it should be offered to any lorry-driver who ran down this particular member of society.

"I got rid of her after that," she confided to her son later on. "I didn't know what I mightn't do if she'd stayed. How anyone can say a creature like that is my equal. . . ."

"On this occasion she seems to have been more than your equal," observed Mr. Stout cruelly. "And she and her horrible daughter may end up in an asylum, but you're more likely to end up in quod. I don't know what you imagine the police will do when they hear all this careless talk."

"Ignore it, if they've any sense." Lady Catherine sounded impatient.

"You might as well try to ignore an elephant in your drawing-room," retorted Mr. Stout, sounding even more impatient than his parent. "The whole village is buzzing with the story that Tom was murdered and the police know who it was but they don't arrest him, because Maggie's a foreigner in German pay and she's making it worth their while to keep their big mouths shut. I've no doubt that by next week they'll have decided she was in the plot—probably for the sake of the pension."

He went very angrily back to town and proceeded to quarrel with all the heads of Government Departments for this reason and that, and having let off steam, turned all the correspondence over to Miss Bennett telling her to smooth the fellows down.

"I do seem a genius at putting my foot into it," he acknowledged ruefully. He was always secretly afraid Sarah's politely concealed contempt would get the better of her and she would vanish to be the prop and stay of some other Member.

Sarah, however, only said nicely, "It's lucky, isn't it, you're not a centipede," and wrote such charming letters that the recipients thought that chap, Stout, had something after all, though they didn't realize that what he had was a secretary with a sense of humor.

Mr. Stout settled down to a short treatise for his local paper entitled "Thank God for the Middle Classes." The middle classes, he said, are the seed of England's greatness. They are forbearing to the frivolous rich, whom they regard as one regards charming children or well-meaning mental deficients, they burn with a sense of injustice on behalf of the downtrodden poor (though in 1943 there were not many of these), they are wet-nursed by Conscience, and Virtue is their godmother. . . .

"What people don't realize is that Virtue is much more a matter of expediency than you'd guess," said Sarah in thoughtful tones, returning the typewritten effusion. "The middle classes have to earn their livings. They don't have Unions and they don't have landed estates. They have only themselves to fend for themselves. I sometimes wonder if they realize how lucky they are."

Mr. Stout liked his article on the whole; so did his readers, but the author's pleasure was torn to rags by the discovery of a letter in an adjacent column, signed *Amor Justitiae*, suggesting that in the name of Truth certain rumors going round the neighborhood should be scotched "like poisonous snakes."

"There is a widespread feeling that something more than accident lies behind the death in the black-out of a local airman," wrote this portentous prig. "If this is so, those responsible should be brought to justice. If it is not the fact, then the police should search out the source of the rumor and destroy it."

"Why can't these chaps learn to write English before they rush into print," grumbled Mr. Stout. But the rest of the paper's readers were far less concerned with the purity of their native tongue than the impression that writer had certainly contrived to convey—that there was something fishy about Tom Robinson's death.

It was hardly to be expected that the police would ignore so open a challenge, and indeed by this time the gossip was so widespread, that, as Lady Catherine remarked, a corpse could hardly have ignored it. The people in Allen's constituency were simple folk. They knew all about pensions, and that the authorities don't give them away for Valentines. It's like a game; the Government does its best to diddle you, and you do your best to put one over on them. If you manage to filch the pension, you've won. No, by the time that letter had been passed round the constituency even a Government Department couldn't have ignored the situation.

"This is all my mother's doing," said Mr. Stout bitterly to his secretary. "The worst of it is that you can't even argue with her. She thinks she's furthered the cause of justice. In fact, I wouldn't be surprised to know she'd written that damned letter herself."

"She ought to have gone into the House," encouraged Miss Bennett. "She'd have been a tremendous success."

Mr. Stout looked at his watch, realized the bar would be open and went to steady himself. He marveled that men, having been provided by Providence with mothers and Female secretaries, should voluntarily take yet more females to their bosom in holy wedlock. And such permanent females as wives, too! It was notorious that there were far more widows than widowers, and the reason wasn't far to seek. He didn't mention this fact to Miss Bennett, who could have told him that most men are bachelors by temperament, but have little chance of remaining so for any great length of time, providence having apparently a great affection for the female sex—for why else reproduce them in such vast numbers? And women being of necessity enterprising and brave, see to it that the percentage of bachelors in any one generation is remarkably small.

Having finished his drink Mr. Stout snapped up a taxi under the nose of a Member he particularly disliked and went to a Shaw revival. This invariably calmed him. If there had been a new Shaw play on every week he would probably have developed into a perfectly tranquil person and the House of Commons would have missed a lot of fun.

Chapter VI

A FEW DAYS after the authorities reluctantly decided they must take action, the policeman on the barrier informed Mr. Stout, coming boisterously out of a telephone booth, that the gentleman in uniform standing near the railway pass office was waiting to see him. Mr. Stout looked across the lobby and saw a tall dark young man of the kind whose face on the films might be his fortune. You could hear thousands of women whispering among themselves, "Of course, dear, I know he's not exactly handsome, but he's got something. . . ." Something, they meant, that Cary Grant had, that Leslie Howard had, something that made women's hearts move in their breasts and set them to wondering, though quite kindly, what it was they'd once seen in John or Alec, and how strange it was that some women married Cary Grant and Leslie Howard and others just got an ordinary man who'd need labeling to distinguish him from anybody else.

The young man, apparently unaware of the effect he was having on a number of A.T.S. who were being taken round the house by a woman Member who called them "chaps" in a resonant voice, stood very stiff and aloof. He was a dark sardonic-looking creature and his face expressed neither pleasure nor interest in his historic surroundings. He might, in fact, have been a Member of Parliament himself for all the emotion they excited in him. Mr. Stout glanced at the card another policeman pushed into his hand and read, "Wing-Commander Lindsay. Business: Private." (But then any Member will tell you that it always is.)

"Lindsay," murmured Mr. Stout. "Lindsay. What does that

remind me of? Why the hell isn't Miss Bennett here? She'd know." He saw Sarah going towards the Post Office and signaled to her violently. Sarah looked at the card, looked at the young man and said, "Didn't Maggie Robinson say she saw a man called Lindsay, the C.O. at the airfield?"

"I knew it would come back to me in a minute," said Mr. Stout and crossed the lobby.

The young man seemed a little on the defensive. "I hope you don't mind my taking up your time," he said abruptly. "I wanted some advice."

"Very happy," murmured Mr. Stout, slightly dazed. He wasn't accustomed to this kind of thing. People wanted definite concrete help, or introductions, they wanted to rid themselves of grievances and suspicions, sometimes they even wanted to make a touch, but they didn't often frankly admit they wanted advice. He led his man away to a corridor where they sat down on green velvet cushions under a brightly-colored mosaic of Henry VIII and one of his spouses.

"I understand you're interested in the Robinson affair," began Wing-Commander Lindsay.

"Tom Robinson was a friend of mine," explained Mr. Stout. "I put up his wife's case for a pension."

"I told her she ought to," muttered the young man. "Now I wish to God I'd left things alone." His expression said it was Mr. Stout's fault that they were in their present pickle. Members of Parliament had, apparently, all powers in heaven and earth, and it seemed unfortunate that they couldn't employ them to better advantage.

"It was thundering bad luck on her," said Mr. Stout.

Hugh Lindsay swung his clasped hands between his knees. "Somehow she doesn't seem to be the sort of woman who'd want anyone's help. I got the impression of an almost frightening amount of strength. Mind you," he added quickly, "I only saw her once. My second in command, Winter, went to see her when we got the news and she came over unexpectedly to the Station and he was on duty. I kept her waiting about half an hour, because I was out when she arrived and when I began to apologize she just said, It is all right. There is no hurry now. It made my blood run cold to hear her."

"She was devoted to Tom," said Mr. Stout, as though that explained everything.

Lindsay nodded. "I wouldn't like to have her on my track. She's the sort of woman who can consume her own smoke till it's time to release it. I wouldn't like to have her for my enemy."

Mr. Stout decided he wouldn't either. "Has she been at you again?" he asked sympathetically.

The young man shook his head. "She hasn't, but the police have, asking a million and one questions. They've been at various other members of the station, too. Heaven knows what they're really after."

Mr. Stout, who could be quite intelligent on occasions, said, "I daresay you could make a guess not too far off the mark, if it comes to that."

"I don't know how much you know," said the young man grimly.

"I know they have an idea a murder's been committed."

The Wing-Commander took all the wind out of Mr. Stout's sails by replying, "They're dead right there. Only this isn't precisely the time to spread the news."

There was a short pause. Then Mr. Stout said, "I suppose you wouldn't like to amplify that a little."

"I don't know how much authority you chaps have with the police, but they may be doing everyone a colossal disservice by poking their long noses into the business just now," said Lindsay. "I mean—everyone, this country, the—the cause." He stopped abruptly.

Mr. Stout felt you could go on like this all night and meet yourself going to bed, so he decided to get down to brass tacks at once. He had plenty of experience at that, because most constituents labor under the delusion that most politicians have all day and nothing to do worth mentioning except listen to themselves.

"Who's Hargreaves?" he asked.

His companion stopped dead, like a great dog tearing out to greet a burglar and discovering he's shackled by a chain.

"What do you know about Hargreaves?" he enquired after a minute.

"Crux of the situation, isn't he?" queried Mr. Stout.

"I'm inclined to think you're right. The devil of it is I don't know the answer any more than you do."

His Member's thick black brows drew together. (One of the young ladies employed by Potts & Owl, the Parliamentary Secretarial Agency, once said she never saw eyebrows so expressive of sex-appeal.) "According to Maggie Robinson, Tom knew. He gave her that last message to send you."

"She didn't know what it was all about, though. I asked her. She just said it's what Tom told her to do."

"Knowing Tom, I can quite believe it," exclaimed Allen.

"Oh, I daresay." The young airman sounded impatient. "Trouble is, that takes us no further."

"What happened when you arrived at the Bird In Hand? Didn't this fellow Hargreaves turn up?"

"If so, he didn't make himself known to me. As a matter of fact, I realized at once there was something queer, the instant I mentioned his name. The girl behind the bar looked at me in a very odd way and said, 'Oh, yes, perhaps he will be coming later.' She asked some chap who was there, who seemed to be the proprietor, if he was expecting Hargreaves, and this fellow said, 'It's a long time since he was here.' I felt as though I were in a trap, and if I could have put Tom off I'd have done it. But, as it happened, it wasn't necessary. Someone forestalled me."

"Someone who knew you were going to be there that night?"

"Someone who knew Tom had found out something it would be damned inconvenient for them to have broadcast. And Tom didn't do things by halves. That's what I can't make the police understand. I've tried to point out to them that this crime isn't isolated, it's just a part of a much bigger and more dangerous crime, a murder attempt not launched against a single man but against the community, the nation, and they shake their thick heads and talk about law and order. And they're going to imperil the very law for which they say they stand. . . ."

"Don't tell me anything you don't want to, will you?" said Mr. Stout, pleasantly ironical.

"Never thought I'd tackle my Member of Parliament for help," murmured Wing-Commander Lindsay, as if he couldn't quite believe the position even now.

"And then you blame your political representative because he doesn't represent your point of view. How do you expect him to interpret it if you never acknowledge his existence? However, that'll do for next time."

"I daresay. You've no influence with the police in your constituency, I suppose?"

"That's simony or something," murmured a shocked Mr. Stout.

"I didn't imagine you would have. Oh, well, perhaps they'll be cleverer than the rest of, after all. The fact is Tom knew something, and he died before he had a chance to pass it on."

"To you?"

"I suppose that's why he wanted me to be at the Bird In Hand that evening. It was a queer place for Tom to choose. Not an honest-to-God pub at all."

"I gather you're not dealing with honest-to-God people. And it probably wasn't the sort of place where you'd meet anyone else you knew. The fellows he was serving with, I mean."

"It was a kind of roadhouse and not first-class at that. Much too much drink going round for the place to be honest. And we were looking for someone so far removed from honesty that he didn't draw the line at murder."

"I hope you told the police all this," said Mr. Stout interestedly.

"Let them find out anything they can. It's not such a simple murder as they suppose."

"My mother's idea is that Tom was engaged on Secret Service."

"She's about right," said Lindsay. "The fact is there were some very odd things, very unpleasant things, too, going on at the airfield. They'd been going on for some months. Chaps went up in machines that had been tested and pronounced O.K. and they crashed for no special reason. Well, you may get a clumsy pilot now and again, you may have bad luck now and again, but you don't get a succession of accidents such as we had at Whipley. I know men are damned careless; my father, who served through the last war in France, said that till you've been with Tommy at the front you don't realize what careless-ness is. He'd fight to the last inch of his bayonet but he wasn't going to make his haversack heavy by carrying an iron ration. He chucked it away and waited for the ravens to bring him bread and meat. But even when you've allowed for all that, there was too much of the trouble. And we're jealous of our reputation at Whipley."

"Meaning someone was playing Hitler's game on his own?"

Lindsay acquiesced sourly. "Not a nice thing to admit about your own people, but you can't shut your eyes to facts. As soon as I tumbled to what was going on I had special overhauls of all the planes before they went up, and the crashes went on. It was an intolerable situation. . . ."

"Meaning one of your own fellows. . . ."

"Someone working on the airfield. The devil of it is to try and pin down a thing like that. Men come and go; they get transferred or—they take a plane and don't come back. We have civilians working on the ground—because like a lot of other places we can't spare our own men for all the repair work that has to be done. That makes for bad blood sometimes. A lot of these chaps believe in Trade Union hours, they expect to sleep between sheets—well, the R.A.F. at Whipley stopped asking for sheets some time ago. Give 'em blankets and they won't complain. We get chaps from other airfields sometimes, lose their way in bad weather, see our flare-path and come down. They think they're lucky if they get a sofa and they don't complain, if it's the floor. Well, we can't O.K. all the civilians. And apart from that it's not nearly so difficult to get on to the premises as it ought to be."

"My nephew got into a heap of trouble when he told an examining Board that if he were a German parachutist and wanted to take a local airfield he'd simply put on a pair of dungarees and walk in."

"They're much more slack than they should be," the officer

agreed. "Planes standing about without adequate guard. Well, they take so many risks, what's one more or less to them? And then we get new chaps who don't know all the ropes or don't think it matters. . . . We're up against trouble in one form or another the whole time."

"And Tom thought he knew something."

"There was a chap there called Miller, a sergeant, one of Tom's special buddies. He got killed in one of these planes that crashed mysteriously ten minutes after taking off, and Tom suggested that if he could get out of uniform for a bit he might be able to unearth something. The Air Ministry didn't want a scandal, naturally, so he was given official compassionate leave. And now Tom's gone with the rest and I'm no nearer knowing who Hargreaves was than at the beginning. But I'm dead sure the Bird In Hand's mixed up in the affair. If I were the Ministry of Food I wouldn't renew its license."

"And if it refuses you'll get an outcry locally that it's an infernal shame if some poor damned service-man can't even get a cup of tea or a bun between trains."

"Tea and a bun!" repeated Lindsay with a dry, scornful laugh. "You're not likely to find those at the Bird In Hand, except behind a glass case as curiosities. I wouldn't be surprised if hooch wasn't the foundation of their fortune and if I could catch them at it just once I'd put the whole Home Office on to them, or whatever Department it is that's concerned with the Poisons Act."

"And what exactly happened that night?" prompted Mr. Stout.

"Oh, I took the car and went over. I took the car because I thought it possible we might want to make a quick getaway. I got there just as the nine o'clock news was beginning and asked for beer. It seemed the safest thing to have. Then I enquired if Hargreaves was anywhere about, and as I say the balloon began to go up. I got the feeling there were eyes in the wall. I took my beer to a small table and waited. There was nothing special on the news that night. Several chaps pushed their way in, but Tom wasn't among them. I waited till 9.30—he'd said don't wait if I'm not there within half-an-hour—and

I got up to go. The girl behind the bar said wouldn't I wait and I said I thought not, it wasn't important. No one tried to stop me going, nothing melodramatic of that kind, and I got into the car and drove off. It's mostly downhill from the Bird In Hand to the R.A.F. Station and I hadn't got far when I realized someone had been tampering with the works. It was rather like our machines. I couldn't get her into control. I did the only possible thing, took a chance and jumped. The car went hell-for-leather down the hill, turned over twice. It would have been kingdom come for me if I'd stayed in her."

"And you think the chaps or chaps who disabled the car are the same chaps who've been monkeying with your machines?"

"I don't swear it, but it seems to add up, doesn't it? I picked myself up and got back—infernally late, of course. Our night patrol had gone out. Presently we heard that two bombers— O. for Orange and T. for Tiger, had crashed over our own territory. You can say that was coincidence, too, if you like, but—there's a damned sight too much coincidence about the whole affair for me. When I got back my second in command, Winter, said they'd been getting damned anxious. Not as anxious as I've been, I said. I felt there was going to be bad news about our planes that night. Some bastard meant me to be out of the way—for good. Well, he didn't pull that off, but—we lost two machines."

Mr. Stout could see from the strain in the young man's face, the tenseness of his bearing, how bitterly he felt the loss not only of machines that could ill be spared but of men who were irreplaceable. Of friends, too, perhaps, but he wouldn't speak of that.

"When did you hear about Tom?" he asked.

"Next morning. As he wasn't in uniform they went to Mrs. Robinson first. That was about six, I understand. They found him done for by the side of the road. Some murderous brute must have ridden him down deliberately in the dark."

"You knew that from the start?" Mr. Stout sounded a little shocked in spite of himself.

"I was pretty certain."

"And you just sat tight and did nothing?"

"I had no proof," the young man explained.

"I don't know what you want a Member of Parliament for," exploded Mr. Stout. "You seem to make your own laws."

"I couldn't have done Tom any good by coming forward just then. Besides . . ." he stopped and Mr. Stout filled in the gap.

"You don't think much of the police's methods."

"It's not that. But—"Wing-Commander Lindsay's voice was suddenly so cold and brittle with hate that even Mr. Stout was struck dumb. "These chaps have sent some of my best men to a rotten and unnecessary death—through treachery. I'd no mind to hand them over to the tender mercies of the police."

"An eye for an eye," nodded Mr. Stout, "and as you say, you'd no proof."

"I've still no proof."

"And you want me to provide it?"

"Not precisely. I don't expect even my Member to go to those lengths. The real reason why I came to you was because you knew Tom a lot better than any of us, and you knew his widow, and it's possible she'll tell you more than she'll tell anyone else."

"I think she's probably telling the truth when she says she knows nothing. But you can be pretty sure she won't want Tom's murderers to get off scot-free. I'll see her, of course, but I doubt if it's much good. I should think, in the circumstances," he added, "she might change her mind about staying."

"She won't have any choice with the police on the warpath. If they put her through what they've put me she's had a pretty grueling time. Why, if they'd suspected me of the murder they couldn't have been more thorough."

Chapter VII

THERE, as they say in legal circles, the matter rested for a while. Mr. Stout, like a good politician, recalled the adage to do the work that's nearest, though it's dull at whiles, and applied himself vigorously to other less entrancing correspondence. All the usual things happened; it was rumored that Mr. Churchill was going to Russia but he turned up at Washington instead; there were bigger and better raids on Germany; there was a Thanksgiving Service for what had been achieved and with a lively sense of divine favors to come. Various Ministers made statements, one Member died of old age and another was killed on active service, a number of White Papers were issued and people began to talk less about the Beveridge Report.

Then, at the end of about a month, the Ministry of Food put their threat to zone potted meat into effect, and the country was instantly in an uproar. As is usual with zoning schemes, it started in confusion. Yarmouth got nothing but bloater paste and people who were accustomed to feed at the cheaper city restaurants had to take their ration in what was euphemistically called "Meat" or go without. There was no doubt in the minds of urban consumers as to the origin of the meat. They pointed out that there was a great shortage of animal feeding-stuffs and that the Government had called up all the able-bodied men and women, so that clearly a lot of animals were "passing on," and they suggested, some deprecatingly, others with good round oaths, where they were passing on to. . . . Mr. Stout got fewer letters than many of his colleagues because his was an agricultural area, but various bodies of philanthropists and every animal

69

society in the country passed resolutions and sent copies to the Minister of Food and the Member for the Division. The Minister let it be known, after a number of questions had been asked in the House and, in the opinion of the enquirers, inadequately answered, that he intended to deal with this burning subject in the general debate on food supplies to be held in secret session on a particular day.

It was noticeable that when such amorphous questions as the future of England and the rehabilitation of those whom the enemy had deprived of their homesteads were under debate, the attendance was earnest and respectful but scanty, but when the food-supplies of the country were at stake every Member buttoned his coat, recalled how much more tightly it had fitted him a year or so back, and went into the fray with all the eagerness and height of purpose of knights cavorting into the jousting heats or gladiators leaping into the ring to dispose of superfluous Christians.

Mr. Stout prepared for the occasion with his usual subtlety. It was his habit to write out a long detailed speech when he intended to intervene in a debate, and he scorned the prevailing modesty of Members who had their notes typed in single spacing on small sheets of headed House papers, and did their utmost to pretend they didn't exist. Mr. Stout had his notes in double spacing on thick foolscap tied with a bit of pink tape. When his opportunity came he flourished them; other Members, hoping for an opportunity to catch the Speaker's eye (and secretly wondering how it was that that fellow, Stout, always managed to say his piece no matter how many Members wanted to intervene), groaned and leaned back, summoning any patience the day had left them. This chap, they decided, was good for half-an-hour. No sense feeling hurried. They folded their arms and clenched their teeth. And then Mr. Stout abandoned his notes, spoke with great fire and passion for not more than ten minutes, and abruptly subsided. In this way, he explained to Miss Bennett, he ensured an absence of that uncomfortable sensation that someone is treading on your heels, which is such a noticeable feature of most public speaking. Men were prepared for ordeal by verbosity and were delighted at his (comparative) terseness.

"Don't they remember that's your technique?" asked Sarah, really interested.

Mr. Stout looked scandalized. "My dear lady, Members' of Parliament have far too many important things on their minds to recall the idosyncrasies of an individual colleague."

On this occasion he dressed handsomely for his ordeal, donning a low-cut waistcoat in air force blue of the kind of material few have seen since the outbreak of war or are likely to see for many years to come. Miss Bennett tried to decide what actually it was and came to the conclusion it was a rich silk poplin. To match this magnificence Mr. Stout added a gray silk four-in-hand and a pearl pin. In short, like the Biblical desert, he blossomed like the rose.

"You can see any constituents who turn up this afternoon," he told Sarah expansively, his sartorial magnificence going to his head. But the only person who came was an elderly lady with a face as plain as the crook-handled umbrella she carried and a heart as golden on the band round it, that was inscribed with her father's name—he had been Colonel C.I.E.—and she had come to ask her Member if he would put down a question on the subject of horseflesh for human consumption.

"So many people buy it to eke out the meat ration," she explained, her fine brown eyes burning behind her glasses. "And of course they don't have to surrender any coupons. Now, my suggestion is that if they buy it they should have to give up coupons just the same as they do at a butcher's for pork, and then they would think twice before they bought it."

"And there'd be ample supplies for animals? Is that your point?"

"Precisely. I sometimes wonder how even Mr. Churchill would solve this problem of feeding pets in war-time. It isn't that I mind making sacrifices for Hector and Othello, and I stand in a queue forty minutes three days a week for them, but it's confusing. The other day when at last it was my turn—it had been raining steadily, and a most disagreeable woman next to me made the most absurd fuss about a few raindrops that ran off my umbrella—I found there'd been a muddle round the corner (because all queues go round corners these days) so I found I was in the rhubarb queue. So tiresome. Hector and Othello don't care for rhubarb, and you can't make dogs understand a thing like war."

Sarah agreed gravely that it must be difficult.

"You see, if you made the people give up coupons for horseflesh," repeated Miss Err-umph (even the competent Sarah couldn't read the name on the card), "they wouldn't buy it and we could. After all," she added, in proud and passionate tones, "it isn't the animals who made this war, though they have to suffer for it."

"I'll suggest the point to Mr. Stout," Sarah promised. "Perhaps he'll put it to the Ministry of Food." It wasn't, after all, much more peculiar than a number of other proposals he had made to that long-suffering Ministry.

"It isn't the queues I mind," urged the constituent. "I'm sure I don't grudge anything I can do in a war, and I suppose it is a great temptation to keep things under the counter. I don't mind so much for myself. My housekeeper would tell you I never complain even though I never see a fish on my table I'd have bowed to before the war, but when it comes to poor Othello getting hysterics because he only has biscuits . . . Some dogs are that way, you know." She blew her nose heartily.

Miss Bennett agreed with sincerity that on the whole dogs were a good deal more attractive than human beings.

"They have such winning ways—certainly my two have," cried Miss Err-umph eagerly. "And they're so sincere. I feel certain that, left to themselves, the dogs of Germany would never have made war on the dogs of Poland. . . ."

Sarah suggested a nice cup of tea, and saw her off the premises.

Some time later Mr. Stout strolled into the lobby with his friend, Mr. Penberthy, both of them hotly contesting the Parliamentary Secretary's statement on the potted meat situation. They talked with such heat that a lady, waiting to see her Member, observed pointedly that careless gossip costs lives, and after all a secret session was a secret session.

"You did damn well," said Mr. Penberthy generously. "Only —did you think it was a fancy dress party?"

Mr. Stout looked surprised. "They always look like that," he said.

"No, no." The Member for South Mould indicated the blue waistcoat. "Stout fellow! No pun intended. Anyone could see Squanderbug hasn't anything on you. I haven't quite got down to robbing the family museum myself. . . ."

"It's a pity you don't give the rest of the House a chance of appreciating your wit," returned Mr. Stout rather coldly. He was an easy-going chap, Heaven knew, but even easy-going chaps have their feelings. He patted the waistcoat in a reassuring sort of way, much as Miss Err-umph patted her dogs when she hadn't been able to get them any horseflesh and they wanted comforting.

Presently, refreshed by tea and the congratulatory remarks of some of his colleagues, he went down, as pleased as Punch, to the Plan Room to collect, if possible, a little adulation from his secretary.

Sarah, however, after the disappointing way of women, failed to realize what was expected of her. She was going methodically through the late afternoon post, carefully slitting envelopes with a penknife, so that by the expenditure of a label, much patience and a certain amount of time, they could be used again.

"Anything important?" asked Mr. Stout benevolently, pulling down the killing blue waistcoat, and preparing to answer questions, and to remind his secretary, quite casually, of course, to send his speech in Hansard to his papers before midday tomorrow.

"A bit disconcerting," said Sarah, and her face was so grave that he forgot the importance of publicity and took alarm at once.

"What is it? Murder? High treason?"

"Both," said Sarah. "The police have arrested Wing-Commander Lindsay for the murder of Tom Robinson."

Such was the effect of this statement on Mr. Stout that even the Potted Meat Controversy no longer seemed important. He stared unbelievingly at the letter his secretary laid before him. It came from his agent and gave him the bare facts. There was another letter—from his mother this time—which clothed the facts in so much comment and speculation and downright assertion that it would have been an example in camouflage to any War Department.

After a tense moment the Member for Malvoisin let fly.

"Of all the flannel-footed, hump-backed, ginger-headed, muckle-mouthed, addle-pated sons of orang-outangs," he exploded. "How exactly like the authorities to pick on the wrong man."

Sarah, always more of a realist than her employer, said gently, "You're sure he is the wrong man?"

To which he replied with what a film audience would have recognized as a sneed, "Of course I'm not sure. It's likely I'd want to defend the man who murdered Tom, isn't it? I believe women think every policeman is a member of the Heavenly Guard. And they're always convinced that whoever is right it isn't their husband or employer." He dropped his long chin into his hands. "Damn!" he said. "I wonder what evidence they've got."

His secretary, undeterred by his fulminations, asked delicately whether the accused man was, in point of fact, Mr. Stout's constituent.

"No," roared Mr. Stout, "most probably he is not. That's another thing about women. They're all born with a book of etiquette stamped on them somewhere like a birthmark." He glared balefully at Miss Bennett but she, who would have confronted Boris Karloff alone and unarmed in the cause of justice, met his gaze unflinchingly. "The fact remains, he needs my help, and if you know your Bible you'll remember the command that from him that asketh of thee turn not thou away. And I daresay his own Member's such a gentleman he won't want to be mixed up in this sort of scandal."

"Where does he come from?" enquired Sarah, doggedly. "Barcheston? Oh, then that's all right. The Member's engaged in post-war planning somewhere in the South Seas—for Mr. and

Mrs. Member and all the little Members. There's no fear of any competition there. So, if you're convinced he's innocent. . . ."

"If you mean, have I any proof, of course I haven't. But have you ever heard of intuition? I know women are supposed to have it all, but now we're getting equality between the sexes, men are gradually catching up with them. No, don't ask. My intuition hasn't yet told me who is responsible. It doesn't work as fast as that—besides, you have to leave something to logic."

"Quite," agreed Miss Bennett, with the composure that is the mark of the perfect secretary as of the perfect wife.

"Wonder if he's got a good solicitor," Mr. Stout continued. "Probably has. He had a very respectable look."

"A respectable solicitor isn't the kind who's going to be much good to him in a case like this," suggested Sarah the Sensible. "I never could see any use in paying a man to stand up in court and repeat the facts you'd given him. Anyone can tell the truth."

"You wouldn't say that if you'd been in the House of Commons as long as I have," returned Mr. Stout, emphatically.

"I didn't say people did, I said anyone could. Naturally most people don't, because truth's often less convenient than camouflage. But in a court of law truth is what you can make the mass of the people believe."

"Were you ever in a solicitor's office?" asked Mr. Stout.

"What you want now—or rather, what Mr. Lindsay wants—is a man who can produce as good evidence as the prosecution and present it even more convincingly."

"Know anyone like that?" asked Mr. Stout, politely. By this time he wouldn't have been surprised if his secretary had opened her handbag and taken a banana out of it.

"There's Mr. Crook. You remember I spoke to you about him once before. He's the man who got Jedburgh pardoned when everyone knew he'd murdered his wife."

"No conscience, in fact," said Mr. Stout judicially.

"A professional conscience," urged Miss Bennett. "He'd tell you his job was to get his man off. That's what he's being paid for. If he fails he's let his side down. You ought to appreciate that."

Mr. Stout, who'd captained the Malvoisin team in his time, felt instantly more kindly towards the unknown Mr. Crook. He was also inclined to be more convinced of his abilities. He would have been shocked had he known that the only cricket that gentleman had ever played had been in an alley at the age of eight.

"How the devil does he do it?" he enquired.

"When he hasn't got enough evidence he manufactures it. I heard him tell the Home Secretary so."

"And the Home Secretary accepts it? Shame on him."

Miss Bennett creased her neat brows. "He hasn't really much choice. All the Ministries are accepting the next-best-thing in this war, what with shipping difficulties and man-power difficulties and so long as it's foolproof he hasn't really anything to complain about. Anyhow, that's what the Ministry of Food tells us when we say we don't like war-time bread or war-time fats."

"It might be worth trying," agreed Mr. Stout, "though it'll have to be put discreetly."

"I shouldn't worry too much about that," Sarah advised him. "I don't think he gives a toss for what anyone else thinks of him. He's one of the few real independents in existence—like fanatics and saints and . . ."

"Did you say you only talked to him for five minutes?" enquired Mr. Stout.

"Don't forget about intuition," Sarah reminded him, registering another bull's-eye.

"May as well take a long shot as a short one," Mr. Stout agreed. "Wonder what evidence the police have got."

"Don't keep a dog and bark yourself," Sarah suggested. "Mr. Crook can probably outbark the whole of the Yard."

"If he takes it on."

"He'll take it on if it looks hopeless enough. He's that sort. You meet them on race courses all the time. They back the spavined outsider at 100 to 1 and the rest of the field are so shocked at finding themselves in such company they just fall back naturally and the outsider wins," a suggestion so original and yet so incontestable in the circumstances that Mr. Stout could only gape.

At last he said, "How do you propose to find this chap?"

"He's a lawyer. We'll look up the directory. His Christian name's Arthur and he lives in London. I heard him say so. He's the sort of man who advertises himself a lot. There are two sorts of men who advertise themselves. The kind that feel they must keep drawing your attention to them or you won't notice they're there, and the kind that do it to reassure you that you've nothing to worry about—like saying, Thank God, we're an island—that sort of thing."

Mr. Stout was by this time pretty well accustomed to his secretary, so he merely said, "When you've found him, what next? Do I write in out of the blue?"

"I should think I'd better prepare the ground," said Sarah thoughtfully. "After all, we haven't been introduced, but we've had some intimate conversation and I should say he's the sort of person with a mind like a cinematographic machine. Everything registers. You can always feel him thinking, Not very promising for my line, but you never know."

At that moment Mr. Stout, remembering his first impressions of her as he crossed the lobby floor, was thinking just the same thing.

Chapter VIII

ARTHUR CROOK experienced no surprise when the bell of his large hideous flat in Earl's Court rang after the 9 o'clock news. He had always had a considerable clientele who preferred to pay their visits in the black-out, and he liked to say of them that they generally paid their bills also, which was more than some of the people who could afford to come by day troubled to do. The front door of the house was left open till 10.30, so all he had to do was open the front door of his own flat and wait for whoever it was to mount the great black staircase. An economical landlord had removed all the electric light bulbs on the ground that they might give warning to enemy aircraft. When he opened his door that night and saw a trim figure on the step his instincts warned him to be careful. Mr. Stout wasn't his match when it came to distrusting women.

"This will seem a very unconventional hour to call," began Miss Bennett sedately, but he silenced her with a hearty, "Not a bit of it. It's what I'm used to," an ambiguous remark that left her for a moment without speech. As soon as he came into the shabby narrow hall and had turned on the dull blue light he added, "Why, it's the lady secretary. Get your job?"

"Yes," said Miss Bennett, rather frostily.

"Quick work," applauded Mr. Crook. "Come inside." He opened a door painted to resemble grained oak and showed her into a room that looked as though a cyclone had swept through it. On an ugly square writing-table the papers lay in piles; they overflowed on to the chairs, where they lay jumbled with tobacco tins, beer bottles and a coat that Mr. Crook had temporarily discarded. The walls were discolored and there was a patch in one place where the house had suffered bomb damage, but Mr. Crook didn't bother his landlord, on the ground that you never could get landlords to do much, and now they had the law to back them up, so why waste your stamps? Anyways, he was nose to grindstone all his waking hours and hadn't time to go staring at flooded cornices. He cleared a chair for Sarah by gathering all the papers off one and dumping them on to another, offered her a cigarette out of a fancy box from Warsaw and a glass of beer. When he saw she took the beer, he nodded approvingly.

"Looks as though you and me might be going to play ball," he remarked. "Whose trouble is it? Yours or the Member's?"

"In a sense, I suppose it's his."

"You know," said Mr. Crook, "if they'd make me Minister without Portfolio for a little while, there's a lot of things I'd like to suggest. You know what I am?"

"A lawyer," hazarded Miss Bennett.

"Right. And what are you? A lady secretary. Well, how did I get my job and how did you get yours? Not standing up on a platform telling people what we were going to do, but going to school and learning how to do it. I don't know a lot about Parliament, but if it's the sort of job a chap can take on without any training, beyond a couple of weeks' coaching by a partisan agent, then it can't be worth much. Of course," he added honestly, "that fact is generally recognized. You can't expect much for £600 a year, with the income tax at ten bob. But I daresay," he added with a shameless wink, "there are little perks on the side."

"If there are," said Sarah coolly, "Mr. Stout pockets them all."

"I'll take you on as bursar when I start my political college," offered Mr. Crook handsomely. "We'd teach 'em what they need to know. They prance into politics as amateurs prance into crime and then they're surprised if they find themselves in jug. What's your chap done?"

"Got himself involved in a murder," returned Sarah, who could be as terse as Crook when occasion demanded.

Crook whistled. "They do think of things, these M.P.'s.

Who's he murdered? A constituent or just another Member of Parliament?"

"One of his constituents has been arrested."

Crook broke into peals of hearty laughter and filled up both glasses.

"Well, well, well," he ejaculated. "One of the conscientious kind. Takes his duties to his constituents as seriously as all that."

"He isn't even a constituent, not the one who's been arrested," explained Sarah, with less than her normal lucidity. "Only the one who's been killed."

"And your man hates his voters so he's prepared to defend the killer?"

"He doesn't think he is the killer," explained Sarah.

"And he wants me to prove he ain't? Well, he's come to the right shop. Any details?"

"Not many." Briefly she outlined the story so far as they knew it.

"Who says the pictures aren't true to life?" was Crook's unfeeling comment. "Is your friend staying out in the cold altogether?"

"If you mean, can you see him, naturally he'd expect it. I thought I'd save time, in case you weren't interested."

"Well," said Crook, to her disgust, "you don't expect me to decide on the spur of the minute, do you?"

That was precisely what Sarah had expected.

"It's not that I'm fussy," Crook was careful to explain, "and I wouldn't hesitate if it was just an ordinary, clean murder. But —sabotaging 'planes—wholesale murder, really—well, that does take a bit of thinking."

"If you become convinced that Wing-Commands Lindsay is the guilty party Mr. Stout's the last person who'd want you to urge his innocence," declared Sarah. "But the police don't make an arrest without something to go on."

"Too true they don't," Mr. Crook agreed. "I don't say the police and me is David and Jonathan, but you have to hand it to them, they sometimes are right."

Thoughtfully he opened another quart of beer.

"Mr. Stout will be responsible for the financial side of the operation, if necessary, he told me to tell you," added Sarah.

Mr. Crook nearly dropped the bottle. "Well," he said, skilfully preventing a tragedy, "I didn't suppose he thought I was the Relieving Officer."

Sarah thought dispassionately it was a pity that brains and breeding weren't more often united, but she supposed it was like brains and beauty. In so imperfect a universe, with too few virtues to go round, no one could really expect more than one.

"All right," added Crook, "you trot back and tell him I'll do it."

He opened his uvula and poured a pint of beer into his roomy stomach.

"One more point," he observed, slamming the tankard down on the table with a noise like a small bomb. "This chap may prefer to carry on with his own defense. I suppose you haven't thought of enquiring?" His expression said that Members of Parliament got so used to poking their noses into the other fellow's affairs they never stopped to ask if they were welcome.

"Mr. Stout appreciates that," Sarah assured him, "but in such a case he thought you might, as it were, hold a watching brief, in case his man's a bit slow off the mark."

"I get you," agreed Mr. Crook. "Pay your twopence and come in and see Arthur Crook, the Human Jackal."

Then he lugged a turnip of a watch out of his pocket and looked at it and announced that it was time to put on the wireless for the Armchair Detective. He said he never missed that if he could help it. Hearing the way authors thought people committed crimes gave him his laugh of the week.

2.

In the average murder the person who gets the least consideration is the corpse, and the person who gets most of the limelight, and a large proportion of public sympathy, is the man in the dock. In the present case, however, the situation was reversed. A rather garbled account of what had happened had percolated into the press, with the result that there were those who said Lindsay was lucky to be under lock and key. It was better than being lynched.

Crook went down to Lestingham, where he was being held, twenty-four hours after his conversation with Miss Bennett. He had an odd preference for doing his own snooping; private investigators, he said, had caught the contemporary disease of being gentlemen. In his young days a chap who'd been at Oxford would have thought it beneath his dignity to look through keyholes or hide behind curtains for a living, but now all these young sprigs of nobility were taking the bread out of honest men's mouths.

"Look at the Stock Exchange," he liked to say. "Sprinkled with Debrett. It's enough to make any chap a socialist."

At Lestingham Gaol they knew him quite well. They get a lot of tough nuts at Lestingham, and the tougher the nut the more pleasure it gave Crook to crack it. And he had a hunch that Hugh Lindsay might prove a very tough nut indeed. The warder who took him along to the prisoner said as much.

"One of these quiet chaps," he said. "Sulky as a bear. That's the kind that gives the most trouble in the end."

When Crook came in he saw a tall dark young man with a face as full of expression as a closed door. This would have discouraged some men, but Crook rather enjoyed closed doors. He said no one troubled to shut them if there wasn't something worth hiding on the other side.

When he saw Crook the young man looked as though something unexpected and unwelcome had come through a crack in the floor.

"Mr. Lindsay?" said Crook, who was a true democrat in the sense that he never bothered about titles.

"Well?"

"Heard of you from Mr. Stout," mumbled Crook.

"Yes," said Mr. Lindsay.

"He don't like the way things have turned out," said Crook.

"No?" said Lindsay.

"Asked me to look into things," amplified the lawyer.

"I see." Lindsay put his hand into his pocket, feeling for the

cigarette-case that was no longer there. Then he remembered
and took it out again.

"Will you be seeing Mr. Stout when you go back to town?"
he enquired.

Crook said he thought that uncommonly likely.

"Then perhaps you could tell him with my compliments
what he ought to know already, that it's not etiquette for one
Member to interest himself in another Member's constituent,"
said Lindsay.

"It's Tom Robinson he's really thinking of," explained Mr.
Crook. "Tom was a friend of his and he wants to see justice
done."

"Can't he leave that to the police?"

Mr. Crook put his bowler hat carefully on the floor. "Mind
you, I wouldn't say this on the steps of St. Paul's Cathedral," he
said confidentially, "but I have known times when the police
were wrong."

He could see he wasn't exactly *persona grata* with the young
man, and with an odd simplicity he put this down to his own
manner and appearance. Obviously, Lindsay was the type that
imagines a solicitor wears white slips to his waistcoat and a
monocle on a black cord, and wouldn't believe that a man with
red hair and the general air of a bookie's tout could impress a
judge and jury.

"I see your point," Crook went on modestly, "but at a time
like this—national peril and all that—ought a chap to put personal feelings first?"

"There are times," said Hugh Lindsay dryly, "when he
hasn't much choice."

"You mean, you think, if you lie low and let everyone
think it was you, these fellows'll be lulled into what's called
false security and hang themselves? Well, it could be, Com-
mander, it could be." His voice was sober enough now. He'd
met all kinds of men in his time, but he hadn't before really
believed in men prepared to die for a cause, against a brick wall,
if need be. It was the brick wall not the fact of death that impressed him here. But he wasn't a sentimentalist, he'd have told
you. His profession soon knocks the nonsense out of a man. He

didn't like this new development, and he knew Stout wouldn't like it either.

"Have it your own way," he said, though he didn't mean it in the least. "Doesn't occur to you you're bein' a bit conceited about the whole thing?"

"Conceited?" Hugh Lindsay was shaken for a moment out of his careful artificial control.

"Imaginin' the experts—as represented by A. W. Stout and Co.—are N.B.G. Besides, in your position (you hold the King's Commission, remember), do you think you've any right to leave these fellows to do a bit more sabotage, kill a few more chaps, if it can be prevented? Unto each man his conscience, unto each his crown. . . . What made the police pitch on you?"

Lindsay still looked stubborn.

"All right," said Crook, pitching away a good trump. "I can find out myself, no doubt. Everything the police know I know already. What I want from you is just that little something that they haven't got. But if you won't give it me I'll have to work on my own account."

"When you say you know what the police know . . . what does that mean?"

"What it sounds like," said Crook, patiently. "Anything you like to add will be gratefully received."

Lindsay suddenly gave way. "All right," he said, "but I can't help you much. You know about the trouble at the aerodrome?"

"As much as you've told anyone," agreed Crook.

"It seems pretty obvious that someone's doing it for one of two reasons, patriotism or money. I don't know which it is. . . ."

"I could make a good guess," said Crook.

Lindsay looked at him enquiringly.

"Well, say that patriotism and thrift sometimes go hand in hand. No suspicions, have you?"

"Not the smallest. I told Stout that. It's almost impossible for a man on the spot, as I was, to see things straight. You need to be a little way off. Tom knew that, and I'll always believe Tom died because he knew too much."

"Why did the police pick you up?" enquired Crook.

"Partly it was the money and partly it was the note they found among my belongings. Of course, they gave me every chance of explaining them both. The trouble was I couldn't do it—at least, no explanations they felt inclined to accept."

"Let's hear about the money first," said Crook, who believed in taking things in their right order.

Lindsay hesitated. "It's a little complicated. The fact is they were making enquiries on all hands and naturally they looked to see whether anybody had suddenly come into some money he couldn't explain away. And there was a sum of five hundred pounds."

Crook nodded. He was accustomed to that kind of argument. Quite a number of his clients admitted with surprise that they couldn't produce any answer the police would take as to their sudden accession to wealth or comparative wealth. Of course, five hundred pounds wasn't much, but Burke and Hare, Crook reminded himself, committed their crimes for about eight pounds a corpse.

"It's odd that they should have placed so much weight on the money," said Lindsay, sounding genuinely astonished. "When you think how little money will buy, how little it's worth these days, you'd hardly believe a man would take such tremendous risks, his own life, in fact, for five hundred."

"From the official point of view you chaps are risking your lives for a damn sight less than that every day of the week," returned Crook in his downright way. "Well, what did you tell them?"

"The trouble was I'd recently drawn out about four hundred pounds for—for a personal debt." He stopped again.

"Any details?" Crook prompted him.

"Well—no. They wouldn't help. It was a debt of sorts."

"Lady?" suggested Crook. "All right. If you ask me, you chaps are brought up on fairy-tales. All this delicacy about a dame. . . . All right, all right. It won't help you to commit a real murder. Carry on. You drew out the money—cash or check?"

"Cash. It was—easier."

"I'll take your word for it," said Crook.

"I suppose I'm a bit careless over money," Lindsay went on. "I always was."

"And if you are it ain't so damn' surprising," reflected Crook. Men who anticipated becoming husbands and fathers, settling down, buying a house, founding a business and a family—money was real to them all right, but you couldn't expect a young man in the R.A.F. to take it very seriously. Anyway, nearly all the answers to this question were *cherchez la femme*. Crook didn't object to clichés, holding, very reasonably, that if they weren't of popular appeal they wouldn't be clichés at all.

"Carry on," he encouraged.

"I wasn't sure how my account stood," the young man continued, "but I hoped it would stand the strain. Unfortunately, I was overoptimistic, and I got a note from the bank manager saying he'd be glad if I'd square the account. They don't like our crowd to run into debt, and you can quite appreciate their point of view. When I got their letter I wrote to my Uncle James. He's a wealthy old bird, with no family, bar his wife, and he feels the war quite a bit. I thought he was a pretty safe bet, but what I hadn't allowed for was his collapsing with an attack of shingles, and my Aunt Cecily dealing with all his correspondence. She's one of these women who know their vocation is to put things right. She does what she can in her own home, and then she turns her attention to the outside world. She sits on Committees and asks questions—you know the kind."

"Not the kind that appreciate debt in the family circle."

"I see you understand," Lindsay agreed in his grim way.

"No sympathy, in short."

"Oh, she had plenty of sympathy, but not with me. No, it was all kept for Uncle James, being bled white by a conscienceless spendthrift. You know, that woman ought to have been Lord Kindersley's private secretary. Between the pair of them no one would dare have half-a-crown left in their bank account by the end of the next Wings for Victory campaign. She wrote that she and Uncle James were having a most expensive time, doctor's bills were enormous, housekeeping expenses up about 100 per cent—though naturally a young man without responsibilities wouldn't understand that. She said she knew that times were abnormal, but with people starving all over the continent, it was difficult to understand how people who were more fortunate could even think of luxuries. She said it was the duty of everyone to give their utmost in this life and death struggle, and she enclosed some savings advertisements."

"Positively no admittance," agreed Crook. "Well? Any other takers?"

"I've got a reversion coming to me when I'm thirty. I tried to raise something on that but—nothing doing."

"Well, it wasn't much security, was it?" observed Crook, bluntly.

"The bank manager began to get unpleasant. I didn't know what the devil to do. It doesn't do a man any good to get into trouble over money especially when he's in charge of a station. This chap seemed my Aunt Cecily's twin. I said would he give me another month to raise the cash and he said he would."

"Any idea where the money was coming from?" asked Crook, quite patient, quite credulous. He knew that optimism is the last and least often mentioned of the deadly virutes.

"Oh, well," said Lindsay, "a month's a long time. Anything might happen."

Meaning, of course, as Crook realized, that by the time the month was over, he might have lost interest in bank accounts and everything else connected with this planet.

"And did you manage to raise the cash after all?" he enquired not without curiosity.

"That's the odd part of it. The story's so flimsy you can hardly blame the police for looking at me sideways. About that time the trouble at the airfield started and drove everything else out of my mind. With some of our best chaps being killed and planes being lost and no evidence that anyone could discover—and naturally we wanted to keep it quiet, if we could—

I hadn't much time to think of my own affairs. Then one morning—this was after Tom had got into civvies and was doing a bit of exploring on his own account—I got a letter from the bank manager thanking me for the remittance which more than squared the account. I didn't know how much I had in hand, so I went down and asked to see my balance sheet, and I found five hundred pounds had been paid in. I thought at once it was Uncle James, though I also thought it a bit queer he shouldn't have written to warn me. Anyway I wrote to say thank you as tactfully as possible, because there's no knowing in that household who opens the letters, and said I was glad he was better and hoped to be able to come over and see him soon."

"And he said. . . ."

"I thought it was a pretty neat letter, seeing Aunt Cecily is reputed to go through his pockets every night. But if she'd read his it wouldn't have told her anything. He simply said he was glad everything was all right and he hoped I'd learnt my lesson and it was all very well to have a stout heart but there was no virtue in recklessness—I could have told him better, but naturally it's no use ever trying to tell relations things, they don't believe you—and besides I was too grateful to him for getting me out of a nasty jam to be touchy. I read between the lines, but it appears I read all wrong. Because it turned out he didn't send the money after all."

"Then where did it come from? Money don't grow on bushes," said the literal Mr. Crook.

"That's what I still don't know, so it stands to reason I couldn't tell the police when they asked me."

"And they wouldn't believe you? Brother, it doesn't surprise me. The police are like that. If they saw a miracle happening under their eyes, they'd refer to their book of statutory regulations to explain it away. That was the beginning of the trouble," continued Lindsay, "but I didn't see then where it was going to lead. I thought it was damned insolent of them to mess about in my affairs in any case. Then they turned up the letter."

"The letter?"

"Yes. It was a message, typewritten on a bit of unheaded

paper. It said: Hargreaves. Bird In Hand nine o'clock to-night. Stage set. Terms satisfactory. Just like something on a film."

"One wonders what sort of letters conspirators wrote before there was a film industry," reflected Crook. "What did Sherlock Holmes say when he wanted to pass the word to Watson that there were dark doings ahead?"

"Played 'em on a violin, I suppose. Naturally, they asked me to explain what the note meant and I said I hadn't ever seen it before. They said that was queer, seeing it was found in my private quarters. I said if it was I hadn't put it there. But I couldn't explain it, any more than I could explain the money."

"You mean you couldn't put a name to it," corrected Crook. "The explanation's simple enough. It's like those things you learn at school. If A. doesn't equal X. then B. equals X. If you're innocent, then someone else is guilty. Q.E.D. And the guilty person put the letter in your room. Does that get us any forrader?"

"I hardly think so," said Lindsey. "Assuming one of the men at the airfield is responsible, it could have been so many people. And I've no other facts to point to any particular person."

"Whereas the police have quite a lot of pointers all traveling back to you. What the police look for first is opportunity—and then motive. How, you had the opportunity all right. You were out the night Tom died. You knew—or were pretty sure—he'd got news at last. He'd passed it on to no one, but when he died—someone was for the high jump. You knew where he was going, you could probably guess the way he came. You were in a car; you could have run him down. You got to the Bird In Hand and Hargreaves didn't turn up—but no one knows who Hargreaves was. You said it might be a name Tom used himself. The police could equally well argue it was a name you used. You didn't get back till late—and two of the 'planes were interfered with."

"And my car?" enquired Hugh Lindsay politely. "Did I buckle her up, too?"

"If you'd been guilty, that's precisely the sort of thing you would do—because people in general would say, 'Well, he might have taken that chance to throw dust in our eyes' and there are even men who would have done it, take my word."

Lindsay maintained a moody silence.

"Then—keep your tomahawk to yourself, won't you?—but you were in a bit of a financial jam and the money turned up damned conveniently, and without any strings tied to it, so far as anyone could see. I get quite a lot of annonymous letters myself, but they don't generally have five hundred pounds inside them. Well, obviously the police will want to know where that came from. You say you can't tell them. It all adds up, you know. Why, when you heard he was run down you kept your mouth shut, though you say now you were always pretty sure it wasn't an accident."

"Tom was dead," said the young man harshly. "I couldn't do anything about that, and these fellows were much too clever to leave any clews. I thought we must give them their head—and that's what I'm doing now."

"Nice sense of values you've got," approved Crook. "Only things don't always turn out the way you expect."

"I've always believed a man's got the right to gamble with his own life, provided he doesn't involve anyone else," observed Lindsay.

"Point is, can you help involvin' anyone else? F'r instance, Stout's pushed his way in, and you're cleverer than I am if you know how to push him out. Now I've pushed in, and you'll be cleverer than Churchill if you know how to push me out." It crossed his mind, though he didn't say so, that a much smaller man than Winston Churchill might be able to push him out—with a knobkerry or a garrotte or just a common-or-garden revolver. Honest men, thought Crook, intelligently following up his own line of thought while Lindsay sat in disapproving silence, looking like a Nonconformist Minister at Phil the Fluter's ball, can't get hold of revolvers easily even in peacetime, and not at all when there's a war on, but the bad hats always know the way round the regulations. The authorities, thought Crook warming to his mental task, do make it difficult for men to be honest. He'd have found himself in agreement with Miss Bennett there, who said that Thrift and Virtue paid the heaviest taxes in the world.

"God," said Mr. Lindsay suddenly, "what I could do to a pint of beer?"

He could have said nothing that would have warmed Crook to him more heartily. No protestations of innocence, backed with the necessary proof, would have been so welcome.

"You'll be having it soon if you take your Uncle Arthur's advice," he said. "By the way, what's a good place round here? I don't mean the Bird In Hand sort, but some place where a plain chap like me won't be run out on sight."

"The Pheasant's not too bad," said the young man consideringly. "And the Walrus and the Carpenter can do you a very pretty line when the Government don't interfere."

"But the Pheasant gets most of your money?"

Lindsay laughed for the first time. He looked a different man when he laughed. Crook supposed that Anonyma must have seen him laughing the first time they met. Up till now he'd thought, if he were a girl, he'd as soon walk out with the rock of Gibraltar.

"It gets most of the chap's money," he agreed.

Crook stood up, collected the brown bowler, brushed it professionally against his loud brown sleeve, put it on at the kind of angle respectable solicitors never affect, and said in a friendly way, "One good turn deserves another. I'll be seeing you," and went.

Lindsay felt for a minute like Sarah, waiting in the lobby of the House of Commons to see Mr. Stout for the first time. Crook was like no one he'd ever met before, but—it was like standing on the edge of a cliff and knowing that any minute you'd crash on to the rocks below, and suddenly realizing there was a wall at your back. And how a fellow with such an appearance could create such an impression was almost enough to make a modern young man believe in miracles.

He had just got to that stage when he was aware that Crook had come back and was standing in the doorway.

"Just a little reminder," he called. "If you should change your mind before my next visit just drop me a post-card."

91

"Change my mind?" There was instant suspicion in the young man's voice. "What do you mean?" The words zipped out like machine gun bullets. You almost expected to see a dent in the opposite wall.

"About you-know-what that you're keeping dark," said Crook, and this time he really did go, making an exit that would have wrung the withers of almost any leading man with envy.

Chapter IX

ON HIS WAY from the prison Crook dropped
in to see the police. He said it would help him a lot if he could
see the actual letter that had done so much to jail Hugh Lindsay. They showed it to him—people always showed things to
Crook sooner or later, and once they'd had dealings with him
it was sooner. It saved so much time. The message was typewritten on a plain piece of paper and was unsigned. It read (as
the young man had declared already):

> Hargreaves. Bird In Hand nine o'clock to-night.
> Stage set. Terms satisfactory.

That was all. Crook copied it down exactly, handed the paper
back and went his way. His next port of call was the accused
man's bank. There were two or three other people on the
premises, on the clients' side of the counter, when he came in.
Two of them were sitting on chairs by the window as if it were
a restaurant and they were waiting for a cup of coffee. Crook's
eye swept the counter. There was one old man counting the
money very slowly and licking his finger with maddening deliberation as he did so, and two women, neither of them young.
He went up to the older and asked if he could see the manager.

"About an account?" asked the woman briskly.

Crook stared. "Urgent private business," he said.

He was beginning to get a curious feeling about this case,
and experienced one of his rare moments of self-consciousness.
In fiction and on the films men who did detective work always
looked exactly like everyone else, little tame rats of men you

wouldn't know if you met them again, but if you'd once seen Crook you'd not forget those beetling red brows, the aggressive tilt of the brown bowler hat, the distinctive suit, the jaunty plump figure. As a rule he thought that if a man was noticeable enough you didn't see him much. Now he began to wonder. This wasn't actually his sort of case.

The woman waited a minute and then went into a room at the back. She returned to say that the manager was engaged.

"I'll give him five minutes," said Crook, and had the odd feeling that he'd made a mistake. He'd made himself more conspicuous than ever. He felt like a man who has never crossed the Channel or learnt any more French than you pick up at an ordinary public school suddenly finding himself in an outlying French district trying to ask the way. He didn't know the right phrases and he couldn't be sure if they understood him or not.

However, he sat down among the pseudo-coffee-drinkers and put his big turnip watch on the table. At the end of five minutes he got up and walked the length of the counter. The plain woman had a customer, a big elderly female with feathers around a cartwheel hat. She seemed to be in trouble about a pension.

"That isn't exactly our Department," the plain woman was saying. Crook marched past in the direction of the door. He thought she gave a sigh of relief but whether it was because she was glad to be rid of a difficult customer or because she saw in him a source of danger that had been damned at the source he couldn't be certain. At the end of the building was a door marked Private and he marched through before anyone realized what he was doing. It was an odd-shaped room in which he found himself, with chairs and a desk at the near end and in a sort of L a well-shaven well-dressed man of about sixty seated at a second desk. When he saw Crook he stood up.

"I beg your pardon?" he said.

"I asked them to let you know I was here," Crook explained. "They seem to have forgotten."

The manager was all courtesy. "I'm sorry you've been kept waiting." You could see he was trying to place Crook and failing completely.

"I'm acting for Wing-Commander Lindsay, the young fellow who's been held for the murder of this chap, Robinson," said Crook, putting down his cards with a bang. You could almost hear them slap the polished surface of the table.

The manager's expression changed. He was still quite polite, but he seemed guarded.

"I understand he drew out a large sum of money some months ago, overdrew his account in fact," continued Crook.

The manager said something about confidence and a client's affairs.

"Well, hell," said Crook, looking hurt, "who's looking after your client's affairs if it isn't me?"

"I understand," said the manager, speaking as though he had a plum in his mouth, "it was a matter of—er—a gambling debt."

Crook exploded. "Upon my Sam, I don't know what the Government expects. Puts these young chaps into the biggest gamble they'll ever have to face, and then look like Mrs. Grundy and Dora rolled into one if they have a flutter in the very little spare time they get in their short lives."

The manager looked uncomfortable. He said, "It's always a pity when young men lose their sense of proportion," to which Crook replied that some people never seemed to have any anyhow. Then he said, "By the way, how did it come? Tens and fives or single notes? The money that was paid in, I mean?"

The manager hesitated again. Then he said, "Tens and fives mostly. We've got the numbers."

"Might be useful," said Crook, taking notes on the back of an envelope. "Did they come by post or—anyone remember?"

"By post."

"Know the postmark?"

The manager said No, he was afraid no one remembered.

"Didn't keep the envelope by any chance?"

"We give all our waste paper to salvage," said the manager primly, as who should say, We old fellows may be past our heyday, but you can count on us to do the patriotic thing.

"Oh, well," said Crook, "if you remember anything else—

by the way what about the numbers of the notes you paid out to Lindsay or on account of his check?"

"He drew it out himself in notes. I may say that if it had not been that most of our experienced staff has been called up for war service the payment of so large a sum would not have been made without reference to the account."

"Don't leave much to chance, do you?" said Crook. "Well, if you've got the numbers of those notes handy. . . . "

The manager was able to supply these also, and Crook swung out of the building, thanking God once more that some heaven-sent genius had evolved the miracle of beer for the solace of the children of men.

2.

It was Crook's boast that he could smell out a pub. as a fox scents a fowl yard. He got into his little red car, that he ran on gas in these days of petrol shortage, with the result that she looked like some monstrosity out of a child's nightmare, and went to the Pheasant. He was a man who didn't arouse much enthusiasm in upper-middle-class breasts, while a good many of his own profession thought he was a pity, but he had a way with barmen. He had them telling him anything he wanted to know within five minutes. He used to say modestly it was because he could absorb a pint at a swallow, a thing common enough in agricultural districts, but one of those things that are seldom achieved by your cosmopolitan town-dweller. He could even, Crook boasted, but only at the end of the evening, get drinks on tick.

He settled down comfortably at the bar of the Pheasant—the public bar, because so-called ladies invaded the Saloon Bar these days, thus ruining it for the very people for whom bars were built, as though, observed the barman, he were settling into his grave, and bought a couple of drinks—one for each of them—and talked of this and that and presently murmured something about Hugh Lindsay. The barman said that was a bad show and they'd often had the Wing-Commander in the bar and it wasn't the sort of thing you'd expect of a chap like that.

Crook said a chap like what, and the barman said it wasn't as if he was one for the girls—too serious altogether—and it was shocking the way young men didn't seem to have the feelings about their own country that they'd had in the last war. Look at Haw-Haw now. Crook asked why, in his blunt fashion, and the barman said well, the police didn't arrest a fellow and a flying officer at that without some reason, and it was his experience there was generally a woman somewhere, and these chaps that weren't used to dames generally took it hardest.

Crook said admiringly he could see the barman knew a thing or two, and the barman said he knew enough to keep clear of skirts himself, even if they wore trousers as a lot of them did these days. Crook said he presumed he was speaking to a bachelor and the barman said he was right every time, and it wasn't because he hadn't had plenty of chances. Crook said how about another pint apiece and he was lucky, too, because most women thought he was a gorilla at a distance and he saw to it they didn't get near enough to find out their mistake. Over a third pint he mentioned Tom Robinson, and the barman waxed enthusiastic at once. Everyone liked Tom, he said. Open-handed, a wizard at darts—generally owed a bit, he added with a grin, but you could trust him to square the account when the next pay-day came round. Crook grinned back and said the best chaps were often like that.

He came away convinced that wherever Lindsay had met the lady who had (apparently) proved his undoing, it hadn't been at the Pheasant. It looked as though he might have quite a job of work ahead of him. He stopped at another local pub for a bite to eat, and decided to end up at the Bird In Hand, though how much he was likely to learn there he couldn't imagine. When he got near the roadhouse he parked his car in the mouth of a little lane; he didn't know what lay ahead, but believed it's always as well to be on the safe side, or, at least, as near it as you can manage. When he walked into the Bird In Hand he saw at once why Lindsay's suspicions had been aroused. He'd never met Tom, but Mr. Stout and the Wing-Commander between them, to say, nothing of the barman at the Pheasant, had given him a pretty accurate picture of the dead man. And he was certain that the Bird In Hand wasn't his particular cup of tea.

It was a gaudy sort of place with a semi-circular bar, painted scarlet, at one end, and a radio blaring away at the other, and already two or three couples were performing, with immense solemnity, some of those slow intricate writhings that pass for dancing nowadays. Crook didn't mind the Lambeth Walk, but this sort of thing gave him a queer feeling in the pit of the stomach. He said the snakes did it so much better. Round the walls were tables with basket chairs, and there was a white pottery vase full of leaves and early blossoms artistically arranged against one of the cream-painted walls, so that the shadow was as lovely as the foliage itself. There were some cocktail stools round the bar, with red leather seats, and some creatures, mostly of indeterminate sex, seated thereon.

Crook made for one of the odious little tables; cocktail stools are not kind to short stout men. A platinum blonde of about forty-five with overdone eyebrows and lashes stood behind the bar, and he noticed that everyone who came in either greeted her familiarly or was ceremoniously introduced. He came in alone and felt like a gate-crasher. The blonde looked at him expectantly; he reflected that the only natural thing about her was her name, which was Maudie. She wore a well-tailored black coat and skirt, that made the best of her ample figure, a white silk blouse and pearls. He had the feeling he was in the one-and-sixpennies at the local Forum. There was a lot of red about everywhere and the ash-trays were very fancy. Crook preferred the bright yellow kind with whiskey advertisements on them. They struck true.

A slender young man in a brown suit, speaking English with a purity that the natives scorn to affect, came up and asked Crook what he would have.

Crook said, "Beer."

The young man said he was very sorry, there was a great shortage and they hadn't any beer that night.

Crook looked disgusted. "Keepin' it under the counter for your regulars?" he asked.

The young man moved his hands in a rather foreign gesture, and said there was whiskey and short drinks but that was all. Crook suggested a gin and tonic, but was told there was no tonic. He asked if there was any stout and was told, No, no, stout. He thought he wasn't surprised that Tom Robinson and his mates didn't come here much.

Finesse not being his strong suit, he decided to lead out trumps.

"Sure there's nothing special for one of Mr. Hargreaves' friends?" he enquired.

Was it imagination or did the young man, whose name proved to be Raoul, exchange a lightning glance with Maudie?

"You are expecting to see Mr. Hargreaves?" asked Raoul politely.

"Rather thought he might drop in," Crook agreed.

"I do not think he is expected," said Raoul.

"Hell, I thought this was a pub," exclaimed Crook. "Do you have to make a date before you can buy a drink?"

Raoul made another rather foreign deprecating gesture. "I understood that you were hoping to meet him. But perhaps," his expression changed, "we are not speaking of the same man. Your Mr. Hargreaves— is he tall or short, dark or fair?"

They'd got him in a cleft stick all right, Crook had to admit. He put his hand in his pocket and pulled out a photograph of Tom Robinson. He hadn't meant to play this high card so early in the game, but it was being forced upon him.

"That anything like your Mr. Hargreaves?" he demanded.

The young man looked at it, shook his head and passed it to Maudie.

"That is not Mr. Hargreaves, is it?"

"Never set eyes on him," said Maudie.

"Well, that's all right," said Crook coolly, putting the photograph back, "because that isn't Hargreaves. That's a chap called Tom Robinson. You know him anyhow."

"Why, it's that airman who was run down in the black-out or something," exclaimed Maudie.

"Something's about right," Crook agreed. "I thought Hargreaves might know something about it."

"Know something?" Raoul sounded mystified.

"Well, he was supposed to be seeing him that night—and Tom never turned up. Too bad if he makes a date with me and then he don't turn up, isn't it?" He pulled out his cigar case. It was difficult to be sure about a joint like this. It might be some foreigner's idea of culture in the English wilds or it might be the sort of place the Home Office should be investigating. One thing, everyone was very cagey, and that was generally a bad sign. Unclassifiable—that was the word. And most of the customers were unclassifiable, too. They were drifting aimlessly round the floor in one another's arms now. He wondered what part Tom Robinson could have played in a fit-up like this. Raoul came over and stood by the table.

"Did Mr. Hargreaves say any particular time?" he asked.

"Nine o'clock. It's his usual hour, isn't it?" Raoul suddenly bent over and began to cough. A nasty tuberculous cough, thought Crook. Maudie hurried up.

"What is it?"

"It is nothing," gasped Raoul.

"I'll bring you something to drink. Won't Mr. . . . " she looked enquiringly at Crook, who became extremely occupied with his cigar.

"You will have a drink on the house?" suggested the proprietor hospitably. He nodded to Maudie. Crook shook out his match and put it in one of the fancy trays. He was thinking about that cough. Was it genuine? He looked a weedy unhealthy sort of fellow. But on the other hand it might well be a signal between them. They were just the sort who would be conspirators. Crook liked honest-to-God criminals, creeping, sneaking subtle criminals, not this flavor of politics, this national treachery. Murder as murder was easy to understand. Men murdered mostly for one of two motives—passion or greed. They weren't pleasant, but they were human. He'd never been scared of murder as most people were; it was a thing that might happen to anyone, even to oneself, and some murderers were good fellows at heart, who happened to have bad luck. But impersonal murder lifted the crime into another category, debased it altogether. He wished heartily that he were outside in his little red car. He hadn't mentioned Hugh Lindsay's name, but the atmosphere hummed with the echo of it, like strings vibrating. The Bird In Hand, he felt, was no place for a middle-aged lawyer of indifferent antecedents and (despite appearances) an unalterably honest disposition.

There was, of course, he reminded himself, a much simpler explanation. Raoul might take him for a policeman in disguise— these odd little shops often infringed a minor law or two. But though he wanted to believe that he couldn't. It surprised him to find that he wasn't enjoying himself at all. He wondered if perhaps he was beginning to feel his age.

Maudie came back with the drinks, and Crook looked at her thoughtfully, trying to assess her, too. She wasn't anything special; he'd met plenty like her in various walks of life. Sometimes they were honest, sometimes not, but he was a lawyer, he'd have told you, not a romantic boy or a novelist, and it's only in novels and plays that barmaids and prostitutes have hearts of gold and beat all the virtuous characters to the Kingdom of Heaven. In real life, they're remarkably like most other people, a bit on the make, learning to look after Number One, knowing that heroes live on celluloid in films. Only—this was more like a film than anything in which he'd so far been involved.

Still, he reminded himself, seeing the two glasses set on the table, you can't force a man to drink any more than you can force a horse. They hadn't asked him what he'd have, he noticed, and only the devil and Maudie knew what was in those glasses. She had gone back now to her job of shaking concoctions behind the bar. A few more people had come in. Unlike most drinking-places these days, there wasn't much uniform here, which was why he so particularly noticed a thin grim young man in Air Force uniform who had just entered, accompanied by a girl, one of the young creatures you saw everywhere before the war, with smooth fair hair like silk falling to her shoulders and curling under. She wore a silk frock and a little bright red coat with buttons as fancy as the ash-trays but not so bogus, and a red silk net like a shrimping net over her hair. She looked about ninteen; he wondered in his methodical way why she wasn't in uniform too.

The couple approached the bar, the young man looking

round him mistrustfully, feeling, it seemed, much as Crook had done on his arrival. The girl looked round as if everything was brand-new and therefore exciting. She had rather a new sort of look herself, as if she'd just been made, an untarnished look. Neither of them appeared to be at home here. For though everything looked so new on the surface, the paint so bright, the chromium fittings so shining, it wasn't new really—it was as old as sin and, he thought, as boring. Strangely, he didn't think of crime as sin—it was a science and you yourself were a research professor.

The newcomers took their places at the bar and the young man murmured something Crook couldn't hear. The girl's voice rang out in clear protest, "But, Charles, I think it's all such fun. I'm glad we came."

Maudie looked at her as she set the drinks down. There was the enmity of ages in that look. The barmaid was painted, plucked, clipped into a good corset, but there was something about her appearance of youth as meretricious as her pearls. This girl was the real thing, and she knew it.

"Go easy," Crook's heart warned him. "You've met dames before." This wasn't an ordinary slice of life, this was riproaring melodrama. The girl might be in it, too, for all he knew. He had reached the stage where he began to suspect anyone going around with a young chap in uniform. The young foreigner was watching them, too. Crook thought the officer looked a bit apprehensive; then the girl spoke to him and he laughed and shrugged and ordered two more drinks.

"On the house," said Raoul gently, indicating his untouched glass. "We know you're an authority, Mr. Crook."

They knew his name, then. Probably knew his business, too.

"No heel-taps," said the soft voice.

Crook put out his hand to shove the table. It was easy to upset those tall glasses. But the young man had seen that move and Crook felt his wrist gripped and held.

"Take care," said Raoul. "You will have it over if you do not look out."

Crook knew then that he was in desperate danger. It wasn't the first time, but it was the first time it had been in circumstances like these. He had been hit over the head, tripped on the stairs, threatened with death by ordinary thieves and murderers, but that was comparatively clear going. This was like walking in a fog. He didn't know who his enemies were, or why exactly he was so dangerous. He didn't know much as yet.

"But I must be on to something," he told himself, "or they wouldn't be so keen to put me out of the way." He drew his hand out of the poung man's clasp. The narrow smiling eyes met his.

"Good luck, Mr. Crook!" he said.

"I notice you haven't begun," said Crook heartily, "and I always distrust a man who won't sample his own drinks."

Raoul laughed; his glance caught Maudie's. In a film, thought Crook, this would be the moment when all the lights would go out and in the darkness, with a dexterity only possible to film heroes, he would change the glasses, and it would never cross the villain's mind that he might be double-crossed and the wrong 'un would drink the poison. . . .

But the lights glared like the dinner-hour on Broadway. Maudie came round with another drink, a little short one.

"I can't take whiskey," explained Raoul. "It makes me as sick as a dog."

Crook wasn't surprised. He imagined that anyone who drank whatever it was in the glasses before him would be lucky if he got off with nothing worse than dog-sickness. He looked back to the bar. The girl was drinking as gaily as though the stuff were lemonade; the young man still looked as if he thought the whole excursion were a mistake. Presently someone turned the knob of the radio so that the music blared through the room. Crook wondered if that were deliberate; you'd hear nothing above that shocking din.

"You do not like your drink, Mr. Crook?" urged the soft insistent voice at his side.

Crook turned foursquare. "Speaking as a lawyer," he said, "I never drink with a man I don't know."

"An excellent rule." The foreigner smiled. There was something silky about him, but something of wire and whipcord, too. "Still, one must always begin a new experience sometime."

"I'm a man of habit," said Crook.

"A habit of peering into another man's affair," his companion agreed. "But that's a thing you can do once too often. You better drink up, Mr. Crook."

"You'll have to fetch a plain van and make me," Crook returned using an idiom familiar to himself, but pointless to his companion, who looked at him speculatively.

"Oh, I don't think we need go to those lengths," he said. He tapped Crook warningly on the knee. Crook looked down. It was becoming like a nightmare, when horror succeeds horror, and there is no logic to clear the air. The hand at his knee held something small and dark. He thought he knew why someone had turned up the radio. He was a man of some experience; he knew what a little pistol like that could do. With all the noise going on and the floor thick with people—for with the blare of sound a number of others who had hitherto refrained had left their seats and were crawling like so many spiders over and round the floor. Crook saw the young girl turn to her companion.

"Oh, Charles, let's," she said.

"There's no room," he objected.

"Of course there is. Charles, don't be a spoilsport."

The young man put down his glass. "I can't think why you wouldn't come to the Glass Slipper," he said. He took her into his arms and they began to move on their few inches of floor with all the rest.

"You haven't long, Mr. Crook," said the warning voice, whose owner appeared to miss nothing.

Crook looked at the drink. Perhaps it only contained a drug. Poison was a dangerous game. But he knew something of the action of hooch and what it can do to a man. He'd sooner die cleanly with a bullet through his heart than be transformed into one of those gibbering, semi-human creatures he'd seen in the course of his business.

"And if I don't?" he asked.

"I don't think you really meant to come here," said the young man. "I think you don't feel very much at home."

"I can't complain of lack of attention," agreed Crook, with a sudden grin.

"You left your car outside, didn't you? Perhaps I'd better see you safely to it. We get some queer people here. They don't like snoopers."

Crook thought how often he'd heard people say that the innocent had nothing to fear; he knew it wasn't true. If you're framed, it's even harder to be innocent, because you don't know anything, and so you can't counter your enemy's moods.

"I can find my own way," he said politely.

"Oh, I think I'd better come with you," said the young man. "It might be safer."

"What is this place?" asked Crook, bluntly. "A thieves' kitchen?"

The young man went on smiling. He didn't say anything. Crook could see exactly what was going to happen. He'd left his car round the corner in a little lane. When he got in, the young man would press the trigger and the silencer and the general sounds of the night would prevent anyone hearing. Besides, he had the idea they'd heard a good many odd sounds before now, and they'd learned that discretion pays higher wages than curiosity. He looked away from his companion at that heterogeneous crowd moving round the floor. They were like a lot of figures out of pictures by the same artist; something indefinable stamped them all. They knew all the tricks, even more than Arthur Crook. I'm used to British crime, he reflected. These damned foreigners. His eyes came back to the patient, smiling face. Nothing to appeal to there at all. It wasn't so much that he'd smothered his conscience as that he couldn't spell the word. A wealth of experience lay behind that calm manner. Probably violent death was nothing to him; he'd seen it so often, inflicted it so often. The hand holding the weapon moved a little.

"Are you coming?" he said.

Crook uncrossed his plump legs. "I don't think so. I think I'll wait a bit longer."

Outside the wind howled uneasily and the windows rattled.

"This looks like a new place, doesn't it?" said Raoul. "Wonderful what a lick of paint can do."

"I thought they wouldn't let you have paint these days," murmured Crook, and the young man smiled.

"You don't really believe that," he said. "You know you can have anything you want. You know." There was an odd emphasis on the last two words. If this is what being sober does to you I'll get tight every evening for the rest of my life, vowed Arthur Crook. "But it's pretty old really," the voice went on inexorably. "Pretty shoddy. When we had a storm like this a fortnight ago something went wrong with the lights."

"How convenient!" There was the threat unveiled. You haven't a dog's chance, smiled those narrow, flickering eyes. Everything comes to him who waits, even a bullet, Crook reminded himself.

"With a crowd like this you can never be sure," the young man agreed. Crook thought, "What punk it all is, the Yard telling you you can't get rid of a body. Sensible men don't try and get rid of them." He could see what would happen if he went out with this fellow. He'd be found in his car in the morning, though not necessarily anywhere near the Bird In Hand. It isn't everyone who'd care about driving a corpse for a companion, but this fellow wouldn't turn a hair. And when Arthur Crook was found—well, hadn't he enemies enough, and why should anyone suspect a young foreigner called Raoul Something who, so far as anyone knew, had never set eyes on the lawyer. It looked like checkmate.

He said, "I wouldn't be too sure. You might even get the House of Commons on your trail."

The young man laughed. "With a series of little pink memos. Passed to you, please." But there wasn't any laughter in Raoul's eyes. "Thirty seconds, Mr. Crook."

"Your bid, partner," said Arthur Crook to his guardian angel.

It was like the genie coming out of the brass bottle. Someone jarred against the little table. Crook turned his head and saw the young flight-lieutenant and the girl. He spoke, like a man inspired.

"Mr. Hargreaves?" he said.

Raoul leaped to his feet. One of the tall glasses overturned, drenching a woman's dress. She broke into loud nasal complaint. Raoul stepped forward. There was a general surging of bodies over the floor. A voice said, "Get me a gin and lime, dear."

"Can't get lime," said Maudie's voice.

Another voice broke in. "That's not true," it said. "You can get anything you like if you want it enough. You know."

It might have been a code-word. The last syllable had scarcely died when all the lights went out.

Chapter X

THERE WAS an instant's silence, and then the sound of footsteps moving over the uncarpeted floor. They seemed to surge like a wave; a table went over with a crash and someone called out, "Why don't they put on those bloody lights?"

Raoul's voice sounded calmly. "One minute please. Do not be alarmed. It is just that a fuse had blown out."

His words made no difference whatsoever. The sound of scuffling continued. Crook realized all the feet were going in one direction, the direction of the door. He recalled seeing a second door, leading presumably to the remainder of the premises, at the farther end of the room and he therefore made for this, keeping close to the wall and thus avoiding contact with the human mass pressing in the opposite direction. He always boasted that, like a cat, he could see in the dark, and it was less than a minute after the lights were extinguished that he softly opened the small door and found himself in a narrow passage running in both directions. Here he paused again. Something Hugh Lindsay had said just befort he left him came into Crook's mind. He had been speaking of his anxiety for his aircraft that did not return to time.

"When you're waiting desperately for the sound of engines, you sometimes hear them when they're not there."

Similarly, reflected Crook, when you're listening for the sound of footsteps, particularly the footsteps of a killer, you sometimes hear feet that don't exist. One way the passage ran to out-of-doors, the other into the more private premises. He mustn't stay more than a second. There was danger all round him. At any moment the lights would come on again. He couldn't even yet make sense of what had happened. The only important thing at the moment was to get himself out of the place alive. He remembered a rhyme he'd once read.

Twice once are two and twice two is four,
But twice two is ninety-six if you know the way to score.

The trouble was he only knew the sort of arithmetic they teach you in the Council schools. And when you added Robinson and Lindsay and the flight-lieutenant and Raoul and Maudie and Hargreaves, whoever he might be, what did all that come to? It would take a cleverer chap than himself to answer that one. Behind him the door opened again, a hand touched his arm. He swerved round quickly.

"This way," said a voice. "They're watching that door."

It was the young airman. "Know the lie of the land?" muttered Crook.

"There's a door leading to the garden; you can get out that way."

They took a couple of steps, then Crook stopped again. "Hold hard."

"What's the matter?"

"Someone's waiting just beyond that entrance."

"But you can't see. . . ."

"I don't have to see. Fact is, they're guarding every entrance, and for myself I'd rather be in the open."

"P'raps you're right. Look here, I'll go on, distract them for a moment. Then you can get by. Go through the garden. . . ."

Crook never wasted words. He nodded apparent acquiescence.

The flight-lieutenant went forward. Crook turned and moved quickly in the other direction. His instinct told him he stood a better chance in the open. He didn't know what was going on in the bar. A case like this was like walking down an endless black passage, pushing open one door after another, never certain what you'd find behind each—a man with a knife, a dangling noose, a cup of cold pizen. It was a pitch-black night,

109

with clouds, dense as soot, rolling across the bitter sky. The world seemed as empty as though it had been made that morning, and God had not yet got down to the job of creating man. Behind in the house he heard a sound of scuffling. He wondered how the airman was faring. He took a turn to the right, was aware of footsteps and dived in the direction of a door. He couldn't see what the place was, but the door opened easily enough, and he could tell from the sense of space round him that it was a large outhouse, probably a garage. As he got accustomed to the blackness he could make out a formidable shape close at home, too big for any car. He moved forward and touched it. It seemed like some sort of carriage. His practised hands moved quickly over the sides. He was frowning. It was cool under his touch, too cool for metal, too cool for wood. Then he knew. It was glass, and he realized it must be a hearse. Cautiously he flashed on a pencil-torch, and the incredible thing was revealed, an old-fashioned high-built hearse, a relic of the horse age, but adapted for modern usage and fitted with an engine.

"Thoughtful of Raoul to keep that on the premises," Crook reflected, grinning inwardly. "Wonder if he uses it much."

The footsteps came nearer, stopped outside the garage. They stopped just outside. Someone spoke; it was the girl he had seen inside the Bird In Hand.

"Charles, I couldn't think what had happened. You disappeared."

"There was such a pack round the door, I got out the other way."

"But what was it?"

"A blown fuse. The lights are on again now. See anyone as you came round?"

"No. But thtn I wouldn't, in the dark."

"You've got your torch."

"I wouldn't flash it in anyone's face."

"You'd know if anyone passed you, though."

"Two or three people were moving about. I didn't notice them particularly."

The man's voice changed. "I'm sorry. I ought to be looking after you better."

A new voice broke in. It belonged to Raoul, and he said, "Please I am so sorry. A little accident. But everything is all right now."

"It's all right, Raoul," said the girl. "I wasn't a bit frightened, but I didn't know what had happened to Charles. I thought he might lose his way."

"We do not keep snakes or tigers on the premises," said Raoul mildly. "You need have had no fear."

"There was a chap bumped into me, looked as though he were making for the cellar or something," said Charles Winter, as Crook presently from the conversation discovered him to be.

"He'll find his way back to the bar," said Raoul, and Crook could imagine the smile with which he would say it.

"Let's get back," said the girl.

"Mr. Winter will take you back," said Raoul. "I must just make sure no one has lost his way in the dark."

It all sounded damned fishy to Crook, who reflected that a man without a gun against a man who's got one hasn't much chance. The armor of righteousness will do a lot but it won't stop a bullet penetrating the vulnerability of flesh and blood. Besides, Crook wasn't altogether sure about the armor of righteousness. The man moved up to the garage; you could hear your heart beat while he hesitated there. He moved off again, but there was nothing to show he hadn't gone to fetch reinforcements. Crook felt his way round to the back of the hearse, opened the door and crawled in. He wouldn't have been enormously surprised to have found it already occupied by a corpse. But there wasn't anyone there now. Still, it had been used not so long ago, because there were flower-petals lying on the floor; one of them clung to his cheek.

He lay quite flat, waiting. The feet came back, went past the door and round the corner. It seemed obvious that Raoul was setting a watch in every direction. Crook lay there a bit longer. There was never any sense getting into a panic and his experience had taught him that for the careful man there are no blind alleys. Either he climbs the wall or he hacks his way through it. And sure enough, about a minute and a half later, common sense pointed out something else. That white petal on his cheek was a symbol. Petals didn't stay white and soft for long, and the fact that this wasn't yet desiccated proved that the hearse had been used very recently, possibly within the past twenty-four hours. In which case, said reason triumphantly, there may well be some petrol in the tank. And if there's petrol the hearse will move, and if you can drive the Scourge you can drive a hearse. (For a good many people with more candor than courtesy had on various occasions referred to Crook's pet car as the unofficial hearse and said she should be permanently labeled To The Cemetery) Crook waited, listened, crawled out of the hearse, and examined the petrol-tank with the aid of the little torch. The petrol gauge showed nearly two gallons.

"Enough to set me on my way," reflected Crook, setting the doors wide. He climbed into the driver's seat. Once he got the hearse under way he'd be pretty safe; they wouldn't want to risk putting a bullet through the glass. There might be awkward questions asked, and the police are regrettably nosey about trifles like gun licenses, particularly in war-time, and even more so when the holder speaks with a slightly foreign accent. The hearse was a good one; it rolled out with practically no sound. Crook put on no lights. If it came to explanations—but it couldn't. What explanation can the wisest man offer in such circumstances? In his mind's eye Crook saw the headlines:

CROOK DRIVES HIS OWN HEARSE.

He'd never live that down, and occupying the unique position he did in his profession, he couldn't afford to become a laughing-stock. Professionally, it would be less damaging to be a corpse.

He passed the Bird In Hand, a great dark bulk rolling through the black night. He reached the corner of the lane where the Scourge was parked, but he didn't stop. The watcher in the ditch heard something go by and peering between leaves and stems saw that it carried no lights. Chaps on manoeuvers, he thought, and wondered if there was anything in that. The history of Europe was chaos; anything might happen. It all depends on me, said the posters up and down the country. The watcher knew better. It depended on a whole lot of people, but he had his share. The dark bulk rolled away and he resumed his vigil. Sooner or later Crook would come back to the car; it was only a matter of patient endurance. You couldn't expect to win without taking some trouble, and even foreigners had heard of Arthur Crook. It was a bad business getting him involved. He wondered who was responsible for that, for though everyone knew that Mr. Stout was making a nuisance of himself you'd hardly expect him to know a fellow like Arthur Crook. Still, when it came to politicians you couldn't tell. That Westminster stable was full of dark horses.

He waited a long time, getting slowly frozen and nipped by the cold night air. At last it occurred to him that some confederate had accounted for Crook. At about the same moment the man on whom his thoughts were so murderously fixed was driving through Beldon, his side-lights cautiously switched on. It was such a dark night no one could see precisely the type of vehicle he drove, and there weren't many people about. Twice he was asked for a lift, but each time he drove straight past. On and on he went into the dark.

A couple of men returning from night shift said later that they saw a vehicle go past and heard someone singing like a bull with a sore throat.

> So now I sings to you   4
>   Of the girl I loved so true.
> She was chief engineer in the White Starch Line,
>   Down in Backyard View.

Questioned by the police, they said they supposed it was one of the Americans, with whom that part of the countryside was honeycombed. Anyway, they'd never heard *that* song on the B.B.C.

2.

The next day was Sunday. Mr. Stout, as usual, was at home for the week-end, and Sarah had also gone away for a couple of nights. Strolling out for a breath of air before breakfast, she was surprised to find a motor hearse parked on the edge of the village green. She looked at it with interest and some curiosity and, being broad-minded, she supposed that this was one of those old English customs of which she had hitherto been unaware. Trained, however, by her political experience, to notice details, she saw that the initials of the number were those of a district more than twenty miles away, and she felt genuine concern at the thought that someone had clearly been driving the hearse during the night. She went back to breakfast and at the end of the meal mentioned casually to the landlord that there was a hearse on the green. The landlord looked superior. "That 'ud be a jeep," he said.

"You tell that to the American Army," suggested Sarah, "or haven't you ever seen a hearse?"

The landlord condescended to come as far as his own front door. "That's a hearse all right," he agreed. "Funny place to leave it but nothing's the same in a war." He went back to the Cock and to the important matters of the day. Sarah, perceiving a telephone booth at the further end of the green, placed there for the benefit of pre-war travelers whose cars might break down here, went inside and put a call through to the police-station. No one else seemed interested and it appeared to her a pity to waste a perfectly good hearse.

At St. Lot's Police Station, P. C. Holloway was holding forth to a colleague called Quilter.

"To an ambitious man," said P. C. Holloway, "there's nothing to the police force. Of course, if he goes on long enough and doesn't fall foul of some of the fellows up above he may get his stripes. There's a nice look-out for an ambitious fellow." And he quoted Burke, "The same sun which gilds all nature and exhilarates the whole creation does not shine upon disappointed ambition."

"Aye," said P. C. Quilter, who hadn't thought much about it.

"When I was at Oxford," continued P. C. Holloway, "I intended to go into Parliament."

His companion looked surprised. He was a product of the church school himself, and had been earning a living in his off time, since he was twelve years old, helping in the fields. He thought of Oxford as a kind of special school where the barmies went, chaps who weren't fit to get a living, even at 19. He didn't feel proud of having a 'Varsity man for his colleague. It seemed to him that anyone who had to stay at school that long must be queer and didn't ought to expect to go far.

"What do we get in these parts?" continued Holloway gloomily. "Not so much as a Fifth Columnist. Not even a case of forgery or theft. Let alone murder."

"You don't want to go getting mixed up with murder," said Quilter in his slow country voice. "Ugly, murder be."

"It gives a fellow a chance," said Holloway. "All we get is a drunk or so every now and again and perhaps a car pinched for a lark. And not much of that now petrol's rationed so severely. The fact is we'd do a lot better if we were the criminals. They. . . ."

"You want to sleep it off," advised Quilter.

"In a big case whose name appears in black type?" demanded the product of Oxford, running his hands through his dark thatch. "Not the fellow who makes the arrest or takes down the statement. The public don't even know his name. No, the fellow who attracts all the attention is the criminal. He gets the limelight."

"Gets the rope, too," said Quilter unemotionally.

"This dead-alive hole," muttered Holloway, in desperation.

Quilter looked at him sympathetically. Town chaps were all alike, didn't know what to make of the country.

"We don't even get raiders," continued Holloway, who saw himself dashing into the flames and unbuckling an unconscious British pilot, dragging him out, regardless of his own safety; perhaps subsequently being awarded the George Medal. Or perhaps the George Cross.

"They have raiders at Whipley Cross," said the tranquil Quilter. "Burnt out Macdonald's place it did. He have to house his hearse at the local. Hearse be supposed to bring bad luck, but—they have a foreigner there. Foreigners don't know a lot."

The telephone rang and Holloway answered it. His face

115

looked first exasperated, then incredulous, then disgusted. After a minute he hung up.

"Your precious hearse seems to gone on the loose," he said. "I wish to God whoever left it at Lot's Green had had the enterprise to leave a body with it."

Quilter looked mildly interested. "Wonder how that got there?"

"Drunk took it for a joke, I should think. Didn't you say it was lodged at a pub?"

"If it be the same hearse. Who rung?"

"A lady visitor scorning the Government ban on week-end travel. Serves her damn well right to find a hearse before breakfast if you ask me. One of these superior females. Has anyone missed a hearse? That's no way to make a report."

"Maybe she haven't seen no hearse before today," said Quilter, consolingly. "She wouldn't know better." His mind registered the probability of her being a foreigner too. As everyone not born within a brief radius of his own village came under this head it will be seen that this supposition cast no aspersions on Sarah's nationality. Holloway took up his helmet and went out. Of all the damned silly things to find! And on a Sunday, too. But he felt better after a little. It was a clear bright morning after a cheerless night, with a silver wash of light in the sky; the air smelt clean and breathed innocence. Holloway thought longingly of the murky city airs where crime lodges with squalor and the two combine to give an ambitious fellow a leg-up.

When he saw the hearse his heart beat a trifle faster. Perhaps it was part of some colossal plot, waiting for some distinguished body to be placed within it. The imaginative Mr. Holloway saw himself saving the life of that distinguished person—the Prime Minister say—foiling the blackguards, winning a nation's gratitude. . . .

After he had interviewed Sarah he would ring up the local and find out if their hearse was missing. He made a careful examination of the hearse, but there wasn't a blood-stained button or a tress of hair torn from a human head to enliven things.

Sarah was, as he had guessed from the telephone message, one of these Miss Know-Alls.

"There's probably some quite simple explanation," he said coldly when he had taken down her statement, which really amounted to nothing—because anyone could have recognized the hearse for what it was. "It's out of petrol. . . ."

"Perhaps the mutes all walked back," suggested Sarah resourcefully. "Only—what were doing so late? Or do they have evening funerals in this part of the world?"

"No saying it was so late as all that," he retorted stiffly, though even he couldn't see how any passer-by could miss the hearse in daylight.

"Surely if they'd come during licensing hours they'd have dropped in for one for luck," Sarah explained. "The Cock shuts at ten. (As if he didn't know and he a representative of the law!) So it looks as though it was after ten. It was very dark last night. . . . Unless of course it had been hired out for an illicit journey and preferred traveling under cover of darkness." Working in the House of Commons made you prepared for all eventualities.

"That'll be for the police to find out," said Holloway repressively.

"That's what I thought," agreed Sarah, lighting a fresh cigarette.

"I'll want your name and address," said P. C. Holloway.

Sarah produced an identity card, smooth and unwrinkled in its cellophane case. The blue card was inside it. When Holloway saw that, he brightened.

"You work in the House of Commons? Funny. I've often thought of going into Parliament myself."

Miss Bennett sighed. "So many people do." He didn't like the way she said it. She had that trim self-confidence you find so much more often in spinsters than in wives, which only goes to show how good marriage is for women. It's a pity on the whole they can't all achieve it.

He went away to telephone the Bird In Hand. The proprietor said there had been a London gentleman there, who had got a bit tiddley (only he said it in a foreign sort of way) and had gone off with the hearse for a joke, after having fused the lights. Holloway rang off, more disgusted than ever. It was just what he thought. A silly practical joke. If only it had been a murder now. . . . He felt he'd have given five years of his life for a body and eighteen months for a blood-stain.

3.

Mr. Crook, having run the hearse out of petrol, philosophically resigned it to its fate and took to the open road. It was now the small hours and much too late to attempt to knock anyone up. He passed one house with a light in the window and an inscription—Hollywood Cafe—over the door—but when he banged on the knocker a man stuck an exasperated head out of a top window and said they hadn't got a night license.

"This so-and-so-Ministry of Food," he said. "I could do quite a nice business in a place like this, but no—they give the license to the station which doesn't use it, but won't pass it on to me. The fact is, I haven't got any relations in Government jobs."

"Oh well, we've all got something to be thankful for," said Crook. "You wouldn't like to rent me a sofa till the next train, I suppose. My conveyance has broken down."

"Car?" asked the man, suspiciously.

"She runs on gas," offered Crook. And he jingled some money in his pocket.

The man withdrew his head and came stumping down the stairs.

"Mind you," he said, "if it wasn't that the wife's away I wouldn't do it."

"Other men's wives have no appeal to me," Crook assured him. "Where am I, by the way, besides being at the Hollywood Cafe, I mean?"

"Three miles out of St. Lots. You can have a bed, if you like. And a cup of tea," he added rather grudgingly.

"That would be a nuisance," said Crook. "Filling a kettle, I mean; and the tea ration's short."

"I haven't got a license for the other sort," said the man.

"No one to prevent you giving your brother-in-law a drink, I suppose," offered Crook.

The man grinned and supposed there wasn't. With the opening of the second quart he unbent a bit. It appeared he was interested in crime, and Crook gave him some useful hints.

"You've got round a bit, haven't you?" said the man, and Crook said he meant to keep on going around as long as people would let him, but there were times when he yearned for the comparative security of the front line.

"Secret Service?" enquired the man, and Crook said, "Careless talk costs lives, and you watch the papers."

The man was so pleased he opened a third quart and fetched a couple of pillows and a rug, and Crook made do with those very nicely. He believed in doing one thing at a time, and sleeping was a whole-time job. It was after seven when he woke and nearly eight when he pushed off. He had to walk to the station and caught the 8.20 train to town, arriving at 10. From Paddington he took a bus and changed and took another bus and so reached his flat in Earl's Court. Almost the first thing he saw was his battered little car standing in the road. His eyes bulged; it seemed too good to be true. He went forward and patted her with more affection than Mr. Stout had lavished on the blue poplin waistcoat.

"Too kind," he said to the shining air all round him, as though it had picked up the little car from its hiding-place in Whipley Cross and wafted it all the way to Earl's Court. He beamed at his little four-wheeled friend. Or perhaps, he reminded himself, someone might have feared he'd notify the police. It could be that.

As he mounted the steps to the front door he heard the notes of an harmonium ascending from the basement. It was Sunday morning and the Troglodyte who lived in the bowels of the house was celebrating the day in music and song.

> Christian, seek not yet repose,
>   Hear thy guardian angel say,
> "Thou art in the midst of foes,
>   "Watch and pray!"

"An omen?" wondered Crook, marching up the stairs like the German army going into Prague.

As he rounded the last corner he saw that, though it was Sunday, he already had a visitor. She was sitting on the top step, her head against the wall. When she saw him she stood up and he recognized the girl who had been in the Bird In Hand a few hours before.

Chapter XI

A MORE romantic man might have thought of a rose growing on a patch of waste ground, to see her, so young, so fresh (despite her troubled night), her gray eyes shining, her yellow hair silken smooth under its red silk net, sitting on that dingy stairway. But Crook had an ingrained mistrust of every-thing female, holding that even the Almighty was occasionally caught napping or he'd not have created anything so rationally uneconomic as a woman. Now, after a suitably brief pause, he tipped his common brown bowler on to the back of his head, and came on up the stairs.

"Hope I haven't kept you waiting long," he suggested. "Fact is, I don't generally see people on Sunday without an appointment. But, of course, if I'd known you were going to be here. . . ."

He couldn't help reflecting he'd sooner she'd come after he'd had breakfast.fl His host at the Hollywood Cafe didn't believe in breakfast on a Sunday, and Crook had had some strong tea and a bit of bread he'd found, but he really needed a more robust diet to dodge murderers and persuade them to drop into the pits they themselves had digged. Still, it wouldn't be the first time he'd missed a meal and his stomach was like the biblical slave who obeyed all orders without demur.

The girl stood up; he noticed one of the red buttons was dangling by a few threads.

"Come in," said Crook, who believed in taking things as you found them, and then twisting them into the most suitable shape. The girl turned in the shabby room and faced him des-perately.

"Mr. Crook," she said. "I want your help. I'm in a jam."

From every corner of the dingy room the whisper came rolling back—memories of all the people who had stood there, shaken as she was shaken now, elderly men faced with dishonor, thieves and coiners, the rich women creeping stealthily up those endless stairs, panic-stricken at the thought of discovery, sober-looking men with responsibilities and city reputations who'd stepped off the grass just once and now found to their horror they couldn't as easily step back, young men with a variety of aliases who could slip through policed streets like shadows, who came dodging like dock-rats round this corner, up that alley, doubling and twisting, to dive at last into this shabby doorway, up the black staircase to see what he could do for them—he, Arthur Crook, the Criminals' Hope and the Judges' Despair. He thought of the Tea-Cosey, that old, old man living in a different age and civilization, of the respectable Miss Bennett, of half a hundred others, all of them with only this one thing in common—their urgent need of him.

The girl spoke again. "Mr. Crook! You'll think I'm mad. But you've got to help me. I tell you, I'm in a jam."

He was surprised to find himself sweating. To save face he dived at a nearby cupboard, saying, "Beer? Nothing like beer for helping the brain to function." He brought out a bottle, but the girl shook her head.

"No, no. I never do. I don't like it."

He looked as if he were going to say something pretty sharp about that, then saw her expression and desisted. There wasn't much you could say to a girl who stood there with the flame of fear burning in her eyes like a candle, and her small brown hands quivering, even though they clutched the table edge.

"I know what you want," said Crook in a fatherly voice. "A nice cup of tea. I'm a bachelor myself and no desire for change but my mother used to say a cup of tea and a kind word at the right moment has saved more marriages than the court missionary."

He went swinging down the shabby passage and she heard a match being struck. She took her hands off the side of the table and clenched them tight. Everything depended now on the next few minutes. Raoul might be right—it was a big risk to take. But at such a moment you couldn't stop and count your coppers.

In the kitchen Crook's line of thought ran side by side with hers. He fished out two cups with green parakeets on them, sitting among rosy may-blossom, and one of them with a handle; there was milk in a bottle and sugar in a tin, and there was a brown tea-pot and a black japanned tray with a pink rose in the middle. In a box in the cupboard he found what looked like some remnants of old Army blanket but that he presumed were meant to be biscuits so he shoveled some of these on to a plate, and added them to his load. When he came back, the girl was leaning against the table staring at a picture that hung above the shabby fireplace. It represented two old men leaning across a table, one fat and furtive the other lean and leering. The execution was so lifelike you could see the lips twitch, the heads nod, visualize the nudge and the mutter that would accompany such shabby transactions.

"Like it?" asked Crook, putting down his tray. "It's called The Conspirators. Same like you and me."

He left the tea to draw for a time. He was of those who like it red as sandstone, thick as treacle and sweet as a wooing woman.

The girl looked at him with quick suspicion. "Conspirators?"

"Well, who knows you came?" parried Crook.

"Raoul."

"Friend of yours?" murmured the lawyer, beginning to pour out the tea and spooning soft sugar into each cup.

"He's a refugee," explained the girl, as though that told him everything.

"I rather thought he might be."

"But it isn't Raoul I've come up about now. At least, not indirectly. It's Hugh—Hugh Lindsay. Mr. Crook, you're probably the only man who can help him—and it's all my fault he's where he is now."

Crook wasn't at all surprised. He held that the minute you got involved with a jane you were heading for trouble. The fact that this one was young, charming and not far from tears didn't move him in the least. He said he'd probably been wept over more than any man in London.

"Is he mixed up with Raoul, too? Here, take your tea. You'll feel a lot better. And sit down. I can see you and me are going into quite a conference."

The girl took the tea and tasted it, grimaced and took another sip.

"I never thought it would turn out like this," she began, and Crook said patiently, "Of course not. They never do." Most women, he thought, were born to be novelists. They had a story they could tell in a couple of paragraphs and they padded it out into 80,000 words.

"Start at the beginning," he said, encouragingly. "When did you meet Lindsay?"

"I've known him most of my life. We're not engaged or anything," she added quickly.

"No," he thought, "but I daresay you could be," and he felt suddenly sick and enraged because another promising murder was going to turn on the hackneyed theme of man's honor and woman's folly.

"And Raoul?" he asked, pouring out another cup of tea. His inside must have been made of asbestos; he could take his drinks red-hot.

"He's a refugee, as I told you before. I met him when I was working at Hill House—that's the Headquarters of the Association for Befriending the Victims of Nazi Aggression. He's part Austrian, part-French, and he managed to get over about a year ago. Things were becoming difficult then, but not so difficult as they are now, when it's practically impossible to get a refugee into the country."

"We are nicely filled up," suggested Crook, rather shamefacedly drawing her attention to the biscuits.

"England for the English and all that," cried the girl, whose name, she told him, was Kay Christie.

"It always surprises me, considerin' what a poor view foreigners take of our hotels and our food and our weather and our manners, how they fall over one another to get here directly there's a bit of trouble abroad."

"It's because we're so safe," said the girl earnestly. "We don't know what danger is."

Crook's gaze moved and fixed itself thoughtfully on the street opposite where the skeletons of three houses lifted their roofless timbers to the sky. A little further down the road an enterprising Council had esconced a family of ducks in an E.W.S.

"Oh, but that's different," said the girl. "That's—impersonal."

"I shouldn't have thought it mattered much whether a bomb was personal or the other thing," objected Crook. "It does just as much damage."

"All the same, it's not so terrifying. Raoul says you can't imagine what life's like out there. You're afraid to speak to your neighbor, afraid of sending a letter, never knowing whether the man standing next to you in the bus or the woman who sells you bread is going to sell your life the next minute. It's natural they shouldn't be so—squeamish—about the individual life as we are. To them the cause matters more than people."

"If you've any pull with your friend, you tell him that won't cut any ice in an English court of law—if he's thinking of murdering anyone, that is."

"Of course he isn't." The girl sounded both indignant and scornful.

"Look here," said Crook. "Let's cut the cackle. Why are you up here? You've got some reason."

The girl went as red as the coat she wore. "I'm sorry. I'm making a long story of it. I'm here because of Hugh, because he isn't really mixed up in this treachery at the airfield, and the evidence the police have got is simply absurd—about the money, I mean. They think he got into a mess and had to have money because of something—shameful. It wasn't like that at all—only now he won't say anything. . . ."

"It's always easier if you begin at Chapter One," pointed out Crook, trying to be patient.

"All right then. I expect first of all you're wondering why I'm not in uniform. But I'm doing something else that they think is just as important. And before that I was working at this refugee headquarters and I got interested—of course—in Raoul's friends and naturally wanted to do all I could for them. Raoul was the moving spirit of the place. He cared—desperately. He was always getting letters smuggled through somehow from men who'd been doing underground work for the Allies on the Continent. They all worked to the last minute, till it got so hot for them they daren't stay any longer. Besides, once their identity was known by the Gestapo they weren't really any use any more."

"How do these chaps manage about ration books and identity cards?" wondered Crook aloud, although he knew all the answers to that one better than she did.

"Oh, there's a sort of organization. They manage it somehow, though naturally it's very dangerous."

"It's generally dangerous to get up against the police," Crook agreed.

"It doesn't seem fair. . . ."

"Be your age," Crook urged her. "Of course they're living here against the law, in defiance of the law. You can be sorry for 'em, if you like, but you can't defend 'em."

"I suppose it's not your fault, you probably can't understand," said the girl.

"That's about the ticket," said Crook. "Put it down to my wooden-headedness. Where does the Bird In Hand come in?"

"Raoul acquired that as a sort of headquarters in the country, an unofficial headquarters where he and his friends could get together unobtrusively. . . ."

Crook tried to think of anything unobtrusive about the Bird In Hand and failed. Still, he thought he could understand why it might be so useful to Raoul.

"A few months ago he came to me and said he'd had an S.O.S. from a man who was in appalling danger. The Nazis had got his picture up everywhere, there was a reward on his head. It wasn't only the Nazis he had to fear. Raoul says that's one of the most terrible things about living in the shadow of fear, that is the way the outlook of perfectly good decent people changes with their circumstances. He says it's imperceptible, that people in our position can hardly be expected to understand."

"I daresay he's right," agreed Crook, kindly.

"You see," Kay labored her point with a young earnestness that had its charming side, "after a time, when you live with death hanging over you, the ordinary things like good faith and courage and standing by one another—don't seem to matter in the same way. Food matters and safety—perhaps safety matters more than anything. You gradually begin to let the other things go. And when you can buy security for yourself with a word about someone else, after a time the temptation may become—overwhelming. And because a man gives himself away to his friends, because he thinks he's safe with them, they become after a time your most dangerous enemies—Raoul says."

"I daresay Raoul knows," agreed Crook unsympathetically. "You mustn't expect me to feel tender-hearted about him. He'd have done for me if he could."

"Because to him the cause is all. Oh, don't think I always agree with Raoul. It's because I don't always that I'm up here now. But I keep reminding myself that he is one of a great army all over Europe working for freedom, and when it comes they are the men who will have won liberty for us and for the rest of the world."

"Don't talk poetry to me," said Crook, unemotionally. "Just you bear in mind that we're the people who've kept alive any freedom there may one of these days be for them to share."

"He says, you see," persisted Kay, "that the real victors in this war are the people who have refused to admit defeat."

"And he got that one off Churchill," said Crook, unsympathetically. "I gather, though, it's Hugh Lindsay he's leaving with the baby now."

"Because I dragged Hugh into it. You see, when Raoul said he had to have five hundred pounds to get this man over—smuggle him by 'plane from Lisbon—it's very dangerous and very expensive and Raoul couldn't raise the money. . . ."

"So he came to you?"

"It was quite natural. He knew I cared. And anyway he doesn't believe in people having things. He believes everything should belong to everyone. And he said what was five hudnred pounds compared with a man's Life?"

127

"Why was it going to cost five hundred pounds?" asked Crook, who believed in attacking the practical problems first.

"Because the authorities at Lisbon are so frightfully careful. The only chance was to find one who, for a sum of money, would take a chance. . . . Oh, we'd tried everything legal first," she added quickly. "I even went up to see Sir Douglas Hardy, who's looking after Daddy's constituency now Daddy's overseas, but he said if the Government had put their foot down about refugees, he couldn't go deliberately against them, though he'd see what he could do. But, of course, he couldn't do anything, and meanwhile Raoul's friend was in danger night and day and I don't come into any money till I'm twenty-one and that's another seven months, so I had to get the five hundred somehow. . . ."

"And you got it off Hugh Lindsay? He doesn't look as if he'd fall for a yarn like that."

"I didn't tell him why I wanted it, of course. How could I? He'd have been just like Sir Douglas—you know—wearing the King's uniform and transgressing the country's laws. Hugh's very old-fashioned."

"It's nice to know there are some of them left," Crook agreed. "What happened?"

"Oh—he gave it me."

"Just like that?"

"I told him I wanted it and he said I could have it. He'd arrange it. And he gave it me."

"What on earth for?" demanded Crook. "Some romantic notion about saving you your honor or something of that kind?"

Kay said nothing. "Sorry if I've said the wrong thing," apologized Crook, when it became obvious she was not going to speak. "Have some more tea."

"No, thank you."

"Well," said Crook, standing up to indicate that the interview was now at an end, "it was nice of you to bring back the car."

The girl rose also. Her face was dumbfounded. "You mean, you won't do anything? But you must."

"And find myself in chokey? I'm not like your hot-headed

friends. When I undertake a job I like a few facts I can verify. You can't expect me to help you if you don't put your cards on the table."

"Oh, all right," said Kay desperately. "You can hear it all, if you like. I thought that would be enough to go on? I suppose you're wondering why Hugh kept his mouth shut about the money. Well, I'll tell you. Because he thought I'd got into a jam and Raoul was making things awkward for me, and nothing but five hundred pounds would satisfy him. It wasn't fair on Raoul, of course, but I couldn't tell the truth, because, if I had, Hugh wouldn't have helped me."

"Not bein' quite so tender-hearted about Raoul as you?"

"He didn't know him. When he asked if it was anything to do with him I said Yes. I was desperate. I begged him not to ask questions. I said I'd got to have five hundred pounds—quickly. He said he'd see what he could do. He didn't give me five hundred, but he gave me four. Raoul said he'd scrape up the rest. I loathed taking it, deceiving Hugh like that. His impulse was to break Raoul's head open. I said for all our sakes he mustn't. Outwardly he mustn't be mixed up in it at all."

"Did he give you a cheque?" asked Crook, breaking through her passionate recital.

"Raoul said he didn't want a cheque. He wanted cash. He could afford to take no risks."

"Meaning he didn't trust your Hugh's cheque?"

"Anyone," said Kay proudly, "could trust Hugh's cheque. Still, I didn't think it would look too good, Hugh giving me a lump of money like that. I mean, supposing he'd been killed or anything, and people started going through his papers—why, they might have thought. . . ."

"Thought?" exclaimed Crook. "They'd have known."

"There wasn't anything to know," flashed the girl.

"Sure there wasn't," Crook agreed. "But everyone would have known just the same. Well, what happened?" He was accustomed to having to get facts out of his clients with a corkscrew, and he sometimes said he had to get his fees with the same instrument.

"As a matter of fact, it was too late," the girl went on.

"By the time I'd got the money the Nazis had got Raoul's friend. A million pounds couldn't have saved him. He told me I could give Hugh the money back, but that wasn't as easy as it sounded. It would have seemed so odd. I'd promised I wouldn't explain the truth, and there wasn't any other story I could tell Hugh. All the same, I knew he wasn't rich. I wanted him to have his money back."

"Nice of you," said Crook. "Didn't occur to you you might owe Lindsay the truth?"

"I'd promised Raoul, and Hugh has such a nonconformist conscience. Why, he'd be capable of letting the authorities know about Raoul smuggling people in. The next thing I heard was that Hugh had been arrested for treachery. Raoul had said there were whispers of trouble at the airfield, but when I asked Charles Winter—he was at the Bird In Hand with me last night—he said he didn't know anything. Naturally, I realize that wasn't true."

"Winter seems to be the only one of the crowd with any sense," observed Crook, drily. "Couldn't you confide in him?"

"Charles doesn't really understand Raoul. Well, you know what Englishmen are when it comes to foreigners. Then I heard about the money and I said to Raoul we must tell the truth now —how the money got paid back, I mean—though why he paid in a hundred pounds more than Hugh had taken out I don't understand. But Raoul said we couldn't speak now. It would ruin Hugh absolutely."

"He's quite right," agreed Crook, looking more sober than he had done since his arrival.

"I don't see why. . . ."

"Think again, honey. Here's your friend wanting money and he can't raise it. Suddenly things began to happen at the aerodrome and without any warning the money's paid into his account. Questions are asked and we find it's paid over by an alien domiciled in this country, who's doing his best to circumvent the country's laws about other aliens. According to you his middle name's Galahad, but the police mightn't be prepared to take your word for it, and if they found out what was goin' on you might find yourself in quite a spot, too."

"It's Hugh I'm thinking of," said the girl.

"They've framed him all right," observed Crook, grimly. "Mind you, I'm not sayin' Raoul meant it to be that way, but it's clear to a blind man that he don't mean to have his little organization disturbed and he's got you both where he wants you. You can't *either* of you speak. Why, what could you say?"

"We could tell the truth," expostulated the girl.

"I wouldn't in your place," Crook warned her. "I mean, I know tissue paper's thin, but even tissue paper isn't as thin as your story."

She looked at him, incredulous anger in her eyes. "Do you mean, you don't believe me?"

"Don't get me wrong," he begged. "What I believe don't matter in the least. I'm nothing and nobody, just a poor yaller dog of a lawyer who's in the trade for his bread ticket. But if you think you can take that story to the police and set your young man free, with all the drums beatin', you think again. Suppose they don't happen to like Raoul, what do you think they're going to say to a chap in R.A.F. uniform who's been havin' money transactions with him? Suppose just for the sake of argument, Raoul's not on the level? It ain't goin' to do a proud young man like Hugh Lindsay any good to be tarred with that brush?"

"But—you can't really believe Hugh had anything to do with Tom Robinson's death? Why, Tom was one of his own men. . . ."

"I know," said Crook.

"You are on his side?" she said with sudden suspicion. "What were you doing in the Bird In Hand last night?"

"What about yourself?" riposted Crook. "Your trouble is you want to run with the hare and hunt with the hounds. Someone's goin' to pay for this mix-up and if it's not to be your friend, Raoul, it'll be Hugh Lindsay."

"I'd give my life to save Hugh," she said, simply.

"I've noticed a lot of people talk like that, as if their lives were worth a million dollars. I don't know how you think it would help him. By the way, does Raoul know you're here?"

"He said I could bring the car back and warn you to keep out?"

"Did he really?"

"He said I was to warn you it was dangerous."

"Bein' alive's always dangerous," said Crook, "and tell Raoul, if you should be seeing him again, that if it meant murder, fire and sword, I wouldn't fall down on a job just because a Franco-Austrian said it was dangerous. How are you going back?"

"I'm going to stay at my Club for a day or two."

"Raoul know?"

"Of course."

"I see," said Crook, moving over to the window and appearing to lose interest in the conversation now that the tea was all gone.

"You will do something?" pleaded the girl.

Crook didn't turn his head. "That a friend of yours, down there?"

"A friend?" She came to his side. A little man in a brown suit was lighting a cigarette. He tossed the match into the gutter and looked up at the window where the two stood. "I've never seen him before."

"I wonder if Raoul has," speculated Crook.

"You mean, he might have followed me? But why?"

"P'raps he thinks you're selling the pass."

"That's absurd."

"I wouldn't say that. In a way, you are, you know."

"I don't understand that." Her voice was sharp and cold.

"You know I'm not on Raoul's side, but you've come to ask me for help."

"Not against Raoul. Just for Hugh."

"It might work out in ways you don't expect. See here, is there any place besides your Club where you could go for two or three days?"

"There's an aunt in Hampstead—but she loathes me—and why should I?"

"What's the good of coming all this way to ask my advice if you don't take it?" enquired Crook testily. "Just you remember that angels wear curious guises and powder your nose and come along."

"You can't mean that something might happen to me?" Her

tone mocked him. But she picked up her little case all the same and accompanied him to the street.

"Be seeing you," said Crook leisurely at the pavement edge. Casually tilting his brown bowler he crossed the road. The little man had moved away. He was looking at a watch as though he were tired of waiting.

"Got a match?" asked Crook.

Rather unwillingly the other produced a box. He looked stealthily over Crook's shoulder. Crook had produced his cigar case. He asked his companion if he'd ever tried this kind of cigar, if he'd like to try one. The first match went out and they had to strike another. By the time Crook's cigar was lighted Kay had disappeared.

A little later Crook, having berthed the car in the garage in the mews, took the tube to South Kensington, where he changed on to the Inner Circle line. At Paddington he was fortunate in finding a train pulling out for Whipley Cross, the best train of the day, that would get him down at noon. In his pleasure at this and having, as he supposed, foiled Raoul by persuading the girl to change her destination, he failed to notice a little man in a brown suit, who having seen the train depart, dodged into a telephone booth and asked for TRUNKS.

Chapter XII

"I'M IN A JAM, Mr. Crook. You've got to get me out."

The words rang through his head like a tune on the slow Sunday journey. She must have said practically the same to Hugh Lindsay, and he'd fallen for it, and where was Lindsay now? In chokey, with worse to come. And if Arthur Crook went bull-headed into this affair it might land him in six feet of earth. It wasn't Raoul's fault or Kay's that he wasn't the next candidate for the hearse.

"And come to that I might be still," he reminded himself, severely. "I might be still."

The weather had changed again when he reached Whipley Cross. The sun had disappeared with the disconcerting suddenness of suns in England and now a steady spiteful rain was falling. He walked from the station to Maggie Robinson's cottage. There were some things he'd got to learn and she might be able to help him. It was the longest walk he'd taken for years, and his shapeless raincoat gleamed with streams of water by the time he reached her gate. As he drew near a car whizzed past him, spattering him with mud. Crook shook his huge black open umbrella after it. He caught sight of the driver, a young man in Air Force uniform, the young man Kay had been with last night.

"Why isn't one of them looking after the girl?" thought Crook irritably, feeling like a mother with two many children, all bent on getting into mischief, and thinking enviously of the methods of the old woman who lived in a shoe.

The condition of the road made him pick his way more carefully. He supposed very little traffic came this way now they'd opened the by-pass two miles further on. He pushed open the little gate and marched up the path between the reeds. The place had a curiously deserted air. The long splinters of rain fell with monotonous rapidity and force into the black waters of the pond, distorting the dark surface; the trees were all bowed in the same direction, for bitter winds blew across the open countryside and they, who protected the house, had no protection for themselves. Even the three drakes were today invisible.

When he reached the little house he saw that all the blinds were drawn.

"For the husband?" he wondered. But surely not, after so many weeks. The bell he rang echoed back forlornly as bells do in empty houses. He rang again, but nothing happened.

"She's gone out," he thought, but it didn't seem the sort of morning that anyone would go out if it could be helped. He tried to think of something important enough to take such a woman out on such a day. Behind him he heard a sudden whispering sound and he turned abruptly. The reeds were moving as though someone crept stealthily through them. But you couldn't hide a child there, he told himself impatiently. The place was beginning to affect his nerves, excellent though these were. The sky darkened, seemed to come down over him like a curtain; the hill beyond the hedge that hid Allen Stout's house from view was black with shadow; there was now no sound at all except the beat of the rain and the rustle of the reeds. Even the trees were still.

"Reeds don't move of themselves," thought Crook, "and the wind's dropped."

He stared intently ahead of him and suddenly a bright eye met his, the reeds parted and the three drakes came steadily towards him. They reminded Crook of the fairy stories with which his mother had tried to entertain him more than forty years ago. He remembered how exasperated sht had been when he said, "I could make better stories than those, because my stories would be true."

She had said (inevitably), "You take after your father" and wouldn't read him any more fairy tales. But there had been one horrific one about a witch in a dark wood. The words ran through his mind—a witch in a dark wood. The three drakes stood in a row and watched him with bright inscrutable eyes. He pealed the bell again—and nothing happened. On an impulse he stooped and looked through the flap of the letter-box. He could see the little hall, rather dark, with a tall flight of steps leading to the upper floor. Something indistinguishable was lying at the foot of the stairs. Behind him the ducks quacked sedately at the sight of that plump figure bent almost at right angles in its tight bright brown suit.

"Enter Arthur Crook," said Arthur Crook grimly, and walked round to the back of the house.

He wasn't as clever as his friend and ally, Bill Parsons, at breaking in through service hatches (in town) and larder windows (in the country), but as it happened there was no need for any amateur acrobatics, for the back door was neither bolted nor locked. Turning for what might be his last glance of the outside world, he saw that the three ducks had followed him round and now stood surveying him gravely from the edge of the path. As he went through the door it occurred to him that whoever was responsible for the heap at the foot of the stairs might still be in the House.

2.

The thing at the foot of the stairs did not stir as he approached When he bent over it and touched it, he understood why. He was still staring stupefied when he heard the unmistakable sound of footsteps coming to the front door. He straightened abruptly, realizing his own situation, and wondering how well his explanation was likely to be received by whoever it was now fitting a key in the lock.

The door opened and a woman stepped into the hall. She was a grave, dark woman, dressed in black, carrying a black book in her hand. When she saw Crook she stood perfectly still, her eyes moving from him to what lay at his feet. Then she closed the door and came forward.

"I do not understand," she said in her quiet way.

"I don't blame you," said Crook heartily. "The Archangel Gabriel might be excused for not understanding. Why, you don't even know who I am."

"I think," said the woman in the same voice, "you must be Mr. Crook. Mr. Stout said I might be hearing from you." She put her dripping umbrella into an old-fashioned stand, took off the long black macintosh she wore, and opened the door of the sitting-room.

"Will you pleast come in?" she said.

Crook followed her, because he had no choice. It wasn't often that he felt at a disadvantage, but he had to admit he felt a prize fool now. What he must have looked like, bent over a long dark curtain that had come down during the storm, and that he had crazily imagined to be a body he didn't care to imagine. Why, in his mind's eye, he'd linked everything up already with the young man in the car who had splashed past him on the road.

Maggie Robinson moved across the room and raised the blinds. "I have to keep them down," she said gravely, "so many people come and peep. You wouldn't think there could be so many in this place. If the blinds are down they cannot see whether I am here, and so if I do not come presently they go away. But if they see me, then they wait."

"I suppose I'm the exception that proves the rule," suggested Crook, ruefully.

She solemnly offered him a chair and he sat down, feeling rather like a mummy himself in this shaded room.

"Matter of fact," he said, "I thought it was your body I saw through the flap, at the foot of the stairs. Honest, it turned me cold. Murder's all very well. . . ."

She looked a him in amazement. "Murder! But why should you think *I* should be in danger?"

Crook set a big hand on either knee. "Never occurred to you your existence might be a bit inconvenient to a certain person?" he suggested.

"Not ever. Why, what could I do?"

"It was all right so long as everyone thought your husband's death was an accident. Now they know the police are on the trial (he was too modest to say Now they know Arthur Crook's got his teeth into it) they'll be more careful."

"But, Mr. Crook." Her fine black brows drew together anxiously. "You cannot mean that. There is nothing I can tell them."

"I suppose you've had the police here," said Crook, abruptly.

She lifted her hands and let them fall again into her lap. "Asking so many questions, looking in every corner. But I am afraid I was not very helpful. I knew so little."

"I don't know. I don't remember. Everything went blank. That's the perfect defence—always. Did they find anything?"

She shook her head. "There was nothing to find."

"I bet you saw to that," agreed Cook. "Well, what did you find?"

But she only repeated. "I knew nothing. I didn't even wish to know, if Tom did not wish it."

"If there were more wives like you," approved Crook, "there'd be more happy marriages."

But the compliment won no answering smile from her. "There are times when it would be better to know. Because a wife at least suspects something, and if she may not ask questions. . . ." Again she repeated that oddly heartrending gesture of the hands lifted in hope, dropping back in impotence. "I knew that night that he was going into danger, that he might never come back. I pleaded with him to stay. I am not well, I told him. He looked troubled. He said, I will send Mrs. McBride up to be with you. It is not Mrs. McBride I want, I told him. It is a man, my own man. There was someone trying to come in the last evening you were away. He seemed a little afraid then, but not, I thought, for me. He caught my wrist; he looked like a man in a trap, feeling the teeth close on him, not able to escape. Is that the truth? he said, and I told him Yes, but it was not, Mr. Crook. But I wanted to save me. Why did you not tell me then? he wanted to know."

"What did you answer to that?" Crook enquired.

"I said, I did not want you to be troubled. There are so

many excuses a wife makes to keep her husband beside her, away from the rest of the world. I meant he should always feel free. He was quiet a minute; then, as though the words were wrenched out of him, he said, You should have told me. Was it someone you were expecting? I asked him, and he cried out in a loud voice, I expected no one—no one. But if it happens again tell me, tell me immediately."

"But he didn't stay?" pursued Crook.

"No. He didn't stay. He said he had received a telephone call. It was important. He would not be long. Shall I wait up? I said. He looked at me so strangely. Not if you are tired, he replied. But I did wait—hour after hour. When they came to me at six o'clock in the morning and said there had been an accident, it was as if my body had known all the time."

"But you didn't say anything."

And again she offered him her first stubborn remorseless answer. "I knew nothing. There was nothing I could say."

"And afterwards—that chap who came to see you from the air field?"

"Mr. Winter."

Crook's red spines rose. "A friend of yours?"

"Not quite a friend. But he knew Tom. He came to say he was sorry."

"Has he been since?" asked Crook.

She shook her head.

Crook frowned. This was leading him nowhere. "Did Tom ever talk about Hargreaves before that night? You told Mr. Stout you had to telephone to Lindsay. . . ."

"He had never spoken of him to me before, but. . . ."

"But you knew he existed?"

"It is not easy, Mr. Crook, to keep everything from a wife. Consider. You are restless. You do not sleep very well. You talk a little perhaps in your sleep. It is quite natural. You whisper a name—once—twice. But, you tell me. Who is this Hargreaves? The police asked me. . . ."

"The police are asking everyone—so am I. So is Stout. You don't know. I don't know. Lindsay don't know. All the same, we shall find out."

An odd expression crossed her pale troubled face.

"Hey!" exclaimed Crook, surprised in his turn. "Don't you want your husband's murderer found?"

"Perhaps—yes. If it is important to anyone else. But there has been enough killing. The air is thick with death."

"Have to do our duty," said Crook sententiously.

"I know. But so often duty leads to death."

"So does everything in the long run. You're sure the police didn't find anything?"

She rose and opened the doors of two cupboards, one on either side of the fireplace. Crook saw a typewriter, a packet of paper, a box of carbons, pencils, rubbers, everything very circumspect, very neat. He rippled his hands casually through the paper. The front of the packet had been torn off and a few sheets extracted; it wouldn't be easy to take out a sheet and put it back again without disturbing the appearance of the whole. Besides, there wouldn't be any sense in it. Maggie Robinson had been through all this before anyone else had the chance. Idly he lifted the lid of the box of carbons. It struck him as odd that Tom should buy a box. Most people who used them seldom bought a folder.

"He didn't write novels by any chance, did he?" he asked. She stared. "Of course not."

Crook took the top carbon out of the box. There was some writing on it, very black and clear. He read it aloud:

Hargreaves. Bird In Hand Nine o'clock to-night.

Stage set. Terms satisfactory.

When he had finished speaking there was a long silence. Both seemed too appalled for words. When at last the man looked up he saw Tom's widow, staring and shaking. She put up a hand and covered her mouth.

Crook remembered something he had read during one of his rare literary bouts.

"Cordite is a touchy substance, impatient of bonds. Free from confinement it will submit to rough treatment; it can be dropped or thrown or tossed about; it will even burn two out of three times without exploding. But if it is compressed or confined it will resent it vigorously."

That was what she reminded him of—cordite. All through the horror of her own secret knowledge, all through the darkness in which Tom's death had plunged her, through doubt and fear and loss, she had maintained her dignity unimpaired. But this suspicion, these privacies violated, was producing an effect that might work havoc for them all. Crook waited, his big impassive face calm again. But behind that sober facade his mind moved like a greyhound after an electric hare. The hare's name was truth, and he had to be cleverer than any greyhound, because he had to nail it before it could go to ground.

At last Maggie spoke. "It is a trick," she said, and he knew the cordite was smouldering. Her face had lost every vestige of color, looked, indeed, like clay, the nostrils pinched, the mouth close-folded. She looked derelict, yet somehow, even at this black hour, not defeated.

"Surely you can see," the words broke from her with a rush, "it was a trick? You were meant to find that. It was not there twenty-four hours ago. I swear it."

Crook was methodically counting the carbons. The box contained 100, in four folders of 25. When he had counted them all he put the box back.

"Yes," he said gently, "it was a trick. Someone was meant to find that."

Her fierce gaze held his for a moment. Then she shook her head.

"Why do you lie to me?" she said. "You don't believe that, you say it to comfort me. But—someone must have known you were coming."

"No one knew," said Crook.

"Someone always knows," she assured him. "There is nothing you can do but people find out. Do you think I don't know that? Do you think I like living with my blinds down? or knowing that wherever I go someone follows me? Now you think I am being hysterical, but I am right. I do not like to shop at the village shops now, and so I went into the town a day or two ago on Friday, the market day. And I was watched and whispered about. I knew it. Every potato I bought was counted as it went into my basket. And even when I am here—they watch me perpetually. They hide among the trees, they are a part of the landscape; they come and they go like mist, but they are always there. I tell you, someone knew you were coming down this morning, someone knew I should go to Mass. But—no one shall say Tom was a traitor."

She reached out suddenly for the sheet of carbon paper, but Crook was before her and whisked it out of her reach.

"Give it to me," she panted. "Give it to me."

"I can't do that," returned Crook, reasonably. "It may be wanted."

"No," she said, "you can't use that.

"But. . . ." she broke in passionately, "do you think I would give you an opportunity—give anyone an opportunity—of saying Tom was a traitor? Do you think I don't know what they whisper as it is? Tom married me because he wanted to be safe. And he shall be safe. With me he shall always be safe."

Crook felt a kind of shock go through him. There were some things you weren't prepared for.

"So you did know more than you told anyone?"

And again she said, "I knew nothing. And you can prove nothing."

"I believe if you thought I could you'd put a bullet in my head before you'd let me leave this house," Crook murmured.

And she said, "I have no gun. Why can they not leave the dead alone?"

"To prevent there being more dead than necessary, I suppose," said Crook.

She put a hand on his arm. "Mr. Crook," she said, "whatever Tom may have done he has paid for it. And if you think he did wrong—well, he can do no more harm now, and the dead are dead. Stop this cruel questioning, stop them breaking into my house. I know you expected to find something, that is why you came when you did. Oh, I say nothing to that. Perhaps you thought it was your duty. One cannot always understand other people's outlook. Tom perhaps did what he thought his duty— we can't tell and we shouldn't judge. But—they may have the pension back, every penny, I will leave this house and go away. . . ."

Crook gently disengaged her fingers. "No good appealing to me," he said. "I'm like the British bulldog. Once I get my teeth into anything they stay fixed, because my jaw's made that way."

But after he had left the cottage he realized he hadn't got very far really. It was easy to say you could manufacture proof when necessary, but he wasn't always pitted against an adversary like Maggie Robinson. For that was how he thought of her now. He'd get no help from her. She regarded him as an enemy, and from her point of view, he admitted, he was. People said they wanted the truth, but what they really wanted was the segment of truth that would frank them. The whole truth was too terrible for most people to contemplate.

Chapter XIII

HE WAS MAKING his way towards Bramham Manor when a rather peculiar thing happened. He heard the roar of a motor-cycle coming round a bend in the road, and drew into the shadow of the hedge. The cyclist, traveling at an appalling rate, tore round the corner and appeared to be making a dead set at him. On such a road in such weather any pace at all was a public danger, and, knowing the irrational habits of the English, the rider, whoever he was, should have realized that one or more of them might be seeking the odd insular pleasure found by the race in walking in rain. The machine seemed to skid and, but for an agility surprising in one of his figure and years, Mr. Crook must have been run down, "just" he reflected uncomfortably, "as Tom must have been run down some weeks ago at a spot not very far from this one." He jumped back into the ditch, lost his balance and, by the time he was on his feet again, the machine had whizzed out of sight. He hadn't caught a glimpse of the driver's face.

"Coincidence," reflected Mr. Crook, smashing through a thin part of the hedge and getting into some woods on the innocent assertion that motor-cycles can't drop out of trees. "Still, coincidence is like elastic. You can stretch it a good way, but if you stretch it too far it snaps."

Even here he proceeded with extreme caution. The ground was soggy and his feet sank perpetually into miniature bogs. It seemed to him, after about a quarter of an hour of dodging through the trees, turning his bullet head suddenly over his shoulder, and ducking to avoid branches, that a desert would be as gay as Piccadilly Circus by comparison. His attention was

144

presently drawn to a small girl who was standing on the bank staring through the tangle of the hedge at his peculiar antics. She held a still smaller boy by the hand.

The child murmured something and his sister replied in the confident maternal tone that men, particularly bachelors, detest, " 'E's silly, that's wot 'e is. Not your kind of silly. You'll 'ave sense one day, we'll 'ope. 'E won't never 'ave sense."

"Kin I play?" demanded the small boy in a shrill voice.

" 'E's not playing. 'E's just silly. I keep telling you."

Crook came plunging through the undergrowth towards the spot where they stood.

"You get be'ind me, Bertie," said the little girl in a dictatorial voice. " 'E's not so bad as a bull and you know bulls don't dare gore me."

Crook felt a pulse of sympathy for the bulls. "I suppose" he observed in a mild voice to the scowling young female, "you aren't carrying a knife or anything?"

"Bertie" said the little girl, hissing like a serpent, "you go right back to your dinner and don't you dare look back once."

"Why not?" whined the little boy, fascinated by the ginger-headed apparition that had materialized out of the ditch.

"You'll be turned into stone if you do, and I'll 'ave all your sweet rations."

The little boy retreated a few reluctant steps. "I wish you'd tell me about the knife," murmured Crook.

"Well, of course I haven't," said the little girl.

"That's all right," said Crook. "I didn't suppose you had. Only there's never any harm in making sure. Which is the way to Mr. Stout's house?"

"You don't want Mr. Stout," said the little girl sceptically. "You're going the wrong way."

"That's what I wanted to know," said Crook, gratefully.

"What do you want with 'im?" asked the precious young female.

"As a matter of fact," replied Crook, sounding almost apologetic, "he wants me."

She didn't pretend to believe him, but she pointed out the way and went back to rejoin her little brother. Crook told himself manfully that motor-cycles can't go careering through fields, but planes can drop bombs, bulls and stallions can be released at will, and there are even such things as land-mines, though that, Crook told himself, was a reflection more worthy of imaginative chaps like Members of Parliament than himself. He was convinced, for all his jaunty air, that he was now up against something very serious indeed. Tom's death hadn't put an end to matters, it had merely accelerated them. The next step would be his own death, if he seemed to know too much, and he was convinced that his discovery in Tom Robinson's cottage this morning had changed him from a common-or-garden Nosey Parker into someone who might prove dangerous. It wasn't, of course, the first time he had gone in danger of his life, but generally there was only an ordinary criminal and his friends to contend with and Crook would just as soon have yielded up the ghost and been done with it as acknowledge that any gang of criminals was his master. Though in that case, he supposed with a grin, he wouldn't have much choice. But he was up against one of the biggest things of his career and though he didn't like making confidence it seemed to him he might as well have a word with Allen Wilkinson Stout and give him some notion how the land lay in case, at the last, the count went against him.

"I needn't give him my deductions," he reflected, "just tell him what I know, and then, if an emergency should arise, he'll be able to carry on."

He had not proceeded more than a few steps when another thought occurred to him. If the motor-cyclist had failed to annihilate him, the odds were he would shortly be returning. It might be possible to get the number of his machine as he flashed past, probably making less pace on the return journey, since he wouldn't now be trying to run a man down.

"I must be damn dangerous," Crook told himself with rather less than his normal complacency, and looking nervously round in case the sharp-eyed little girl was still somewhere on the skyline, "or this chap wouldn't be taking these risks."

He considered his position without much enthusiasm. There didn't seem to be any cover anywhere. From the bit of rising ground where he stood he must be as obvious as a bull outlined against the sky. He turned and sloped back to the ditch. This had been cut, doubtless for a good purpose, earlier in the war by the War Department for their manoeuvers, and now, the fields of activities having shifted, representations were being made to that Department to fill it up. It wasn't a pleasant place in which to hide, but conscientious men have to stifle personal scruples, as Crook knew, and he scrambled down, hoping nobody could see him. Dying in duty's cause is one thing, but looking a fool is quite another. There's no glory about that at all. Still, even the Enemy, as Crook called him, would hardly come charging into a ditch, because much as he might want to kill Crook, and Crook had few illusions on this point, he would be even more anxious to preserve his own life in order to work yet greater havoc among the fighting forces.

"Lucky I ain't one of those nobs who're fussy about their continuations," he told himself, moving a bit of twig that looked like putting out one's eyes. "They'll send me round to the back door when I get to Lady Catherine's place."

Not that he minded. He said there was as good company be- low stairs as above it, and indeed he was more likely to be appreciated there. He had phenomenally good eyesight; his enemies said he could even see what wasn't there, to which Crook generally replied that if it wasn't there originally it damn well was when he'd seen it. And the evidence was inclined to support him. His instinct was right on this occasion also. He had only been in the ditch long enough for the thick mud to ooze into his boots and make his trousers cling to his stout legs like tights when he heard the chug-chug of a motor-cycle returning up the hill. He had been holding the offending twigs away from his face, but now he let them go and arranged himself so that he could get a glimpse of what went by without himself being seen. The rider came round the corner and went straight ahead. Crook got one clear glimpse of him and there wasn't any doubt in his mind as to his identity. It was Raoul of the Bird In Hand and the picture assumed a yet more sinister aspect. He also managed to read the number on the back of the machine and realized it was a local one.

ANTHONY GILBERT

"If I could link that up with some fellow at the airfield I'd be a long way on," he reflected. 'Anyway, I'd get somewhere."

Anyone seeing him crawl out of the ditch would have supposed he'd got somewhere in any case.

When he got to Mr. Stout's house they let him into the morning-room at once. No one visiting below stairs would have dared to look like that.

"Been swimming?" asked Mr. Stout good-naturedly. He was writing his weekly article, this time entitled "What the House of Commons means to me." Crook came to stand behind his shoulder and when he saw the heading he grinned. Mr. Stout had written a couple of paragraphs and had now come to a standstill.

"You chaps do like to spread yourselves," said Crook in his candid way. "I could have answered that in four words. Six—hundred—a year."

"You'd better have a drink," said Mr. Stout, who noticed more than most people realized.

"I could do with it," agreed Crook, taking a whiskey-and-soda with real enthusiasm. "Heard from your secretary this morning?"

"She doesn't work on Sundays," returned Mr. Stout gloomily. "I wouldn't be writing this thing by hand if she did."

"Good," said Mr. Crook. "There's one woman waiting to put a knife in my back, as it is. Listen. I've got a story to make your hair curl."

He began with the story of his adventure at the Bird In Hand.

"I wish I'd seen you driving that hearse," said Mr. Stout, wistfully. "I say, they seem to think you're pretty important."

"Don't make the mistake of thinking you're up against a lot of fools," said Crook, sharply. "They're smart, a lot smarter than you and your friends would think it gentlemanly to be."

Mr. Stout sobered. "Seriously, you're on to something. Even a Member of Parliament can see that. Any idea what it is?"

Crook passed on to Chapter II, which was the visit of the girl to the flat, and Chapter III, which was his own visit to Maggie Robinson's cottage.

148

"Remember that note they found in Hugh Lindsay's room?" he demanded. "Well—I can tell you where that was typed—in Tom Robinson's cottage."

Mr. Stout didn't look amused. "That's not a good joke," he said.

"Nothing that happens from now on is going to be a joke to you or me," observed Mr. Crook, grimly. "You watch your step. You've got that little something the others haven't got—the something in this case being the extra bit of information it is so important you shouldn't have."

Mr. Stout still refused to take the story at face value.

"It's incomprehensible," he protested. "Maggie's right. It's a trick to put us off the scent."

"It adds up," said Crook, sadly. He didn't much like the solution himself, though he'd not have admitted to a soft streak in his nature.

Mr. Stout was silent for some time. Then he said, "But you still don't know who Hargreaves is?"

"Not yet," said Crook. "But—I'll find out."

"Take care you don't find out too late," said Stout, uncontrollably. "That is. . . ." But he stopped, because it really wasn't necessary to complete that sentence. It was too obvious what he meant.

Crook, however, never crossed bridges till he came to them.

"We'll have to go on now," said Mr. Stout restively, "but I tell you, there are times when I wish to God we'd never begun."

"Forgetting Hugh Lindsay?" Crook's face twisted wryly.

The door opened abruptly and Lady Catherine came in.

"This is Mr. Crook," said Allen, and from his voice you'd never have guessed he was a Member of Parliament.

Crook stood up. He'd have made any provincial audience roar its head off, he looked so odd, but Lady Catherine didn't seem to notice anything amiss.

"I can't tell you what a relief it is we've got you on our side," said Lady Catherine, offering her hand. "Allen's so impulsive, and whereas that mayn't matter so much at Westminster, when you're up against real brains—you see what I mean, Mr. Crook."

"Sure I do," agreed Crook. "I'm warning him to watch his step." He considered for a moment, then asked suddenly, "Ever met a young lady called Kay Christie?"

"That child!" said Lady Catherine. "She's going through the phase when she thinks it's patriotic to be rude to everyone who isn't one of the working-classes. And of course her political views are as red as her coat."

"Socialist?" said Crook, intelligently.

"I see you understand," nodded her ladyship. "England's to blame for everything that's gone wrong in the last hundred years. It's her fault the Jews are being persecuted and Europe's short of food. Of course, she's terribly taken up with these refugees."

"Chap called Raoul?" enquired Crook. "Bit under his thumb, what?"

"She thinks it would be Tory-minded to believe your own country might be right," explained Lady Catherine. "If you say something about the Empire, she counters with something about Russia."

"Friend of Maggie's, is she?" asked Crook.

"You couldn't exactly say Maggie had friends," returned Lady Catherine. "When Tom was killed everyone was sorry, but not many people wrote. There's something about Maggie that stops you."

"I'll say," murmured Crook. "Y'know, I haven't much taken to that friend of hers—Raoul. Does she go about with him a lot?"

"It'll wear off," said Lady Catherine soothingly.

"Soon, one hopes," murmured Crook. "I'm not good enough to die."

"Die?" said her audience.

"It won't be Raoul's fault if I'm here to kiss all the girls under the mistletoe," returned Mr. Crook in his usual sprightly way. "What about the other chap—the one at the airfield."

"You mean Hugh Lindsay?"

"I said the airfield, not quod."

"Charles Winter. I don't think there's anything in that. Hugh always meant to marry her."

"What does Winter think about it?"

"If he chooses to fall in love with his superior officer's choice, that's his affair," said Lady Catherine bluntly. "Still, one can't altogether blame him. She's an attractive chit."

"She gave me the impression it was Lindsay she was after," Crook acknowledged. "Still, any woman can put on an act, as we all know. And the arguments they'll use. Do you know, I had a dame once who put her husband out with rat poison? Told me so straight. What do you expect me to do? I asked her. You admit you put the stuff in his gruel. And what do you think she replied? 'If he hadn't been a rat it wouldn't have hurt him.' Fact. And she expected an acquittal on that."

"Did she get it?" asked Lady Catherine, fascinated by the story.

Crook came nearer simpering than he'd ever done in his life. "Well, I was frankin' her," he pointed out.

Then he asked where Kay Christie lived.

"Are you going to visit her?" asked Mr. Stout, looking a little startled.

"Don't tell me you've got leanin's in that direction, too?" exclaimed Mr. Crook, as gossipy as an old maid.

"I haven't the slightest hope of getting Allen off," said Lady Catherine. "And of course you can visit Kay, if you like."

"Thanks a million," said Crook in gracious tones. Lady Catherine might, as her son said, had coats of arms embroidered on her underwear, but she was his cup of tea just the same. "I left the lady—or rather, she left me in London this morning goin' to Hampstead. Just wondered if she'd changed her mind. You never can tell with these females." And he winced, remembering the little girl in the field.

Kay, it appeared, worked at a local arms factory. "So Russian" sighed Lady Catherine. "But, of course, nothing else would be in the picture." They supplied Crook with the address and he asked dubiously if it was a long way to walk.

"I could lend you a bicycle," offered the resourceful Mr. Stout.

Crook accepted the offer unemotionally. "And this Charles Winter?" he enquired. "Will they let me through if I mention your name?"

"You're much likely to get in on your own account," said Mr. Stout.

"One chore for you," said Crook. "P'raps you could find out who owns a motor-cycle with this number."

He handed a slip of paper across and Mr. Stout pocketed it, thinking, Motor Spirit Minister, I suppose, but not quite certain. Still, Miss Bennett would be sure to know.

"Come and have a look at the bicycle," he offered, feeling this conversation, enlightening though it had been, had gone on long enough.

Crook surveyed the machine with a polite lack of enthusiasm.

"Leave it at the station," said Mr. Stout. "We'll send for it tomorrow."

"Did you think I was going back to London on that?" demanded Crook in horror.

"It's rather small," agreed Lady Catherine.

"Not so far to fall," her son pointed out.

"Do you usually fall off, Mr. Crook?" asked Lady Catherine who, unlike her son, didn't feel this conversation could go on long enough.

Crook, that incalculable mortal, suddenly grinned and struck an attitude.

" 'The harder you fall the higher you bounce,
    Be proud of that blackened eye.
    It isn't the fact that you're hurt that counts,
    It's how did you fall and why.'

One of my aunts gave me that, or something mighty like it, printed on a card, to hang up in my day nursery," he explained.

Then he jumped on to the machine, looking more than ever like someone from the Coliseum, and wobbled carefully round the yard. After a moment the bicycle, realizing that it had met its match, gave up its attempt to throw him and sailed, like a ship before a spanking breeze, as Crook put it, round the corner of the house, down the drive and into the lane.

"No coward soul is mine," said Mr. Stout very humbly, watching his visitor depart, "but when Crook girds on his battle-axe, my impulse is to go under the table and pull down the cloth all round."

"He looked just like the original of a Walt Disney cartoon," whispered his mother, entranced. "I'm afraid, Allen, you have a very mean nature."

"I know," said Allen swiftly. "I take after my father. You haven't reminded me of that for a fortnight. Why mean?"

"You bring your friends down from Friday to Monday when they look like rehearsals for the old family butler," said his mother, viciously, obviously referring to the Honorable Mr. Smythe, "but when it's an entertaining vulgarian like Mr. Crook you keep him for yourself. They say politics is like marriage— it brings out the worst in everyone. I'm going to make the gooseberry jam." And she was gone like Nellie Wallace doing her witch act through the trapdoor in the stage.

Mr. Stout went back to his article, and thought what a pity it is that truth should be so potent you daren't offer it un-diluted to a mixed public.

Mr. Crook, like the great apostle concerned only with those things that lie before and forgetful of what lies behind, was pressing forward, pedal by sturdy pedal to his goal.

Mrs. Tom Robinson was sitting dumbly in her front parlor, her hands folded, her face impassive, her mind working with the desperation and ferocity of some creature toiling in the dark.

Miss Bennett, who had the Heaven-sent gift of dividing up life into water-tight compartments, having dealt with the matter of the hearse, was coiled in an armchair devouring an enchant-ing book called "Blood on the Doorstep."

Raoul was making a telephone call to town, Hugh Lindsay waited in prison in a kind of crazy hopelessness, more concerned even now for the havoc being wrought at the Station than with his own future; though when he could sleep no more of nights, every hag and horror of the dark would come to perch on his pillow. And when he could put the airfield out of his troubled thoughts he was haunted by visions of Kay who was somehow in that refugee bounder's power.

Charles Winter thought about the wreckage at the airfield, but he was a taciturn young man and gave his confidence to no one.

As for the girl, Kay, no one could tell what she was doing or thinking because, having received an urgent telephone call at the house at Hampstead soon after her arrival there, she had walked out into the cheerless morning without a word to anyone as to her destination, and to those anxious for her whereabouts it seemed a very long time before she was heard of again.

Chapter XIV

IT WAS ABOUT the lovely close of a warm summer day that someone tried to kill Mr. Stout.

All through the afternoon the House had hummed with activity. The Goverment had been debating one of those great moral issues that feed the twin flames of curiosity and self-righteousness, and constituents had swarmed like bees in June. They formed a double queue at the Admission Order office, and were marshalled with as much tact and wisdom as a fruit or dog meat queue by the policeman on duty. The Purity League could be recognized everywhere by their practice of wearing a small cardboard shield as a badge, inscribed "Virtue lives when Beauty dies," and to see the representatives of the League grouped solidly in the lobby was to believe it. The "Bless the Bairns" Association was also very much in evidence, and deputations from the Happy Home Society, the Moral Martys (who were talking of forming a Trade Union on their own account) and the Penitence Propaganda Party, with their motto "Sin and Suffer" embroidered in red on black bands worn round their arms, tackled Members without ruth. The Members indeed were like rabbits in a warren, fascinated by the army of ferrets who approached from every direction.

Mr. Stout had early taught his constituents not to send deputations to the House, particularly on moral subjects.

"If you've got morals you don't need to come to the House of Commons to demonstrate the fact," he pointed out, "and if you haven't got 'em you're not likely to pick 'em up in Westminster."

While the crowds swirled restlessly to and fro, filling in

cards, examining statues and restraining their children, of whom there were a great many, children and virtuous campaigns being inextricably interwoven in the public mind, Mr. Stout sat on the Whips Seat dictating to Miss Bennett. He was the type of man who could have gone on dictating even if the Speaker had passed by, and it's not possible to say more than that in the House.

"Women are winning the war," he said. "Will they win the Peace?"

He wasn't writing for his local paper this time, but for one of those hopelessly optimistic evening journals who believe that an article by a Member of Parliament will increase their reputation. Mr. Stout didn't, to do him justice, care a jot whether women won the peace or not. He was convinced that if they wanted it they'd get it, women not relying on logic or what men consider justice and common sense but on instinct and individuality.

He was in fine fettle, in spite of the fact that the Robinson affair wasn't progressing too well. "You know," he said, pausing in the middle of the article, "this thing is beginning to make me look ridiculous. I mean, an empty hearse is all right—that 'ud be a good title for a thriller, by the way—The Empty Hearse—but a disappearing girl's quite a different thing."

"The Vanishing Virgin," murmured Sarah, not wishing to be outdone. "That's quite a good title, too."

"Sounds like something off the halls to me, and not very classy halls at that. Or rather like Crook himself. You know, there is something about that chap so incredibly vulgar that it's almost endearing. He made the most tremendous hit with my mother. If it weren't that Crook's so obviously married to his work and would consider any other sort of marriage a rupture of the seventh commandment, I might have been presented with a step-papa by now. All the same, I don't understand the way he's taking this. Altogether too calm to please me."

"Perhaps he's like that river—I've forgotten its name—that runs under Fleet Street."

"Underground worker, eh? It could be, you know. Good Lord, that's the way he talks. I'm picking it up already. Well, he's tunnelled himself in pretty far, and if you say anything to him he tells you he doesn't keep a dog to bark himself."

"Of course," suggested Sarah, "there are times when it suits a girl to go to ground."

Mr. Stout looked shocked. "I don't think Miss Christie's that sort of girl," he said in his primmest tones.

"I can't imagine what you mean," returned Sarah, inaccurately. "All the same, there is something mysterious about her. She may be devoted to the Wing-Commander, but she hasn't dropped Raoul either, and I should think it would be a bit difficult to keep the balance true between the pair of them. It might suit her book better to go to ground for a bit."

"There is that," Mr. Stout agreed. He was a fair-minded man. "It's true someone must have warned Raoul that Crook was going down to Whipley Cross, and he doesn't seem to have confided in anyone else."

"Is is certain that he even confided in the girl?" asked Sarah. "He doesn't give me the impression of being a confiding sort of man."

"That's true," agreed Mr. Stout again. "Then who?"

"There is the man who was watching the flat. Perhaps it was Mr. Crook he was watching, not the girl. She couldn't, after all, do any more harm than tell Mr. Crook what she knew, and after that he would be the villain's mark, so to speak."

"That's all very well," grumbled Mr. Stout, "but it isn't Mr. Crook who's disappeared. It's the girl. We don't even know for certain who telephoned. It appears that she hadn't been long at the House at Hampstead when she announced she'd had an emergency call and had to go, and off she went without leaving any messages and no one seems to have seen her since—no one on our side, that is."

"Surely the authorities can find out if the call came from a trunk number," said sensible Sarah.

"It didn't. The aunt answered the phone, and said it was a man's voice asking for Miss Christie."

"Then it was either toll or local. Whipley Cross is trunk, isn't it?"

"You know perfectly well it is," said Mr. Stout a trifle

sulkily. "Though only the P.M.G. knows why when Brighton's on the toll, and. . . ."

"If it had been a trunk call," said Sarah, interrupting him ruthlessly, "the operator would have said, Hold on, So-and-So. There's a trunk on the line."

"That's another good title," observed Mr. Stout in a gloomy voice. "When my constituents chuck me out because I can't even solve a simple murder, I shall set up an author's assistance agency. Most authors' titles are beneath contempt. Now A Trunk on the Line suggests vast possibilities."

"What I can never understand," pursued the single-minded Sarah, "is how girls get themselves abducted in broad daylight, but perhaps Raoul's movement has a London headquarters and she was told to go there, and when she arrived someone was waiting behind the door with a hatchet or the famous chloroformed scarf and. . . ."

"I wish you wouldn't be so heartless," said Mr. Stout. "I don't like the thought of any girl being at that scoundrel's mercy. They've no use for him down at Whipley Cross. Why didn't you say all this before?"

"Because I imagine Mr. Crook's thought of it all himself, and doesn't look to me the sort of person who cares for people poaching on his preserves."

"All the same, he might have unearthed something about the telephone. . . ."

As though that were the key word a policeman came across and told Mr. Stout that he was wanted in one of the Members' boxes. Sarah said she'd go across to the Sales Office and get a copy of the Bendix Report (Agriculture) and the Ministry of Food's white paper on "Edible Vermin."

She was not away long, only long enough to get the two publications and exchange views with the man who gave her change on the Kitchen Front recipes, which had that morning dealt with rabbit, the most important, said the speaker, of the edible vermin—but by the time she came back something had happened.

With so many people moving about, so much noise going on, so many children straying where they ought not, so many

mothers exclaiming, "Give *over*, Ernie," so many fathers remarking, "Cheese it, son," the policeman trying to keep order
and good humor simultaneously, it was an ideal situation for a
bold man. When the authorities began to make enquiries, all
that the police could tell them was that Mr. Stout had entered
one of the Members' Telephone Boxes and taken up the receiver
and that about a minute later someone—a stranger—had exclaimed, "There is a gentleman there, I think he has been taken
ill." The policeman went to the box and saw Mr. Stout leaning
sideways on the stool against the wall of the narrow compart-
ment. The policeman thought he must have had a fit or something and called for a doctor. The crowd immediately sensing
something more interesting than either politics or morals,
crowded round to deprive the injured man of the small amount
of air he might be able to inhale, and had to be pushed back
again, to the accompaniment of growls from the bolder spirits
in their midst about democracy and privilege and a free country.

"You're not free to go round murdering," expostulated one
of the police.

"Murder?" The crowd thrilled. This was better than they
had anticipated.

"If you go taking all the air off him that's what it'll be,"
said the policeman sternly.

But it was very nearly murder, after all.

2.

It had been most cunningly devised and carried out with an
audicious simplicity that aroused admiration even from Crook.
Someone must have been watching Mr. Stout, waiting for an
opportunity. When the attention generally was distracted from
the individual he had moved across to the telephone box (Crook
said the call was obviously a faked one), pulled open the door
before Mr. Stout had time to realize what was happening, and
had endeavored to kill his man by driving an outsize carpet
tack into the vertebrae of the neck. It was a delicate operation
in which an instant's bungling or a scrap of bad luck would defeat its object, and in this instance the murderer had had bad
luck rather than bad judgment. Or you could say, as Mr. Stout
did later, that his guardian angel was on the *qui vive*, and on

such an occasion, when the country in general was parading for morality and demonstrating its virtuous tone within a foot of him, he could not allow vice so blatant a triumph. At all events, some instinct made him dodge, with the result that though the needle pierced his neck it did not have fatal results.

Naturally, when the policeman looked for the man who had raised the alarm, he had disappeared.

"It's a very rash way of procuring death surely," protested Sarah to Mr. Crook to whom she reported the incident the same night.

"I've known it to come off," said Crook. "And these chaps don't seem to mind what risks they run. Mind you, in a way it's a compliment to Mr. Stout," he added in serious tones.

"You must be sure to tell him that when you see him," returned Sarah. "In the meantime, he's asking if there's any news of Miss Christie."

"Who the hell does he think I am?" demanded Crook. "Maskelyne and Devant? I can't produce a missing female out of my trouser-pocket like a conjuror producing a rabbit out of a hat."

"Do you think," enquired Sarah, putting her fears into words and endeavoring not to sound melodramatic, "that she's been. . . .?"

"Murdered? Well, that all depends."

"On what?"

"Whether she's more useful to them living or dead. How much she knows. What hold they've got over her."

"If she's dead," continued Sarah, "there's no reason why she should be found for ages, is there? Oh, I know what they say about the impossibility of concealing bodies, but history doesn't bear that out. There was that woman whose skeleton was found in a tree in a wood eighteen months after she was missed, and the soldier whose mummified body was discovered in an empty house by its owner more than four months after he disappeared."

"And there are all the bodies that won't be found till the sea gives up its dead," added Crook, grimly. "Quarries and disused wells. She doesn't seem to have left so much as a hair-pin as a clue."

He had indeed done everything he could to solve the mystery. The aunt in Hampstead to which the girl had gone in desperation (and when he saw the aunt Crook understood the desperation) had been resigned to her niece's disappearance but exasperated by the circumstances, as they affected herself, that had led up to it.

"She was always inconsiderate," she said, nodding a red-gray poll crowned with a bandeau of flowers on a black satin foundation. "She comes without warning and she goes without apology. That may be the freedom for which we're fighting, but *I* don't consider it's worth two world wars. She treats my house just as if it were an hotel, though, of course, nowadays, you couldn't behave like that in hotels. They all have such long waiting-lists that if you're out to a meal without warning, they put your luggage in the passage, and let your room for an extra half-guinea a week, and when you come back they say they thought you'd left and it's no use arguing with them because hotels always get the best of it."

Crook thought she might be rather like a hotel herself in that.

"Didn't she tell you anything?" he insisted. "Not a single word?"

"She didn't think women of my age had any right to be alive," snapped the aunt, who was glad that Mr. Bevin was going to call up women of forty-nine, because then she'd be able to talk about being registered, and with a bit of luck could pass herself off as forty. "Besides, what good would a single word be?"

"You'd be surprised," said Mr. Crook in oracular tones.

"Anyway, she didn't," continued the aunt in her flat rapid voice, walking up and down the room on her flat, rapid feet. "She came without a scrap of warning, just as though she didn't know what daily women are like. Why, they can get anything, just anything—by asking for it—and you can't expect to have visitors without asking them first if they mind—but my niece never thought of things like that, and I was just coaxing the

161

ANTHONY GILBERT

woman round—I have a rather sweet marabout cape that belonged to my mother that she fancied. The Foreign Office don't need as much tact to manage those two French generals who never seem able to agree as housewives need to manage women who oblige. Though you'd never guess they were doing it—obliging, I mean. And just as she was agreeing she might be able to manage an extra person if I lent a hand, Kay marched in and said she'd had a message and she'd got to go. Someone was ill. I said Who? and she just said, Someone, and out she went."

"Your daily must have been pleased," suggested Crook in soothing tones, but Kay Christie's aunt said, "Pleased? Of course she wasn't. She said she couldn't be expected to go on working in a household where there wasn't any security and she put on her hat and went out, and so far as I'm concerned she's vanished as completely as Kay."

Crook supposed charitably that it wasn't altogether surprising that the lady mourned her char more than her niece. But when he realized he wasn't going to get any more help from that quarter—because she could add nothing about the mysterious person who telephoned—he prepared to go.

"It's too bad," he agreed.

"I never have anything to do with my nice that doesn't lead to trouble," continued Miss Worrall emphatically. "There's that young man she was always going about with—the Air Force one —he rang up that afternoon and asked for her. Where is she? he said when I told him she wasn't here. How should I know? I asked him. Who do you think I am, Santa Claus? I said. He asked no end of questions. Who rang her up? where had she gone? was I expecting to hear from her? I never expect to hear from her, I told him. She comes like an un-birthday present. I knew how it would be if her father let her go rampaging around as he did ever since she was seventeen. Things were different when I was a girl."

Crook thought the later issue an improvement but he didn't say so.

The aunt was insatiable. "If she'd married Mr. Bompas this would never have happened."

162

"Who?" enquired Crook, who believed that if you comb a haystack carefully enough you may find the needle, "was Mr. Bompas? Or is?"

"Is," said the aunt. "He's a God-fearing man and any girl would be lucky who got him. And when I was young it wasn't considered polite to laugh at a man who was earning two thousand a year on Government contracts, and a traveling allowance —and Mr. Bompas is so clever about his traveling—just because he has the kind of hair that grows far back on his head. And I've always thought myself that plump men make the best husbands."

Crook looked at her the instant suspicion of a born bachelor. He didn't ask what she meant by that, because he didn't want to know; and how she knew anything about husbands, she who must have been written down in the Recording Angel's Book of Life as "Spinster" from the hour of her birth, Crook didn't care to enquire. He wouldn't have been surprised if she'd suddenly behaved like the broomstick in Hans Andersen and started beating him to draw blood. He skipped nimbly away before she had the chance.

"Mr. Stout," said Sarah, recalling him to the present, "is worried about this girl. He wonders whether the police. . . ."

"The police," snapped Crook, "can't do any more than I can. In fact, they can't do as much, because they're like Cabinet Ministers, governed by statutory regulations. Either this girl's in the racket and she's hiding because it suits her book, or it suits somebody else's book that she shouldn't make a public appearance at the moment. Don't say it," he added quickly. "What you're afraid of is it may suit them that she shall never make another public appearance. I don't mind admittin' it's what I'm afraid of, too."

Then, remembering his manners, he asked how Mr. Stout was going on and if he was thinking of applying for the Chiltern Hundreds. Sarah, astonished, said, No, of course not, why should he?

"Might be safer," murmured Mr. Crook, to which Sarah retorted that if "they" meant to get him they wouldn't let a little thing like his resignation from Parliament stop them.

163

And Mr. Stout had a conscience and felt like Horatius that man couldn't die better than facing fearful odds. She asked what chance there was of running the would-be assassin to earth, and Crook said they'd have to wait till he made another shot and maybe they'd be lucky then.

"And Mr. Stout? How about his luck?" Sarah's voice was very dry.

Crook's exasperated expression said it stood to reason everyone couldn't be lucky, and he hadn't been called in to save the life of a Member of Parliament, no matter how valuable, but to get Hugh Lindsay out of jug. What he wanted was opportunity.

He needn't have worried about Opportunity. Anyone who knew Mr. Stout could have told you he'd dash his head against the next brick wall that offered. What his enemies didn't guess was that his head could be even harder than the wall.

Chapter XV

IT WAS one of those whom Victorian Members still like to refer to as the fair sex who proposed, with apparent gravity, the staggering suggestion that the House of Commons might stage a dance or a pageant of some kind to raise funds for Oppressed Bolivian Animals. She was a member of the oldest of all parties and didn't see why the Russian Horses should have everything their own way.

"The woman's insane," said various Members, the braver of them to her face. "What do you suppose we should look like in fancy dress in the middle of a war?"

"Not so very different from usual," returned the lady, who was the Under-Secretary to the Ministry of Plain Speaking. "Anyway, what does it matter? You're all prepared to say how wrong it is that animals should have to suffer for the sins of man but when you have a chance of showing your sympathy in a practical way you all put forward such selfish considerations I should think you'd be ashamed to acknowledge them. Oh, I don't mean," she added with that royal disregard for the laws of slander that had won her her present position, "that some of you won't write cheques—small cheques—and mark them Political Account—but that's no better than lip service really, actually not so good, because only the bank manager sees your signatures, whereas if you thump a tub in Marble Arch you do attract some attention."

"We should look a precious lot of fools," said the Financial Secretary to the Ministry of Suppression.

The lady, who was small, golden-haired and would have had a brilliant career if she had taken to heart St. Paul's warning that the tongue is a little member but is set on fire of hell, remarked, "Political people are fair game anyway, and at least you could reflect you'd done some active good for once. The country would realize you were in earnest about something if you were prepared to make that sort of sacrifice."

It looked for a long time, however, as though the Members were unprepared to do anything of the sort.

Miss Whistler, who wrote the political column for one of the Mirthshire papers, utilized all her space the week the suggestion was made, with a bold headline—

MORAL COURAGE. THE GREAT ISSUE.

Various readers chimed in, offering their views. One school thought it absurd in war-time and an unnecessary luxury when our poor boys were suffering such hardships overseas.

"Give me the trenches any day," said some of the harassed Members, aware that already the idea was catching on, not only in constituences but even in the House, the politicians for the most part mercifully unaware of their own deficiencies, and all thinking the game of seeing what their colleagues made of fancy dress worth the candle of personal absurdity.

A second school of thought was all in favor of the idea, provided the public were admitted on payment of a net fee— like Madam Tussauds. And a third party scoffed openly, with Mrs. Barchester, the originator of the scheme, at those who couldn't face a little friendly, and doubtless timely, chaff in a good cause. The pressmen in the lobby were wild with enthusiasm. It wasn't often a grand chance like that came their way.

"If that woman gets scragged during the dance or whatever it is I hope the jury bring it in justifiable homicide," said Mr. Stout viciously to his secretary. "One thing, her husband's what they call a funeral upholder, so he'd see to it she was laid out handsomely."

"What shall you wear?" enquired Miss Barrett who, like all the other secretaries, found this an enthralling topic.

Mr. Stout said he didn't for one moment suppose he'd go.

"I expect you're wise," Sarah agreed.

Mr. Stout bristled. "I can't imagine what you mean."

"We-ell, one never knows what may not happen. Mind you, I don't say Mrs. Barchester is a Fifth Columnist in disguise anxious to admit her anarchical friends to the House in a good cause, because she'd think it bad form to bow to an anarchist, but it would be perfect opportunity for getting rid of someone who stood in your way. Everyone will be wearing masks, they'll all be disguised, most of them will be unrecognizable. Suppose, let's say, Mrs. Barchester wants to become the Secretary of State for Plain Speaking instead of just the Under-Secretary—what a chance. And her husband would get the business of laying him out professionally after her friends had done the unprofessional part of it—so she'd be killing two birds with one stone."

"Thank God there aren't more women in Parliament," ejaculated Mr. Stout sincerely, but Sarah knew the seed had been sown. If there was the remotest chance of anything melo-dramatic happening, Allen Wilkinson Stout wasn't going to be left at the post. His constituents would never forgive him if someone got murdered and he wasn't there, and he was a con-scientious Member who liked to please the men and women who'd sent him to Parliament. Within five minutes he had an-nounced casually that, if he went at all, he'd go as Dick Whit-tington, thus proving himself a man of rapid decisions, since he hadn't really meant to go at all.

Sarah looked suitably demure.

"Go on," said her employer savagely. "Say it. You think I'm too fat, too old, don't you? Well, let me tell you, you're damn well wrong. You've taken your ideas of Richard Whittington from some silly pantomime where a young woman with a pigeon breast and velvet tights came on and warbled until the hero, in pity for his audience, stopped her mouth in the only way matinee audiences understand. But let me remind you, Whittington was three times Lord Mayor of London. He must have been a stout fellow of middle-age the third time, and that's the chap I'm going to be. And let me tell you," he added, raising his voice impressively, to the enchantment of the Potts & Owl staff, all of whom ceased typing in order to hear him, "those were the days when men were men. Your pigeon-breasted female wouldn't have got far—no further than the Maternity Ward anyway."

"And what will you wear?" asked Miss Bennett in composed tones, prepared to let him win the first round, since, after all, he was more likely to know than she what would happen to a pigeon-breasted female let loose on a ravening world where men were men, with no better chaperone than a cat, and a tom-cat at that.

"I shall go in modern dress, of course," said Mr. Stout readily "and don't imagine I shall carry a bundle wrapped in a red-spotted handkerchief. I should only be taken for the leader of the Labor Party if I did. No, if my clothes are modern, my baggage is going to be modern, too. But I shall wear a whacking great gold chain and seals inherited from my Uncle Albert, who made a fortune and lost it later in ways that smudged the family scutcheon, though what they were I could never persuade my mother to tell me,—that will mark me as a Lord Mayor, and of course I shall have a cat. I shall ask the Minister for Progress and Social Hygiene if he'll oblige. He'll love it."

"Will he?" Sarah sounded a little skeptical.

"Of course. Nature obviously intended him for a cat and changed her mind at the last minute. I never see him without expecting to hear him purr. He can tie on a hearthrug—in fact I don't mind lending him my mother's, since costumes are limited to ten bob, including hiring, and he can rent a cat's head from that place in Cambridge Circus; or there used to be a shop opposite Olympia that sold them for about half-a-crown. After the party he can keep it against the invasion. It 'ud frighten any German from here to Russia."

"Who else is coming?" asked Sarah.

"My mother. She's going to be Epstein's Inspiration of Womanhood," returned Mr. Stout, so overcast by this thought that he didn't realize how tremendously he'd given himself away. "The devil of it is she'll look exactly like something chunked out by Epstein and she'll also make everybody wonder how it is they've never seen anything in his stuff before."

"It ought to be very good value for the money," murmured Miss Bennett.

"You'd better come, too," said Mr. Stout in a burst of generosity, thereby turning all the staff of Potts and Owl green with jealousy, because though all their Members were going none of them had been invited.

"I thought," observed Sarah in her sedate way, "tickets were only for Members and their relatives and close friends."

"Well," exclaimed Mr. Stout testily, "you can come as an unmarried wife, can't you?—my wife, if you like. And you needn't look coy about it either. It's perfectly respectable. Why, the Government pays you for not being married."

"It doesn't pay you for being virtuous, though," Sarah pointed out.

Mr. Stout looked scandalized. "Why the devil should it? Things have come to a pretty pass if you've got to pay people to behave themselves. Well come anyhow as my bodyguard. I daresay I shall need it. All these females about in tights and whatnot. . . ."

All bachelors think they're irresistible, reflected Sarah, thinking that the choice of Dick Whittington was a remarkably apt one. A portly gentleman was Mr. Stout, ruddy, prosperous, self-opinionated, all the things the original Whittington must have been. He dictated a letter to the Ministry of Agriculture, warning the Parliamentary Secretary of a number of questions he proposed to put down the following week, then jumped out, blowing a lot of papers about, and rushed off to find the Minister of Progress and Social Hygiene, to whom he proposed his plan. The Minister, as he had anticipated, was delighted at the suggestion, and spent the rest of the evening purring and miaowing in front of his domestic mirror, surrounded by his numerous critical adoring family, all of whom, down to the youngest, aged four, demanded tickets to see Daddy in the Zoo.

2.

Mr. Stout having departed, the Potts and Owl staff surged over to Miss Bennett to ask if she were really going to the party and what she would wear. Sarah who, like Mr. Stout, believed in being prepared said cordially she knew all right but she mustn't tell, because there was going to be a prize for the most original costume and she didn't want anyone else to choose the same disguise. One Potts and Owl secretary observed to another that she'd been talking to Sir Douglas that afternoon and he was going as Sir Francis Drake because he'd grown the right sort of beard, but all the others said there wouldn't be any disguise about that at all, and he'd much better shave it off and borrow his wife's carving-knife (it was well-known that he had married his cook and most of his political colleagues envied such foresight) and go as Jack the Giant-killer.

"Oh, I don't think he should shave his beard," said the No. 1 secretary. "He's never looked so well before."

"Besides, there's something so distinguished about a beard," said the No. 2 secretary. "That is, you feel if a man with a beard makes a pass at you, well, you can't help thinking you must have got *something*."

The No. 3 secretary who was married to a man who only had to shave twice a week said that in her experience the only men who grew beards were men with no chins.

The No. 5 secretary, speaking out of turn, said that if you hadn't got a chin you obviously couldn't grow a beard because you wouldn't have anywhere to park it.

The No. 4 secretary, a contemporary of Miss Bennett's, said that the No. 3 secretary wouldn't have said what she had if she'd seen Lord Louis Mountbatten or Edward the Peace-Maker.

Quick as light the No. 3 secretary said well, she was afraid they were both before her time.

The No. 4 secretary said Yes, that was a pity. They didn't seem to have men like that nowadays and added a Latin tag that was meant to be *Barbae tenus sapientes*.

Before she could offer to translate for the benefit of her less-educated colleagues the No. 5 secretary said, "Talking of Latin, do you know what the Colonel said to me today? He was writing to the Minister of War Transport and he used the expression "en route" and then he stopped and said—E-N—en—R-O-U-T-E—route—that's French."

"He must have forgotten you were a trained secretary and confused you with another Member," said the No. 1 secretary, kindly.

And then the door opened and Mr. Potts came in, looking like Napoleon, 1943 vintage, and they all went back to their machines.

The plans for the pageant, which was the shape the charity entertainment finally assumed, went on apace. Mr. Stout bought a number of tickets, distributing them to (among others) his mother, his secretary and Mr. Crook. Crook didn't waste any time on fancy dress. He borrowed a Henry Heath model hat from a client and came as an English Gentleman, a disguise no one penetrated. Other guests were equally enterprising. The Minister of Food disguised himself as Old Mother Hubbard, in a white bonnet of crinkled paper that had come out of a cracker box the previous Christmas, his housekeeper's black bodice, a bleak skirt belonging to his wife's mother that conveniently hid his rather spindly shanks, and a white apron belonging to the cook, who handed it over, saying in sepulchral tones, "Don't forget that's three coupons"; and he brought his Parliamentary Secretary as the dog. The Minister for Social Hygiene was so enchanted to see another Member in a hearth-rug that he indulged in a great deal of most entertaining byplay on his own account, dropping on to all-fours, arching his back as far as his rotundities would permit, spitting and hissing. It was particularly delightful because he and the Parliamentary Secretary were always at daggers drawn and the Minister had often wanted to spit at him, but the decorum of the House of Commons had always forbidden it hitherto. The Parliamentary Secretary had prepared a number of typical antics on his own account, and it was particularly annoying when the cat leaped on him, batted him with more violence than the onlookers realized with his padded paws and finally tore off his tail, a feat which brought down the house. The Minister's wife—the Food Minister's wife, that is—took the agrieved Secretary away and

sewed his tail on in a quiet corner, and his antagonist, deprived
of his pleasure, prowled round avoiding other Members so
sedulously that nearly everyone put him down as The Cat That
Walked Alone and considered they'd scored a bull's-eye. This
was hard on Mr. Stout, who was counting on the cat to give
the audience the necessary clue. He was feeling rather annoyed
in any case, because one of the Members had thought it a good
joke to come disguised as Mr. Stout—though he was grateful
enough later on. Mr. Crook also attracted some attention, several people mistaking him for a Cabinet Minister, many of whom
he resembled. One of the Potts and Owl members, a large pallid
man the same shape the whole way down, came in white satin,
intending to represent someone out of Congreve's plays, at that
time enjoying great success in the metropolis, and was uni-
versally listed as a specimen from the Ministry of Agriculture's
exhibition at the Charing Cross Station of Farm Pests.

Miss Bennett went as Squander-bug in a dust-sheet decorated
(by hand) with Nazi swastikas and attracted more attention
than any other female present, besides doing a really good piece
of propaganda by representing the little fellow as a really forbidding creature; but though from temperament and lack of
skill she eschewed the dancing, she sat out to the great satisfaction of all her partners. Since a number of Members felt—quite
rightly—that their dancing days were over—a number of competitions had been arranged, with prizes of half-crown savings
stamps for each winner and runner-up. The Members displayed
a great deal of ingenuity in attempting to acquire these, most of
them never having owned one, for Members of Parliament only
buy Savings Certificates for their children and then in good
round numbers. A single stamp was something they'd never
owned in their lives. The results of these competitions would
have interested a psychologist, had any been present. The Rolling the Umbrella competition was won by the second richest
man in the House of Commons who was accustomtd to have
his umbrella slung on his arm by one of his staff before he left
his house in the morning, perfectly rolled and the gold band
shining like a halo. He observed, however, that you were never
respected by your employees unless you could do everything

they did at least as well, and since it wasn't expected that you should know how to do it the impression you created was that you could do it even better than the expert. The most entertaining of the competitions was the spat-buttoning one, in which a number of stout gentlemen (thin Members being excluded by the judge), accustomed to the services of valets, buttonhooks and wives—wrestled valiantly, even to the extent of bursting the buttons from their holdings (a proceeding that automatically disqualified the competitor), and a spelling bee (won by the only Potts and Owl secretary who had been able to inveigle a ticket out of a Member) in which Mr. Stout distinguished himself by spelling "BOWL" B-O-W-E-L.

"That was a bit of a bloomer," he confessed to Miss Bennett in rueful tones, but Sarah, with the ready tact that distinguished political secretaries, replied, "Oh, but it's so original to spell it like that. Most people have to get their spelling out of the dictionary."

Lady Catherine, who overheard her, said, "That woman's much too clever to be content to be a secretary all her days," and viewed her with great suspicion, but Sarah, who had not heard her and would have been quite unmoved if she had, was sought out by Mr. Crook and the two of them went down to the bar where they had a pleasant time with several pints of beer.

In order to identify the Members from their guests, a more difficult proceeding that you might imagine, the former were requested to wear a white gardenia, and one of the Members with a hothouse had produced a regular florists' shop for the occasion. This decision seriously distressed the Honorable Mr. Smythe, who had come as Galahad, wearing the white flower of a blameless life, and found himself generally mistaken for the Black Prince in modern dress. (Modern dress incidentally was very popular with the gentlemen, while most of the ladies present had got as near to Nature as they possibly could. Crook counted four Godivas in bathing tights and horsehair.) Mr. Smythe discarded his gift gardenia as quickly as possible, and had no notion that thereby he was assisting at a murder.

A few of the Members who had the right idea about fancy

dress, had togged themselves out as replicas of the statues that line the corridor leading to the lobby to remind England's sons of England's greatness. This fact was noted by most of their colleagues, but the trouble was that they had seen these effigies so often they couldn't remember which was which, and though they might agree that Bell was meant for the chap with his arm outstretched standing on the left as you go in, they couldn't be sure if it was Mansfield or Chatham or that fellow whose name begins with D. It was then that the indefatigable Mrs. Barchester, who had every intention of winning the whole National Savings Certificate offered as a reward for this competition, suggested that it would be a good wind-up to a most original entertainment if they all proceeded to the House of Commons by moonlight to verify their suspicions. The party by this time had attained such zest that if she had proposed going to the moon they would have agreed, and though most Members secretly wondered how their friends could contemplate being seen even by moonlight parading from the Durban Hotel, where the affair was being held, to New Palace Yard, they none of them experienced any qualms on their own accounts. In velvets, silks, dolmans, cardboard armor, hearthrugs, battle-dress, pre-war Savile Row and the Sixty-Five Shilling Tailor—everything indeed short of woad, they came surging into the street, giving a late bus-driver such a turn that he resolved to sign the pledge, poured down Parliament Street and took the House of Commons by storm. Here and in the corridors all the lights had been extinguished and the black-out curtains drawn, so that the only illumination came from a number of small torches placed on the floor for the benefit of the Home Guard and those Members of the House who might be on fire-watch duty that evening. The guests urged to be shown everything, from the Plan Room to the Council Chamber, and at least twenty voices could be heard saying, as they approached the lobby, "Now this is where the Speaker's Chair was placed until. . . ." Two or three men from Overseas Forces managed to get in, too, and the policemen on duty didn't like to ask to see blue admission tickets because they might at any moment hold up the Prime Minister (always supposing he was there), and though they didn't mind incendiaries and regarded high explosive bombs with a stolidity that did them credit, there are some things no wise man is going to risk.

"Busman's holiday for you," observed Mr. Crook cheerfully to Miss Bennett, as they went through St. Stephen's Door—Miss Bennett being a stickler for the proprieties even at that hour and even in fancy-dress—accompanied by a bearded lady whose deep voice (said Lady Catherine) was her undoing, and the ubiquitous cat. By this time, owing to heat, libations and the sudden plunge into the cool night air, some of the Members' disguises were beginning to become unstuck. One Member, creditably disguised as Widow Twankey, had lost the heel off his housemaid's shoe (Number Ten feet in that household, whispered Crook) and as he stooped to rescue it he cannoned against the Bearded Woman, whose bag was knocked out of her hand, spilling its contents in all directions. People dived for this and that—a powder-box, money, a red button, a latch-key, a yellow pencil; Mr. Crook contented himself with rescuing the button. Sarah picked up the pencil that had fallen at her feet.

"You must have a good time here in the ordinary way," suggested Crook, approvingly.

"Well, of course it's not always so lively as this," Sarah assured him, hitching her own wickedly expensive-looking gold-bag, labelled "With Squander-Bug's Compliments" under her capable arm.

"Pity Hitler don't know about this," continued Mr. Crook. "Drop a bomb and what price England's hopes?"

Miss Bennett, moving towards the lobby, said she would leave Mr. Crook to think out the reply to that one, while she went up the four or five steps opposite the Admission Order Office to powder her nose. Mr. Crook improved the shining hour by chatting to a nearby policeman.

"Sidelights on the world war," he said cheerfully.

"Wonderful what they'll do for animals," agreed the policeman. "No wonder Hitler does not understand the English."

He was a tall young man with a heavy golden mustache. There was something odd about him but for the minute Crook couldn't identify it. Behind him Sarah said, "Mr. Crook" and he turned quickly. It says a good deal for her that at such a moment he saw nothing ridiculous in the juxtaposition of her urgent voice and her grotesque appearance in her Squanderbug disguise.

"I think there's been an accident," said Sarah in the same steady voice.

Mr. Crook jumped the steps and turned sharp left. On the floor a man was lying, a man in a dark blue uniform.

"He's still breathing," said Sarah, kneeling down. "There was a gag. I've removed that."

Crook who believed in first things first explored the big head from which the helmet had fallen, with expert fingers.

"Someone's given him a healthy crump," he said with lower middle-class directness. "Big as an egg. In fact, the war-time hen who could produce eggs that size would deserve a medal from Mr. Hudson."

"He's not going to die—not yet, I mean—is she?" enquired Sarah.

"The papers will enjoy this," said Mr. Crook irrelevantly, "and what a chance for all the old women who don't think Members of Parliament should have any fun in a war." Then he smote his own head and stood up, exclaiming, "Of all the marrow-heads. I know there was something wrong with that bobby."

"Which one?" asked Sarah, patiently.

"The one outside, the one I was talking to when you distracted my attention."

"What was wrong?" asked the patient Sarah, accustomed after several months of Parliamentary work to extricating information with a corkscrew.

"Well, tell me this," returned Mr. Crook belligerently. "Did you ever see a policeman wearing a white gardenia?"

Sarah jumped quickly to that implication. "Meaning he wasn't a policeman at all but a Member of Parliament."

"Meaning he wasn't a policeman. No man on duty in the House would dare sport that sort of mustache. The M.P.'s wouldn't stand for it. Put 'em right in the shade."

He went to the top of the stairs. For the moment the corridor was empty, but the sound of voices warned him that some-one was coming. The policeman had disappeared, but that was only to be expected.

He turned to Sarah. "You can let that chap be for the moment," he said. "He ain't going out this trip. We'll call out the House Heavy Rescue Squad when we've got a minute. In the meantime, we've other fish to fry."

Sarah stood up and joined him. Her face was very thought-ful.

"Doin' a bit of arithmetic?" demanded Crook, smiling kindly.

"I think so," Sarah agreed. "You mean, there was one police-man too many."

"Got it the first time. And what I'm beginning to be afraid of is there's going to be one corpse too many, too."

Chapter XVI

THE VOICES CAME nearer; seen in shadow the newcomers seemed like part of some monstrous frieze, old Mother Hubbard, the torches throwing a gigantic pattern of his frilled cap on the walls, Epstein's Inspiration of Womanhood, a Harlequin with dancing pompoms in his dunce's cap, a stout Merry Monarch, the Bearded Woman, and after her the faithful Minister of Social Progress who, tiring of being taken for The Cat that Walked Alone, cherished a hope that by sticking closer than a brother he and she might be taken for *La Mère Michel et Son Chat*, that delightful classic only familiar to those who grew up before the First World War.

"Damn that policeman!" said Crook, drawing Sarah back a little.

"That one of course," Sarah nodded towards the ungainly lump on the floor, "is Fellows, the man on duty. He was knocked out by your friend with the mustache, who wanted to take his place because he had to be on the spot and didn't want to attract attention, and knew that policemen like postmen and private secretaries don't count as human beings that is, no one notices them until it's time to pay income tax and then they're just like everyone else. But he hung on to the gardenia—or stole it—because the other regular policemen would know he wasn't one of them, but would think he was a Member and. . . ."

"A was an Archer who shot at a frog," said Mr. Crook impatiently. "What do you think you're doing? Teaching me my alphabet?"

Sarah realized that inwardly he held himself responsible for the corpse they hadn't yet found. If you'd asked him who

Shelley was he'd have frowned a minute and said, "Wasn't that the chap they didn't get for the Bank hold-up in '38?" but he'd have agreed with the poet that conscience is a serpent in the breast, and at this moment she was calling her venomous brood to their nocturnal task. He didn't know who had been murdered, though he could guess, he didn't even know if anyone had been murdered, though he was pretty sure, and he felt illogically and probably vainly that he should somehow have prevented it.

They didn't, after all, have to look far for the body. As they passed the statue of Mansfield, looking with a sober benevolence at the representatives of a lighter age, one hand outstretched, the noble head framed in his judge's wig, Mr. Crook's pencil torch picked up a gentleman, no longer young and very quietly dressed, who had apparently fallen asleep on the dark velvet cushion that covers the stone seats lining the corridor. He might have been there a long while without being noticed. And if anyone did see him the obvious deduction would be that the evening had been too much for him; and in the House of Commons policemen are slow to move Members on. Crook went nearer followed by Sarah. The gentleman's head had fallen on his breast, in the lapel of his dark coat he wore a white gardenia. Crook put an arm round his shoulders, then withdrew it hastily, but not before Sarah had seen the hilt of the common-or-garden knife between the shoulder-blades.

"It's Mr. Stout," whispered Sarah, in a voice ice-edged with horror. Then she bent closer, drew back again. "No," she corrected herself, "it isn't. It's the one who came disguised as Mr. Stout and everyone said how good he was. Mr. Stout was rather annoyed."

"He seems a difficult chap to please," said Crook, testily. "If this fellow hadn't aped his colleague he'd probably be walking the earth a living man instead of something only the mortuary will welcome. Who is he, anyway?"

"Mr. Darell, the Member for Seven Kings. I suppose it was really Mr. Stout they were after."

"I don't know," said Crook. "I don't know how many people had it in for Mr. Darell. I daresay every Member's got a per-

centage of constituents who'd like to knife him. And for all
I know, they're right."

He beckoned to one of the legitimate policemen, and said in
a grim voice, "This is the sort of thing you're used to in the
House, I suppose, with half the Metropolitan Police Force standing round."

It says worlds for the shocks to which Members of Parliament have accustomed their servitors that the policeman retained his normal stolidity of expression.

"Might have expected something of this sort, all this larkin'
about," he said. "It's Mr. Darell, isn't it? You mark my words,
the Government won't hold that seat. Put himself on the wrong
side of the fence over the Pensions Measure, Mr. Darell did."

"I come to bury Caesar not to praise him," said Sarah unexpectedly, rather shocked to find her nerves not equal to those
of the men. "What about the rest of the party?"

"They must stay till they've been questioned," said the
policeman, aware that this was a matter for a superior. He looked
worried. No one was quite sure when death had taken place,
and there had been opportunity for any number of people to
slip out under cover of darkness and their own disguise during
the interval.

"Take it easy, honey," said Mr. Crook to Sarah, in what he
intended to be a soothing voice. "There can't be many of them
willing to go to these lengths even for their country's sake. And
knowin' what you and me know, I should guess they'd got the
wrong man." He turned to the policeman again. "See a bobby
go past you?" he enquired. "Tallish chap with a big fair mustache?"

"That's none of ours," said the policeman decisively.

"I know that. Anyway, he was wearing a white gardenia."

The policeman said rather sloofly he wouldn't be noticing
what the Members were doing, and calling another policeman
to mount guard over the body, as if he thought Crook quite
capable of wrapping it up in his handkerchief and whisking it
away when no one was looking, he went out to set in motion the
ponderous machinery of the law.

A number of guests had materialized with the speed of the

British race, out of the dark air and were standing about in small uncomfortable groups, talking in low tones as though, if they raised their voices, they might disturb the dead man.

"Darell," said a voice. "God knows why."

The Minister for Social Hygiene, as a mark of respect, removed his cat's head.

"Meant it for Stout, I should say, whoever the fellow was. There'd be some reason in that. Stout is the sort of chap a lot of men might want to murder. You can't imagine anyone thinking Darell worth the risk."

"One of the things that might have been put more happily," said an austere voice behind him.

"Nonsense," said Mrs. Barchester, seizing the opportunity for a little propaganda. "Plain speaking is the only hope posterity has left," a pessimistic point of view which few people fortunately shared.

The Minister turned and looked at her reproachfully. "The chap's dead," he muttered. Still, the general view was that though the murdered man had been a pretty decent short of chap—well, naturally, or he'd never have been put up by the Party—but dull, as decent fellows so often are. This was, in fact, the first time in his political career that he'd attracted any attention at all.

The Members parted to let an Inspector—no less for an M.P.—come through. The onlookers were herded away for questioning. Someone mounted guard over the body. Crook touched Miss Bennett on the arm.

"Can you get out of that skin-tight outfit at short notice?" he demanded.

"In about thirty seconds," said Miss Bennett, who was obviously designed for perpetual spinsterhood, so prepared was she for all emergencies. Wives are, naturally, not so prepared, believing that one of the functions of husbands is to be on tap at awkward moments.

"Then come on," said Mr. Crook.

The police had been told to let no one leave the place, but of course they were a bit late. Several people had gone since Darell's death,—even since it was discovered—and since many of the roisterers were not Members it was clearly going to be difficult to trace them all.

"They can check up on the lists they'll get from the Members," suggested Sarah, unzipping the Squander-bug disguise in a dark corner of Westminster Hall, and pulling off the home-made headdress, which she tucked neatly out of sight behind a convenient door. She looked, within the specified half-minute, as neat as though she were ready to take dictation on the spot. She took it, too, with an accuracy and directness that enchanted Mr. Crook. When he said, "Now then, remember that game of Follow My Leader? You do as I do and you'll do right. That's your cue from now on," she didn't ask any questions but plunged into the game with more zest than the average child of today would think it good form to show. They came down the Hall, Crook flashing his little torch this way and that, looking for something. When they reached the steps leading to the Fees Office he paused. Even Sarah saw nothing that first moment, but Crook was more used to finding clews when he'd made up his mind he needed them. He bounced down the stairs and came back with something dark in his hand—dark and shapeless and soft.

"The Bearded Lady's Beard," exclaimed Sarah. "Is that what you were looking for?"

"Thought it might be lying about somewhere," agreed Crook, modestly. "Well, Chesterton may be right saying you can eat a penny bun in the London streets without anybody noticing you, but you can't go round in that sort of beard without someone callin' Beaver and attracting one hell of a lot of attention."

"You realized she was mixed up in it?"

"Remember the red button I picked up at the Pass Office. It didn't say anything to you, I know, but—I'd seen that button before, and I saw it on the coat belongin' to Miss Kay Christie."

"Then you mean the Bearded Lady murdered Mr. Darell?"

"Be your age," reflected Crook, sensibly, shoving open the swing doors and stepping into the Yard. No policeman stopped them, because there was no policeman posted there. There are a number of exits from New Palace Yard to the outside world, including a passage that, so long as the House is sitting, runs to Westminster Underground Station. No one is allowed to use that passage who does not possess a blue pass, and an hour after it is known that the House has risen the wrought-iron gates are locked until next morning. All the same, on the chance that someone would not know this, a constable had been stationed in the passage, and there was another watching the body, and others were wanted to help with the examination of the guests, so they were a bit short out here, and only one man stood between Crook and Liberty. This man kept guard at the gate through which taxis (mostly containing Members) are wont to drive. When they drew near him, Crook seized Sarah by the elbow and began to run. The constable turned.

"Not so fast!" he said.

Crook indicated a man standing by the curb, obviously hunting a stray taxi. Taxis in Westminster are not very common at about 11.30 P.M., but, it having been rumored that the House was going gay that night, a number of drivers had saved their petrol in the hope of making double fares. Because, though a Member of Parliament may feel a dashing success dressed as the Reluctant Dragon so long as he's under cover and people are enviously hazarding guesses as to his identity, he's going to feel precious silly walking through Westminster by moonlight with little horns and a long spiked tail. And not every Member owns a car and enough petrol to go joyriding in fancy dress after official hours. The drivers were good judges of psychology and they hung about the House long after they were usually all abed. The man on the curb wore an ordinary suit and a hat crammed over his eyes. As the policeman halted Crook and his companion a taxi drew up rather reluctantly. This wasn't the sort of fare the driver wanted. You couldn't bargain with so unexceptional looking a creature. The only way out would be to ask where he wanted to go and say you hadn't the petrol. Apparently, however, this man wasn't going far, because after an instant the driver sulkily put out a hand backwards and turned down the flag.

"Stop him!" yelled Crook. "Stop that man! You damned

fool, look at this," and into the astonished policeman's hands he thrust the astounding beard.

The policeman looked at it, looked at the man as he crashed the taxi-door to and dropped back into darkness, linked up the one with the other, like bacon-and-eggs, said Crook—and leaped forward.

"Here, you!" he bawled. "Hi, driver!"

"Get on," shouted the passenger. "I'll miss my train. I tell you. . . ."

The policeman shouted again. The driver happily turned the wheels of the cab and came to rest beside the curb. The policeman went forward. Crook put out his hand to catch Sarah's arm and found she'd gone on ahead of him.

"Good girl!" he said. In an instant they were round the corner and across the road. Crook knew too much to hail a taxi. Drivers can be questioned by the police. He dived into Westminster Underground, blessing the forethought of the L.P.T.B. that lets the trains run till midnight, slammed some coppers into an automatic machine and then he and Sarah were through the barrier and down the steps, chuckling at one another, neither aware, it appeared, for the moment of the dangers ahead, a hundredfold more powerful than those they had already faced. Luck was with Crook as usual. After about a minute an almost empty train came in. Crook was taking no chances, however, and at South Kensington he bustled them both out on to the platform and went on by tube. At Earl's Court they came up by escalator, and went round to the lock-ups where Crook kept the Scourge. All this time Sarah had been thinking and now she could answer her own question. Of course the Bearded Lady hadn't committed the murder. She and the Cat, who doubtless would be called as an alibi in an emergency, had entered the House only just in front of Crook and his companion. The real murderer had gone on ahead. The Bearded Lady was probably there to keep an eye on Crook and see he didn't get in the way at an inconvenient moment. Now, seeing Crook prepare for an all-night session, she only enquired, "Do I come with you?"

"You'd better," said Crook. "In case they bump me off or anything, you'll be a witness."

"They might, of course, bump me off, too," suggested Sarah getting into the seat alongside the driver.

"Damned careless if you let 'em do that," said Crook severely. "Still, it's not very likely. They know I usually work alone. Ho, they'll split their sides when they hear of Arthur Crook working with a jane. And anyway," he added, driving into the moonlit street, "they'll probably think I'm still locked in that mausoleum of Government."

"Who was that man you put the police on to?" Sarah enquired.

"Heaven knows," said Crook, carelessly. "And that's more than I do. Though by this time," he added, shaving a corner, "I daresay the police have got it out of him."

"He wasn't actually at the party at all, then?"

"Oh, I shouldn't think so," said Crook, in a tone that suggested that was quite enough about a necessary but anonymous cog in an intricate machine. "One thing about being a secretary —I hand it to you there," he added, after a long silence. "They do teach you to jump to it."

Sarah was so offended she didn't even reply.

"That chap" Crook went on presently, "has had the devil of a start, and it's only in books that the villain's car breaks down. In real life the Good Man—that's me—has to do all the running."

They tore through Hammersmith Broadway and made for the Great West Road. Sarah didn't ask where they were going; she supposed sooner or later Crook would tell her anything she needed to know. No one stopped them, despite their reckless pace, with the little car eating up the miles with a gluttony you'd not have expected, for the police hesitate to challenge a car not running on petrol. Sarah reflected that the man they were after wouldn't have stopped to change out of uniform. A car with a policeman at the wheel will get where a car driven by a Savile Row suit and a rakish Homburg will get stopped every dozen miles. Sure enough Sarah presently began to recognize her surroundings. They were drawing near Whipley Cross.

"So it is Raoul," she thought. "Do we just ring the bell of the Bird In Hand or go in by the window?"

It occurred to her that no one knew where they were or what their intentions had been and if, as Crook had originally surmised, they were up against a gang, there was no reason why they shouldn't disappear as efficiently and possibly as permanently as Kay Christie. Crook drove down the long quiet road that passed Maggie Robinson's cottage and, to his companion's surprise, stopped the car in a patch of black shadow. It was a still night, so still that the faint sounds in the undergrowth, the faraway jarring of an airplane engine as it floated invisibly through the sky, the whisper of some creature stirring in the ditch, sounded loud and sinister. Crook opened the door of the car and got out.

"Do you drive?" he enquired.

Sarah nodded.

"Good. Look here, we're going in, and if by any chance there should be any trouble and I don't come out, take my place and make for Lady Catherine's house. You can 'phone the police from there, it's nearer and they may not think you'll make for the Manor. Besides, Lady C. 'ull believe you without wanting chapter and verse and the police had better believe her on the same terms or she'll know the reason why. You can talk all you like about democracy," said Crook, moving in a catlike fashion towards the gate, "but when it comes to the police, they'll believe an unlikely yarn from a dame with a handle to her name more sooner than they'll believe it from you or me."

Sarah wanted to say "Is it really so dangerous?" but knowing this to be an idiotic question she crushed it down and prepared to follow Crook through the little gate. The lawyer had pulled out his pocket torch again and was examining the ground with interest. He had to stoop low and appeared to have no realization of the undignified picture he presented, squatting almost to the earth. After an instant he looked over his shoulder.

"Take a look," he said. "This may be useful later on."

Sarah stooped and saw by the light of the little torch several imprints of shoes in the light dust.

"Of course, if I was a sleuth on the films I'd have a pocket camera and a pocket receiving-set and possibly a dictaphone,"

Crook remarked, "but being just a poor yellow dog of a lawyer I haven't even got a yard-measure."

Sarah snapped open the ridiculous Squanderbug bag and took out a little folding-rule. She measured the footprint and told Crook the result; then she sketched a light outline of it on the back of her entrance card to the party, that she'd been keeping as a souvenir, putting in the little peculiarities that made that particular print different from all the other prints in the world.

"One man only," said Crook, "and—the feet only go in one direction. See where that lands us?"

"That whoever made those prints is still inside?"

"It could be," agreed Crook. "It could be. Point is, who else is there?"

He opened the gate and they went through. Sarah had that sense of the unfamiliar and therefore the perilous that all city dwellers know at night in a wide country landscape. The moon was temporarily obscured by cloud; the trees were dark towering shapes; the ducks were invisible. If they watched at all, they watched unseen. The house itself was completely black, every window blinded; a faint perfume of flowers rose from the dark beds and borders. Only the reeds rustled together, whispering in the dark. Overhead the sky arched as wide and impersonal as the world. Crook and she seemed no more significant than two blades of grass on a prairie. They passed through the reeds, stood under the little porch. The watch on Sarah's wrist said one o'clock, but Crook unhesitatingly applied his pudgy finger to the bell. There wasn't any electricity in the cottage but Mr. Stout had fixed up an electric battery. They heard the bell peal, but no one moved, no board creaked, no step advanced to admit them. Sarah felt her heart—that orderly machine—beating like a trip-hammer; she'd never before known the meaning of the phrase choked with apprehension, but she thought that if she lived to be a centenarian she'd never forget this instant. She turned her head over her shoulder expecting to see some human shape materialize by the gate, but nothing happened. Nothing at all.

"Mr. Crook," she began, but he silenced her with a hand on

her arm. He was listening intently, and she had the curious feeling that he could hear what was inaudible even to ears as sharp as her own, as though the silence that engulfed them had its own voice and he knew what it was saying. Her heart thudded louder and louder, like the throbbing of an airplane engine. Another plane went by, as aloof and self-absorbed as the first, speeding forth on its dangerous errand, guessing nothing of, caring nothing for the grim relentless drama of death and treachery at that moment being enacted 3,000 feet below.

"They're not going to open," said Crook, stepping back. He shook the door very gently, then put his hand in his pocket.

"Bolted as well as locked," he said. "We'll try the back."

Sarah followed him round the corner of the house. To her surprise he made no attempt now to deaden his footsteps.

"If he went in and didn't come out he must be there still," she whispered.

"It could be," said Crook again.

"But what else . . . ?" But she stopped there. Because once again she'd supplied the answer to her own question. Only this time it didn't seem possible that she was right.

As they drew to the turn of the wall Crook stopped. "This is zero hour," he said, drawing her back against the wall. Sarah crouched beside him, expecting she knew not what. But still nothing at all happened. It was completely anti-climax. No lean shadow darted round the corner flourishing a thin knife; no revolver-shot rang out, no hands, strong and ruthless as a gorilla's, clutched at their wind-pipes. Everything was motionless until the cloud slid away from the moon and showed them the level landscape bathed in its clear silver light.

"Come on," said Crook, and even his voice sounded more taut than usual, "either the back door's open or . . . !"

But the back door was open and they came in without encountering any opposition. And now Sarah for the first time felt real fear grip her heart. She knew why terrified people scream, why they reveal their whereabouts when it is of paramount importance that they shall remain concealed, how when success seems within their grasp they will fling it all away because their nerve fails them. She felt panic stealing over her as water gradually rises in a bowl. The interior of the cottage was pitch-black now that Crook had shut the door. She felt her ears terribly astrain for the smallest sound—for a breath, a whisper, a stealthy movement, perhaps even for the steady drip-drip of blood. And again nothing happened; still the most deathly silence reigned. She choked back a wild laugh. Deathly silence, she thought, deathly—deathly. . . . She felt Crook's big hand, hard as leather, close over hers.

"Don't you let me down, sugar," he said.

She drew a long breath, was almost afraid to draw it in the silence; let it go fearfully.

They edged forward step by step, not knowing what might be waiting for them no more than a foot ahead, what might be watching from the stairs, listening behind the close-shut door. Suddenly Crook flashed on his torch. Sarah's eyes followed its rapid beam, as it moved over walls and floor and then up the stairs.

There was no one to be seen, not even a mouse. The place might have been deserted—but there were those footprints going and never coming back. Sarah remembered that grim and ghastly masterpiece—Flannan's Isle.

> We seemed to stand for an endless while,
> Though still no word was said.

"Come on," said Crook, and opened the living-room door. He pushed in first and when he saw what was inside he would have kept her in the hall, but she was too quick for him. Her eyes took in the horror at their feet, but before the deathly sickness that threatened to overwhelm her had done its work, she felt a big rough arm come round her waist, while a common voice said, "Twice in one evening. It's a bit thick. I ought to have warned you."

"Who is it?" whispered Sarah. "Not . . . ?"

"Maggie Robinson. Yes. I had a sort of feeling it might be."

"But why?"

"Raoul don't like people when they know too much. Here, come outside."

But Sarah was her own mistress again now. Probably her senses were partially numbed by the series of sensations they had experienced. Later she might realize the full horror of the event. Tonight she had seen two people who had been violently killed. But a peculiar tense calmness was the unexpected result. She knew already that this mood must pass; but she knew, too, that it must not give way to the inevitable reaction until she had accomplished whatever it was that Crook demanded of her. It did not even seem strange that she, the self-reliant, should admit herself for the moment dominated by this man with whom, she'd have said, she had nothing in common. Crook, for all his scorn of psychology, knew more of human nature than she. He had known from the start that it was she, the deliberate and the cynical, and not Stout, the generous and the impulsive, who could help him best at this crisis.

"You've got to be damned careful from now on," said Crook.

"Yes," Sarah agreed. "I think, I think I understand. You mean I've joined the class of people who know too much. All the same what did Maggie Robinson know?"

He flung her an odd glance. "I fancy she had a very good idea who killed Tom Robinson, and I should say she would be pretty certain who killed Darell. She was clever but not quite clever enough. A cleverer woman would have realized hers was bound to be the next death." He looked down at the body again. "Strangled," he said. "It's as good a way as any. No weapon needed, you see, and everyone has hands."

Sarah shivered. "It must have been horrible—unless she was expecting it. Only—she let him in, whoever he was, didn't she?"

"Looks like it," Crook agreed. "Anything else strike you?"

Sarah looked down again. After all, she'd seen uglier sights in the blitz.

"She generally wore earrings, didn't she?" she said.

Crook looked pleased. "Good girl! You do use your eyes."

"Her ears are pierced," Sarah explained. "Besides, the lobes have that rather dragged appearance you notice in women who wear rather heavy earrings. Mr. Crook."

"Well?"

"I've just remembered. Those footprints—all going one way. . . ."

"Yes," agreed her companion. "We'd better find out about that."

There was nowhere in the room where a man could hide, so they came back to the hall. As he drew the door to Crook's sharp eyes saw something else. He stooped.

"Nothing like signing your masterpieces," he observed in a dry voice. He held out what he'd found. It was a trampled muddy gardenia.

Chapter XVII

"IF YOU'D RATHER stay down here," he said, as they reached the foot of the stairs, "you're welcome. Then if you hear any rough stuff going on overhead you could bolt for it."

But though Sarah was doing her best to be brave she wasn't brave enough to be left alone in that house of horror. And though she faced the possibility—remote though it appeared—that there was yet another body upstairs, she clung to Crook like a human leech as he made his quick uncannily-quiet way up the steep little staircase. It was so steep that she instinctively put out her hand for the rope that was stapled to the wall. The stairs were old and discreet; no creaking boards here betrayed their advent. But Sarah had wit enough to realize that similarly they would screen a would-be murderer waiting at the stairhead. Crook's torch, however, revealed a small bare landing and two closed doors. Crook opened the one on the left and Sarah saw they were in Maggie's bedrom. Everything was simple, rather old, though no one would reap a fortune from the sale of those homely furnishings. A china toilet set painted with roses stood on an old-fashioned black stand, there was a big bed, two chairs, a cupboard, a patch-work rug. The curtains had been painstakingly lined with scraps of varied material. It was the room of a careful and thrifty woman. It didn't fit with the diamond earrings.

Crook looked around appraisingly. "No rough business here," he remarked. "Whatever he wanted wasn't in this room."

"You think the motive was robbery?" Sarah sounded surprised.

"I didn't say so. But—what happened to all that money? You remember Maggie said she knew there was something in the wind because Tom had so much money. Well, he didn't leave it in a bank and he didn't leave it in a Post Office, because I've enquired. And he didn't invest it in War Savings Certificates. Besides, there are the earrings. I know something about stones. They cost quite a nice little bit."

He walked across to the cupboard and opened one of the small drawers. Inside he found a little case.

"They're there all right," he said, opening the lid for Sarah to see the stones. "So robbery wasn't the idea."

"Perhaps her husband gave her the money to keep," suggested Sarah. "She was a foreigner, or partly so, and they haven't the same feeling about banks as we have."

"And if you knew as much about banks as I do you might applaud their common sense," said Crook, a little nettled by the unconscious superiority of her voice. Women of her kind always spoke as though they were first cousins to the Almighty, and yet half the time a mouse could put them out of countenance. But he remembered that she'd had a trying evening, so he closed the drawer again and crossed the passage. The second room surprised them by being in pitch darkness. It surprised them because the one they had just left had the curtains drawn back and the shutters were unfastened. Crook's little torch came into play again and showed a scene of considerable disorder. There was a bed against the wall, and the clothes on it were rumpled as though someone very restless had lain there. There was a cup and a plate on a wooden ladderback chair. Crook went over to the windows. The apple-green shutters were not only in place; they had been carefully screwed down.

"That's odd," murmured Sarah, inadequately.

"Only just beginning to filter through that this is a damned odd case altogether?" demanded Crook, with what seemed to her unnecessary rudeness. Then she remembered that he, too, had had a trying evening and she held her peace.

In one corner of the room was a long cupboard painted applegreen and Crook next approached this, opening it gingerly as though he feared what he might find dangling from the hooks within. But there were only some suits belonging to the late Tom Robinson, a raincoat and a gas-mask in a blue waterproof cover hanging there. Crook felt rapidly through the pockets of the clothes, frowned, pushed the gas-mask out of his way, paused, took the box from its place and snapped open the fastener. It was a cheap sort of cover, selling for a few pence at a time when it was *de regle* to carry masks. Inside the cover was the usual cardboard container marked L. but inside the container there was only some paper. Crook and Sarah both stood looking at it an instant in silence.

"So that's where all the money went," said Crook. "I thought the box was damned light."

"There's a small fortune there," Sarah muttered.

"And no one to inherit it. That's a bit of luck for the State."

"Do you know where it came from?" asked Sarah, risking a second rebuff.

"Not all of it," acknowledged Crook, "though I could make a dam' good guess. But some of these notes were drawn out of the bank by Hugh Lindsay and given to Miss Christie."

"So she was in it?" Unromantic Sarah felt a throb of acute disappointment.

"Oh, she was in it all right. Look at that bed. See those cords. What do you think they were there for?"

Sarah looked, feeling horror prick her skin. Some thin stout cord was attached to the bed-frame a number of places. It had been cut through with a knife very recently, too recently for any fraying to have taken place.

"Do you mean *she* . . . ?"

"Come on," said Crook, "we've got some telephoning to do!" He hustled down the stairs again. He seemed, oddly enough, to find some stimulation in the thought that he and she might provide the next excitement for the coroner. Sarah decided she was, after all, a mid-Victorian at heart. She might enjoy Wild Western stories and mystery films, but once she was personally involved in an ugly cycle of crime she wanted nothing but Jane Austen and a tortoise shell cat for company round a safe fireside. Anyone could have corpses, cops and Crooks, for her.

Crook paused at the door and looked round once again as if he expected a serpent to push its head through one of the roses on the flowered wall.

"It is like a film," she heard herself say.

Crook scowled. "Trouble with you addicts is that you imagine the things you see on the pictures never happened before. Can't you understand they're nothing but photographs of what's already happened somewhere else."

Sarah let that pass. "Do you think then it was Kay Christie who was tied to that bed?"

"Well, she was the only one, so far as we know, who's disappeared."

"And Maggie knew? They had some hold over Maggie."

"Maggie knew a lot. And—yes, they had some hold over her. But not so much as she had over them. You know, people talk a lot of hifalutin stuff about the beauty of knowledge, but you take it from me, if you want to stay the right side of the churchyard wall never know anything. You may be glad to remember that yourself one of these days."

Sarah thought that more than likely. She also thought a more tactful man might have refrained from mentioning it at that particular juncture.

"Do we ring the police?" she asked as they made their way down the stairs. If she had ever imagined herself playing a part in a murder mystery she would certainly have seen herself calling the police at once, but Crook broke all the accepted rules and substituted his own so naturally that you found yourself accepting them even if you couldn't see an inch in front of your face.

"All in good time," said Crook. "We've got to do everything in the right order. I daresay you don't know so much about the police as I do. Logic's their middle name. Motive don't worry them, and if they find you and me and a corpse and a bunch of money in an empty house, they'll put two and two together and make it five hundred and ninety-six."

Sarah, who was becoming accustomed to her companion's verbal extravagances, said, "Meaning they'll think we might have had a hand in it? But why?"

"I've told you, you don't have to prove a motive under British law. Of course, if you can throw one in for a makeweight it all helps, but they get along quite nicely without it. What we've got to show is that someone else was here. And though a gardenia petal might satisfy you and me, the police will point out—logic again—that we were both at the party tonight and could have taken a dozen gardenias off some of the gentlemen present without their noticing it. Now, the first thing for us to do is to find out whether Raoul's back at the Bird In Hand. That should be simple."

"Should it?" murmured Sarah, thinking that he could make a fortune holding correspondence classes for Members of Parliament, who found it hard enough to deal with their constituents and one another, let alone bodies in empty houses and gas-mask containers stuffed with wanted notes.

"Of course. We'll just ring up and ask."

"Do you suppose they'll tell you?"

"They'll tell me all right," returned Crook, "even if they don't know they're doing it."

The telephone was in the parlor where the body of the murdered woman lay. Crook opened the door and went in. Sarah followed rather gingerly.

"Good thing she had a deep voice," said Crook unshipping the telephone.

"It was characteristic of the man that he knew the number of the Bird In Hand without having to consult a directory, characteristic, too, that he was convinced he'd get an answer though the time was now one a.m.

It was equally obvious that no one was expecting the call. The operator said sleepily, "No reply" but Crook said, "Ring again. It's a matter of life and death."

The operator who, like the man at the other end of the wire, seemed beyond surprise, did what he was bid. This time he was more successful. A feminine voice said, "Who's that?"

Crook spoke suddenly in a voice Sarah didn't know. "Hargreaves?" he enquired.

Sarah heard a sudden intake of breath at the other end of the wire. She could hear a female voice squeaking.

"Who is it?"

"Mrs. Robinson. Tell Raoul to be careful. Someone has talked. The girl has gone."

The voice at the other end of the line jabbered shrilly.

"I can tell you nothing," said Crook in the same assumed tones. "I was out. You knew that? But of course. Raoul? But he should have been back. Unless something has happened to him also."

Something clicked in Sarah's brain. She began to feel like the child, Alice, when the playing-cards began to rain on face and shoulders and hair.

She saw Crook replace the receiver. "They're coming right along. Raoul hasn't turned up. Hullo, you look all in."

"I'm beginning to put two and two together," said Sarah. "Where is Raoul?"

"That's one of the things we've got to find out. And find out pretty damn quick, before they know we're on the track. One thing," his brow wrinkled like corrugated cardboard, "she must be more useful to them alive than dead or they'd have put her out before now."

"Who answered the telephone?" enquired Sarah.

"The blonde—Sadie, Maudie, whatever her name is."

"And—she's coming over now?"

"They're coming over."

"They? Who's the second one?"

"That's one of the things we're going to stay and find out. This," he added warningly, "is where the thickish part of the evening begins. It's been plain sailing up to now."

"Plain sailing? A man's been killed in the House of Commons and a woman's been brutally murdered here—and you talk about plain sailing?"

"What I mean is motive and all that's obvious. Why do you suppose I said Hargreaves just now?"

"I suppose it's a code word of some sort."

"Quite right. Well, how d'you imagine Maggie Robinson knew it?"

"She'd heard her husband use it. We don't know that she knew. . . ."

"Happen to notice that Maudie wasn't one little bit surprised at gettin' a message from Maggie Robinson?"

"It would save a lot of time," said Sarah with some heat, "if you told me what all this is about. I suppose you mean that Maggie Robinson was in it—Maggie Robinson." She paused for a moment; Crook watched her alertly without speaking. "It doesn't make sense," she confessed. "It was Maggie's husband . . ."

"You're like all these spinsters," said Crook, without offence. "You think marriage is something like the Kingdom of Heaven. Husbands and wives make just as good enemies as next-door-neighbors. Never read a history of crime? Never heard of Crippen or Armstrong or Buck Ruxton? To say nothing of all the cases that never come to light."

"And you've known—how long?"

"I had my suspicions from the first," Crook confessed. "That day I broke in here, that Sunday, and she knew at once who I was, sayin' Stout had told her I'd be payin' her a little visit. And then I saw Stout and he said he'd been meanin' to warn her about me and somehow he'd forgotten. Well, that was queer, but there was something queerer still. Think a minute. Someone was makin' a whale of a lot of money in a hole-and-corner way. Maggie said it was Tom, but if so, how was it he owed something at a pub and never seemed to have a bob to bless himself with? Besides, fellows like Tom don't buy their wives diamond earrings. He'd have known she couldn't wear 'em here. He might have bought her some fal-lal but not that. But suppose part of your payment came in diamond earrings? That 'ud mean something to a woman. And, of course, there was the carbon."

"I don't think I know about the carbon," murmured Sarah.

"There was a typewritten message found in Lindsay's room making a date at the Bird In Hand on the night Tom was killed. And when I was last here there was a single carbon used out of a box of 100 with very much the same message on it. But—why take a copy of a damn' dangerous message like that? And who had the copy? Besides—why didn't the police find that carbon? And wasn't it pretty queer just one carbon out of a hundred? Why should he choose a new one just for that."

"It's not proof," said Sarah, hardly recognizing her own voice.

"But this is," said Crook, and he sounded as grim as the Particular Judgment. "I told you the messages were very much the same. But if they'd been typed simultaneously they'd have been exactly the same. Well, you're a lady secretary. You know that."

"Of course," Sarah agreed.

"Well," said Crook simply, "they weren't. The paper they found in Lindsay's room said" (he took a slip of paper and a pencil from his pocket and scribbled the message down for her):

> Hargreaves. Bird In Hand. Nine
> o'clock tonight. Stage set. Terms
> satsifactory.

Then he said, "See anything queer about that?"

"The S and the I are transposed in "Satisfactory," remarked Sarah.

"Exactly. I suppose that's a thing a careless typist working in a hurry under strain might easily do."

"Quite easily," agreed Sarah in slightly forbidding tones.

"Well," said Crook, "on the carbon the word was spelled right. How does that add up to you?"

Crook elaborated the point. "Anyone making a fake carbon would be very careful not to make a mistake," he said, "but if you hadn't got the message with you you'd not remember that typing bloomer. Anyway, I daresay she never noticed it."

"You mean, she sent the original message? Tom had nothing to do with it."

"You're getting warm," Crook approved.

"And—how did the paper get into Lindsay's room? Did she . . . ?"

"She went up to see him at the airfield after Tom's death—remember? A clever woman like Maggie Robinson, who's been throwing dust all this time in the eyes of a Member of Parliament —fancy!—and even more in the eyes of his lady mother who's forgotten more common sense than her son will ever possess—

would make short work of palming a piece of paper where it 'ud do most harm."

"And that slip is going to prove the vital clew?"

"I don't depend on vital clews," said Crook. "I like as much as I can get as strong as I can get it. All the same, it's the little things that matter in the end." He hauled out his great turnip watch and picked up the receiver again.

"Get me police," he commanded. When he was connected he said, "There's been a murder at Myrtle Cottage. You'd better come right away," and he rang off before anyone could ask any questions.

"We'll get cracking," he said, with a final glance round to make sure they had disturbed nothing and had left no trace of their intrusion. They went out the back way as they had come.

"We haven't much time to spare," remarked Crook cheerfully. "We don't want them to know we're here."

"Are we getting out?" Sarah enquired.

She was surprised that her voice should sound so decently casual.

"Not very far," Crook assured her. "Here, help me shove the car back a bit."

Shoulders to wheel they got her into a patch of yet denser shadow, and on Crook's instructions concealed themselves behind her.

A wind had sprung up, rustling the leaves quite horribly, so that even to the unimaginative Sarah it was as though ghostly feet were creeping up behind them. Once she barely suppressed a scream as something cool touched the nape of her neck. It took an instant to realize it was only a wet leaf.

"I've just thought of something," she exclaimed suddenly. "Why didn't we find any footsteps leaving the Cottage?"

"Old trick," said Crook. "Fellow walked backwards, and I'd say he was carrying something heavy."

A gleam of light appeared very low on the ground quite close to them. Sarah shrank a little closer to her companion, one warning hand on his arm. Crook glanced in the direction she indicated, flashed on his torch and there was a quick, stealthy movement and more rustling, as a great tortoise-shell-colored cat, who had been out hunting, slid into the darkness.

"Good luck!" muttered Crook. "Well, it's what we want ourselves."

The cold seemed eating into Sarah's vitals. It all seemed unreal, and yet her common sense told her it was as real as anything that had ever happened. It is difficult even for the perfect secretary to assimilate two murders in one evening, with the prospect of more ahead. For the first time since she left the House of Commons she thought of Mr. Stout, probably wanting her to make notes for him, since he'd surely want to send an account to his papers—and she wouldn't be there to oblige.

Thoughts began slipping crazily through her head. She had applied for the post of private secretary to a Member of Parliament and she had been prepared, she thought, for an elastic program, but it hadn't included murder (possibly one's own), crouching behind a hidden car waiting for the criminals to arrive or whatever might be going to follow.

Crook's hand suddenly closed on her arm. "Here they come!" he said. "Now, if you don't want to make the third of the corpses that lay out on the shining sands, keep down."

Sarah needed no such injunction. The little dark car coming up the road slid into the shadow of the bank and two people emerged. It was difficult to see very much, except that one was plump and the other a slender fellow. Both wore trousers.

There was something uncanny about the way those two moved. Without a word being spoken, flitting like shadows, with apparently no more substance than shadows, they approached the gate. It opened noiselessly; and they were through and lost almost at once in the black immensity of night. A muffled sound warned the listeners that the front door was being attacked.

"They'll think it's fishy if she doesn't come," whispered Sarah.

Crook said nothing. He was like some squat hideous idol, with an idol's immobility. After a number of efforts the newcomers went round the corner of the house. A rift in the clouds that had closed again showed their indistinct shapes, though the light was too faltering to disclose their identity. The two in the hedge waited. Time seemed to stretch like a piece of elastic, longer and longer. Presently surely it would snap with an explosion like a revolver shot. Crook pulled out his big watch again; the figures were outlined in luminous paint.

"Damn those police!" he said heartily. "Do they keep Trade Union hours too?"

Sarah had been smitten by a similar doubt. Both realized that the two in the cottage would not remain long with their grim discovery. The brilliant simplicity of the notion Crook had had—of decanting the police on to the scene of the crime with two of the gang also on the premises—promised to fizzle out like a damp squib. Crook began to ease himself out of the bushes and long grass.

"I'm going in," he said. "We can't take any more chances. Give me ten minutes. If I haven't appeared and they haven't at the end of that time, go hell-for-leather for the police. In any case, get the number of their car."

"Will they be able to learn much from that?" wondered Sarah.

"Only the name of the chap who licensed her," returned Crook dryly. "It might be a help. And anyway it's up to them to earn their bread and skilly, though, come to that, we're giving 'em butter *and* jam, and what Lord Woolton would say about that wouldn't be passed by the B.B.C. So long."

"Won't they have guns or something?" asked Sarah quickly, surprised at the gush of almost maternal tenderness she felt for the absurd creature who had inveigled her into this most unenviable situation. It wasn't just fear for her own safety that made her wish Mr. Crook wasn't going to push his obstinate bull head into the noose.

"Thrice is he armed that hath his quarrel just," Mr. Crook reminded her. "Here," he pushed his watch into her hands, "you might want that. Besides, it'll be a passport for you. One of these days," he added managing to look more like a shadow that you'd have thought possible for a man of his bulk, "they'll put that with the Crown Jewels I shouldn't wonder. So take care of it. Remember, you hold history in your hands."

The next instant he simply wasn't there. Sarah felt as she

supposed a widow might feel waking to an empty bed. It wasn't a nice feeling, but it didn't occur to her she had any choice of action. Crook had said, "Get the number of that car, and if anything happens to me get in touch with the police." He hadn't used any more emphasis than Mr. Stout when he said, "Ring up the Board of Trade and ask them what they're doing in the case of X.Y.Z." and though it might be simpler to unship the telephone and ask for the Minister's secretary than to go round the country after dark foiling villains, one thing equaled another apparently when it came to the point. You remember, Crook had said, this is your chance to keep British justice alive. And in spite of the mockery of his tone when he said it (they were waiting then for the car with the gang in it to come like a spirit of evil speeding through the night) she'd got a sense of an undercurrent of feeling as strong as a wind. While she had concentrated on the two dead people he'd been thinking of all those young men who had been killed by treachery. There was no need for him to say so (and wild horses wouldn't have got it out of him) but Sarah knew it was so. It occurred to her that he'd have made a good theologian if his tastes had happened to lie that way. He got down to bedrock and stayed there, like a diver on the ocean floor. As conscientious people will read a dull book to the last word for no better reason than that they have begun it, and mean people will sit through to the last line of a play they don't enjoy simply because they've paid for the tickets, so Sarah intended to see this adventure out, even though it might involve a short cut to the cemetery.

The slow minutes ticked away. She toyed with the idea that the police car had been tampered with, that a number of stout blueclad corpses strewed the road from Whipley Cross to the cottage, or, in a way worse still, that they had taken the S.O.S. for a joke. She waited six minutes by Crook's watch, then stole out of her hiding-place. The cottage was in pitchy darkness. There might be four corpses there instead of one; and indeed, she thought, it was quite on the cards there were two, and the living couple were busily disposing of their prey.

Moving as though the very shadows had life and might pounce upon her, for in so eerie an atmosphere anything was possible, she reached the little black car. She dared not switch on the torch, lest she attract attention from the wrong quarter, but with her fingers she felt round the outlines of the letters and figures and committed the result to memory. ARCS. 425. That was easy enough to remember. ARCS. A Really Curious Situation. 425. Her own age, 42 years and 5 months. She was about to steal back to the little red car, prepared for pursuit if need be, when she was aware that someone was moving not far away. There was the sound of a door closing. Probably it was closed with some care, but to her ears it was as startling as a revolver shot. A torch shone. Madness, thought Sarah, but it seemed proof that Crook's famous luck had failed him at last, and they couldn't be expected to know that he had left a second-in-command outside—the merest cabin boy, no doubt, but nevertheless, a creature trained to take orders, no matter how absurd they might seem to the lay mind, to keep watch and wait and use its discretion and do what it was told and not count risks or rely on anything as banal as common sense and self-preservation. Guarding the convoy, thought Sarah. And then as the feet came nearer it occurred to her she was in an uncommonly awkward situation. Because she was practically certainly to be found out—there wasn't much cover here—and people as thorough-going as Raoul and his friends weren't likely to stop short of a third or possibly fourth murder in one night. She might explain till she was blue in the face, but most likely they'd prefer their own explanation, which would certainly be nearer the truth and in the end she might easily be blue in the face. It was an undignified way to end one's life, she who liked neatness and formality. She stifled a natural and quite unworthy desire to scamper off like a rabbit and leave Crook and the girl and the country generally to take a chance and acting on impulse she put out her hand and tried the rear door of the car. The handle turned, the door swung open. A moment later she was crouched in great discomfort and no dignity at all in the back of the killers' car.

Chapter XVIII

THERE WAS, fortunately, a rug beneath which she could conceal herself. If the new arrivals were suspicious and looked under the rug they could drive a knife between her shoulder-blades in less time than it would take her to turn her head, but she reminded herself that life's a risky business at best and in peace time there are Green Line coaches and mad dogs and in war-time there are air-raids and sausages that ought never to have slipped past the Ministry of Food, and one danger's as great as another—and in any case no one thought of looking under the rug. Indeed, her invisible companion seemed as eager as she was to get away from the place. Sarah's only trouble was that she wanted to go in the opposite direction. She was surprised to realize that though two people had left the car only one returned to it. She had visions of Crook and the other unknown locked Laocoon-like in a death struggle on the dark floor of Myrtle Cottage, but even if she'd wanted to get out then it was too late, because the driver had slipped in the clutch and they were moving away into the dark.

"I hope someone gets this story straight," reflected Sarah, the perfect secretary, as they went round a curve into the Unknown. "Then perhaps we'll hear a little less talk of the lack of enterprise of Members of Parliament. For what could be more enterprising than getting involved in a series of murders and leaving the outcome to the underlings who'll never be missed so long as there's a Ministry of Labor functioning in Merrie England. She thought of Mr. Stout again, badgered by inconvenient questions. At crucial moments he always turned over tiresome visitors and silly letters to his secretary, saying,

"You can deal with this lot. I want to try and get in on this Debate (or it might be, I've got a question down, starred, and I must be there). If he couldn't at all times deal with constituents and correspondence, how much more deadly are the incomparable British police?

The car went on and on. Sarah had no notion of the road they were taking, and she was afraid to move, though she was uncomfortably cramped, in case she let the driver suspect that he was carrying a stowaway. She did ask herself, common sense winning the battle with loyalty, what she thought she could do when the car did stop, but remembered the famous adage about not crossing bridges till you come to them and exerted all her energies to conquering an overwhelming desire to sneeze. And conquer it she did, by the will-power that had brought Mr. Stout so often to his metaphorical knees. Presently the car began to slow down. Sarah dared not lift her head to look out of the window, but by parting the rug a cautious inch she saw that the moon had re-emerged. She couldn't imagine why they were stopping. They didn't seem to have reached a town or any human habitation.

The night seemed deathly still. They might have been on some desert island with a sea of darkness lapping all around them. As soon as the car stopped the driver jumped out, leaving the door swinging. He made for the side of the road. Sarah peered cautiously after him. She saw that his objective was one of those yellow-painted telephone booths that belong to the R.A.C., and the stranger was unlocking the door. At once she realized that here was her opportunity to discover her destination. Clearly X. had to get in touch with Headquarters (presumably Raoul) and equally obviously Raoul wasn't altogether aware of some unexpected change of plan. She told herself sensibly that if she was destined to join the number of corpses in this case it was useless to kick against the pricks, but at least she could be killed doing something useful. Carefully she worked at the door of the car, disentangled herself from the rug and crept out on to the road. The driver had disappeared inside the box but had left the door open. He wasn't taking any chances. At the first alarm he'd leap back into the car and swoop off into the night. Sarah, her heart pounding, crept a little nearer to the box, nearer still, near enough to hear what was being said.

It was clear that the speaker was having difficulty in obtaining his connection.

"Stoneford two-four," he said in the exasperated tone kept for repetition of a number when time is the essence of the situation. "How much?"

There was a brief pause while he fumbled for the requisite coins. Sarah had half a minute in which to make up her mind as to her best course of action. Surely her best plan would be to wait until he had gone and then try to get in touch with the police. It would be easier if she had some idea where she was and how far away the nearest Police Station. There was also the reflection that by the time she had warned the police that a vague murder was probably going to be committed and that someone whose telephone number was Stoneford two-four was involved, and they had verified the information, it would be too late to do anything. She recalled the long delay there had been in the arrival of the police at Maggie Robinson's cottage. But what finally decided her was the reflection that though she hadn't much chance in any case, she had no chance at all if she stayed where she was, because she hadn't dared shut the door of the car, and the driver would know car-doors don't open themselves.

He had got through at last and was speaking loudly enough for her to make out what he said.

"This damned line!" he exclaimed. And then, "Winter here."

A pang went through Sarah like a knife. Winter! Kay's friend, Hugh Lindsay's friend, a man they'd all trusted. . . . It didn't seem possible. "Something's gone wrong," she heard him say. "The police are at the cottage. What the devil happened?"

It was only possible, of course, to guess at the other half of the conversation.

"Well, of course she was dangerous. I told you that from the start. But did you have to murder her? And if you did couldn't you have contrived it on the way down instead of in her own house?"

Sarah experienced another shock. Of course. Everything was falling into place now. Maggie had been at the pageant. Maggie had dropped the red button. Sarah remembered that she and Crook had come in just behind—behind the Bearded Lady. So that was the significance of the pierced ears and the absence of rings. Crook, of course, had recognized that. Nothing much escaped him. Maggie had been there to distract Crook's attention, if necessary, while Raoul disposed of the main enemy. She came back from her momentary reverie to hear Winter say, "No, I tell you it won't be safe to wait till morning. If we can't get the information out of the girl we must do without it. I'll be down in less than an hour."

The other voice was apparently still talking, but Sarah didn't dare wait. She couldn't risk being left behind, still less being discovered. She stole back to the car, shut the door without a sound and returned to the dubious refuge of the rug. She was only just in time. An instant later a door closed and footsteps came in her direction. The driver got in, slammed his door and they went off again at a fine pace. Sarah felt a mingling of emotions, the sum total of which was peculiarly joyless. It wasn't only that she was probably going to be killed in some ig-nominious and quite disgusting fashion, she was going to be made to look an unmitigated fool when she was discovered and while, as anyone who has been through a big blitz can assure you, violent death can be taken in one's stride, being made an object of ridicule is quite another matter.

She knew that if she had been the heroine of a film she would have known nothing but a selfless exaltation. Film heroines are never afraid. She wouldn't have seen death as something ugly and undistinguished and accompanied by every circumstance of beastliness; she'd have experienced a noble joy in the thought that she might be the chosen weapon to save a young girl. But then the heroine of a film would never be forty-two, and even if she were she would know perfectly well that in spite of all the odds and the loaded dice, she was going to come out on top, uncover a Nazi plot, win her country's gratitude and get either an offer to appear at the Chiswick Empire or the M.B.E. In real life things didn't happen that way.

She was listening hopefully for any sound of passing traffic or footsteps ringing on a pavement. She even played with the idea of smashing the window and shouting for assistance. But again, life and the films didn't coincide. On the pictures the passer-by (always assuming that a spinster past her fortieth birthday was allowed to occupy the limelight at all) would be a dashing and distinguished bachelor, the faint gray streaking the thick dark hair, who would instantly understand the position and would take charge. But in real life they'd merely think she was lit up, and if they—or he—spoke to her at all it would simply be to tell her she ought to be ashamed of herself in a world at war—and a woman of her age was old enough to know better. She knew all the phrases that would roll off the ready tongue. She had done notes for Mr. Stout's speeches too often not to have them all by heart.

2.

She felt suddenly that she was going to sleep. It was incredible, and she was tempted to blame the beer with which Mr. Crook had so generously plied her, no doubt putting the expense down to his client's account. She fought against the impulse. Sleep would be fatal. One might move unconsciously, one might even—though nobody believed this about themselves—even snore. Very cautiously she moved; instantly something chinked faintly. at once she was rigid; it hadn't been much of a sound but to her attentive ear it was as sudden as a chime of bells. The driver, however, was immersed in his own thoughts. He heard nothing.

"I do begin to have bloody thoughts," reflected Sarah, who was apt to go Shakespearian in a crisis. It was odd to realize that if she came through this ordeal the probability was that ten years hence she'd be a neat, stereotyped spinster living in a small flat, watering the tomato plants on the window-sill, putting down moth-balls, checking the telephone account. Life went by so fast, so remorselessly, rolling along, incidents becoming absorbed in the whole, even the sensational ones disappearing like bumps under a garden-roller. She contrived a glimpse at Crook's watch and saw that it was fifty minutes since that nightmare conversation in the telephone box. If Winter had been speaking the truth they were near their destination by now. Now her heart began to race again, her nerves were as twisted as railway lines after the night raiders have been over. She told herself sternly that she could panic as much as she liked afterwards, but now there was more to be considered than her own safety or even the girl's. It wasn't the personal issue that mattered in a crisis; one had to see the larger plan. . . . And that came out of one of Mr. Stout's speeches, too.

The car took a turn to the right and stopped almost immediately in front of a large house screened with trees. Sarah waited for the driver to get down, but he remained where he was. Evidently someone had been watching out for him, for an instant later footsteps could be heard and then a voice speaking English with a slight accent said, "Here is a nice surprise for you. Your friend," there was unmistakable emphasis on the last word, "is going to take you for a pleasant drive. You will like some fresh air, I think."

A girl's voice, obviously laboring under almost unbearable strain, said with a pathetic attempt at jauntiness, "I never want to find myself under a roof again."

The man laughed. A shudder of terror ran through the unseen listener. It wasn't merely that the man who laughed was ruthless; he was enjoying the situation, the opportunity it afforded him to show how ruthless he could be.

"That is an unwise thing to say," he warned her. "Suppose the gods were to overhear. Or do you really mean you never really wish to find yourself under a roof again?"

"What are you going to do with me?" asked the girl. They might have done their utmost, but they hadn't broken her. Perhaps there's something in the human spirit you can't break.

"We will ask your friend here." The gate creaked as it swung open. The man in the driving seat struck a lighter to kindle a cigarette. The little flame showed his face, thin, hawklike, as hard as a stone. There was a moment's breathless silence. Then:

"But, Charles—oh, Charles, it's you. I don't understand."

"Charles will explain to you as you go," said the soft, foreign voice. "But come—we have not much time. It will soon be morning."

"Not much time? But—oh, why? I love the morning."

(Sarah remembered Crook's description of the girl. Like something new, he'd said. And you couldn't call him a sentimental man.)

"That is a pity," said Raoul's voice. Just that. No more. It was a pity. He didn't say why. But if the girl didn't know Sarah did. And was afraid, not for herself any more, but in case her courage wasn't up to scratch. You couldn't tell till your hour was upon you.

Charles Winter extinguished the lighter. "Get in," he said, briefly.

The girl seemed to be overcoming her fear. "Shall I sit beside you, Charles?"

"Yes, yes," thought Sarah. But she wasn't really afraid, because it was much safer for Charles to have the girl beside him under his eye. He'd know that.

"Yes, come in beside me." Charles Winter leaned across and opened the door. The girl got in.

"You will be careful," said Raoul, and Charles said, I'll be careful." Sarah noted that he locked the door after the girl had got in.

For a few minutes after they had driven away no one spoke. Then to Sarah's horror a new sound broke the quiet of the night —the sound of desperate, tearless sobbing. It tore at a heart that she had thought remarkably well-armored. Winter might have been an automaton. He paid no attention whatsoever. After about three minutes the sounds died away.

"I'm sorry, Charles," whispered the young voice. "Awful of me to give way like that. I got frightened, thinking you'd all forgotten. It was such a long time—days and days. I lost count. Raoul said people would think I'd gone away of my own accord. He said you wouldn't be looking for me. He spoke almost— almost as if you were an accomplice."

Winter turned the car round a sharp corner and they sped on. You could tell the pace they were going by the rush of the wind past them. "You worked it very cleverly," continued the

211

girl. "You—quite took him in. But I suppose you're good at that sort of thing—aren't you, Charles. You have to keep a poker face—don't you, Charles? Charles, why don't you say something?"

"I shouldn't talk," Winter advised her in a hard voice. "It doesn't help."

"I only want you to know how thankful I am to be with you, to be safe at last, when I thought I'd done with safety for ever. You knew what he was like, didn't you? You never really trusted him. I ought to have listened to you earlier."

Winter sighed impatiently. Sarah got the impression that his nerves, too, were affected by the events of the evening. He had a job ahead and he wanted to get it over with. It didn't occur to him to waver, but it was asking too much to expect that he would enjoy it. Still, he wouldn't want to prolong the agony. Besides, he wasn't so safe himself as he'd have liked. Men in his job never are.

"You don't know what they did to me at the cottage to make me speak," whispered Kay. "What they threatened to do if I made a sound." She was silent a moment, battling with those terrible memories. "I'd never guessed that in England—I suppose now I know a bit of what concentration camps are like."

Sarah felt sick. What had they done? It didn't do any good to probe too deep, not at this moment. There are so many things two people without conscience can do to an unprotected girl. "And they tricked me so easily," the restless voice went on. "When I got a telephone message telling me there'd been an accident and I must come at once, it never occurred to me it didn't come from you. And that man who met me with a car and said he'd drive me down—of course, I ought to have suspected. Honest people don't have all that petrol."

"I've told you, there's no sense talking," said Winter roughly.

"It's so lovely to be able to talk, when for weeks every word has been so—expensive. I've been so afraid—you don't know— It wasn't only me—truly it wasn't—I thought of you and Hugh and all the others. He'd have let Hugh die, too. You don't know what Raoul is, not even you, Charles."

"I know exactly what he is." Winter's voice was as iron as his name. "You can't blame him."

"Not blame him?" Her voice was unsteady with surprise.

"He's a patriot."

She laughed, for the moment on the verge of hysteria. "That proves you don't know. Why, he's in enemy pay. All the stories he told me were lies. All the people I helped him to get over here with English money, using English names—they were all our enemies. In a way, I'm a traitor, too, plotting with the enemy, that's what I've been doing. They shoot traitors, don't they? Or do they hang them?"

"Be quiet," said Winter savagely. "To hear you talk one would think there was only one nation in the world. You can't expect Raoul to see this thing from your point of view. Other countries have their patriots, too. Raoul wasn't an Englishman, and he plotted and risked his life for his country just as Lindsay chanced his life for his—only that wasn't so dangerous, and he might have got a medal. There are no medals for people like Raoul."

"But, Charles," her voice was normal now but stark with amazement. "You're defending him. You speak as if you sympathized with him!"

"I'm simply pointing out that the English are such fools they never believe—there's more than one country can produce heroes."

"You think of Raoul—like that?"

"If he'd been a British Secret Service man that's what you'd say."

"And you knew about him all the time, and—did you know what was going on at the airfield? Did you know, when those 'planes went up, the crews were going to certain death? But you couldn't, because if you had. . . ."

Winter moved impatiently. "Women's arguments," he said. "Can't you understand? In a war personalities don't exist, nothing matters but the cause. Everyone's subservient to that. They're only valuable in relation to it. When they cease to be of use, then they're—eliminated. Because they become a source of danger. They know too much, you see. Raoul knows that.

He knows he takes his life in his hands. One day it'll be his turn. He knows that, too."

"I believe I'm beginning to understand," whispered the girl. But she didn't believe it. There are some things you can't believe.

"You should have kept out from the start," said the man, harshly. "If you come into a war you take the same chances as men. Sex, personality, nothing counts. Money doesn't count, honor doesn't count, your own family doesn't count. Nothing counts but that you shall win. What sacrifices are involved, you have to win. That's the essence of war."

"I do see," whispered Kay. "I see now you've been tricking me all the time. You were hand in glove with Raoul. A traitor, too. And I thought you were my friend. But, of course, people like you don't have friends."

"No," agreed Winter. "Only civilians can afford luxuries like that."

"Any more than you have honor—or chivalry. All the time when you seemed so interested, when you seemed to care, it was never really me, only because I had information that might be useful. And I didn't guess."

"You work in your uncle's factory," agreed Winter. "You know things we need to know. You could help us if you like."

"Help you? I?"

"Someone will tell us in the end. It might as well be you. Listen. I'll make a bargain with you. You've seen the designs of the new machine, haven't you? I happen to know Sir Alan showed them to you. You're working in that Department."

"You mean, if I tell you what you want to know, you'll give me money?" Even now she didn't seem able to accept the implications of the peril in which she was.

"Not money. Your life."

Now at last she understood. The brutality of the words stamped their meaning on her horrified mind. She began to speak urgently, not panicstricken, but not displaying that noble calm shown by the true heroine in the face of imminent and deliberate death.

"Charles, I can't really believe this is happening. It's a joke, isn't it? Only it's rather a horrible one. You didn't fetch me away from that house to—to . . . I mean, why not let Raoul. . . . Oh, but I must be mad. Things like that don't happen, not in England."

.Charles Winter drove doggedly on. There was no suggestion that he was torn by some frightful inner conflict; he wasn't struggling with his own better nature or with a love that duty commanded him to ignore. He wasn't tormented by the anguish of making an appalling decision. To him the issue was perfectly clear. He was the fanatic, *pur et simple,* the type that it is so difficult for the English to understand, since they breed so few of them.

"Did you mean what you said just now?" Kay, urged with a horrible sense that in a moment she might whimper for her life.

"Those are my terms. It's no use arguing or thinking you can make me change my mind. I've told you already people don't matter in a war, you don't matter, or I, or Raoul or Lindsay—no one person matters. Only the cause."

Sarah groaned. The groan was due partly to a sense of helplessness, because you can fight Goliath if you have to, but you can't fight a mad beast, because it's beyond reason, and partly due to sheer physical wretchedness. She ached in every muscle, her eyes burned, her heart was choking her. She thought of this plan and that and discarded them all, because this was one of those situations where a single false step meant death for them both. It was, of course, quite on the cards that any sort of step meant death for them both, but she resolved with a savage satisfaction that at least she'd see to it they took Charles Winter with them.

"I couldn't do it, of course," said Kay in a dead, dreadful voice. "That new plane may be the turning-point of the war."

"It can't make any difference," exclaimed Winter in a voice of mingled contempt and excitement. "The Allies are going to lose the war in any case. If we have these plans we shall win a little sooner, and a few less of your people will be killed. That's all. It won't affect the final issue. Nothing can affect that."

"And even if I did what you ask," continued the girl, as if he hadn't spoken, "you wouldn't keep your word. As soon as

215

you had the information you'd get rid of me. You'd have to. I should be—a danger, too."

"I am glad you see that," said Charles Winter.

Silence came down again, stifling as the rug that was smothering Sarah in the back of the car. They seemed to be rushing through an empty world. Perhaps they passed houses, or even ran through towns but, if so, not a stir of life penetrated the darkness.

After a long time the girl spoke again. "What—are you—going—to do with me?" she asked.

Winter had no reply for that. On and on they sped. The silence seemed to drive Kay frantic—or perhaps the depths of her own peril was only just making itself known. Flinging out her hand she tore at the catch of the door beside her.

"There's no sense doing that," said the driver. "It's locked."

She lifted her clenched fist and began to beat on the glass window.

"It's unbreakable glass," Charles warned her. "It's no good. You should have kept out of this from the first. You admitted yourself you're too—dangerous—to be allowed to go on. I've no choice. Surely you can see that."

"They'll trace the car," stammered Kay.

"They won't find the car," returned Charles Winter. "Not in a recognizable state."

"You mean, you're going to—Charles, what are you going to do? You're going to burn it, and I—and I—"

"Be quiet," said the man. "Nothing can change things now. You've said it yourself. You know much too much."

"I can't really believe it, even now. You're taking me away —to kill me. I've danced with you and had drinks with you, and even shown you Father's letters. And now you're taking me for a ride—that's what they say in America, isn't it? Taking a man for a ride means . . ."

"If you don't shut up I'll gag you," said Winter, savagely.

It seemed to Sarah, who liked to boast that she at least wasn't sentimental, that she would never forgive this night for being so wide, so tranquil, so utterly untouched by the horror and fear that enfolded them. The imperturbability of the world, its complete indifference to their peril, made her feel almost as frantic as the girl in the front of the car. She lay there, tense as a violin string, hands clenched, brain aflame, convinced now that such slender chance as remained to them, depended on her—her courage, her wisdom, her quickness of hand and brain. And yet any movement of hers might be too late. Winter might draw a revolver and shoot—he wouldn't need more than one bullet. If she, Sarah, was even a little clumsy and he suspected her presence here, he wouldn't hesitate; only he would need two bullets instead of one. Then, as Kay Christie had suggested, he could fire the car and make his own getaway. He was clever enough to have fixed some alibi. Probably the blonde, Maudie, would give evidence to cover his absence over the essential time. In books, of course, the criminal was always caught red-handed. In books it was easier. There was a loophole, because the writer knew that virtue had got to triumph. "I suppose" thought Sarah, the thoughts wheeling in her head like birds that are never for an instant still, "people like that sort of book because it's so unlike real life. They feel virtue ought to triumph, and it's so often defeated. They get a sort of compensation out of reading stories where evil is confounded."

She was about to make a last desperate move when the car suddenly jerked itself to a standstill in a deep patch of shadow cast by a bunch of tall trees.

"Is it now?" asked the girl, and there was a shriller note in her voice. It was no use, reflected Sarah, pretending you weren't afraid when you were in desperate danger. You were afraid to your very soul.

"Be still," repeated the young man. "Do you *want* to be gagged?"

Sarah listened intently. This was zero hour. In an instant they'd be going over the top. All the old phrases she'd heard as a schoolgirl in the last war poured through her mind. Then—like a miracle, like light flooding into a darkened mind, came reprieve. A sound had reached her ears sweeter than any angel's chorus. Along the dark road ahead a procession of vehicles was moving to a new destination under cover of night. Sarah heard the noise, could hazard its nature. In any case, the position was now so desperate she dared not let this opportunity slip. The same notion had occurred to the girl. She threw back her head, opened her mouth to scream—but no sound came forth, because Charles Winter, realizing her intention, took his hands off the wheel, covered her lips, at the same time crushing down her head into the curve of his arm.

"You would, would you?" And now there was naked murder in his voice. "Be still, you fool. It's too late to do anything."

Rising like a cautious Jack-in-the-Box from her enveloping rug Sarah put up a ruffled head. The procession of Service vehicles rumbled on, unconscious of the little dark car so close at hand. The girl in front gave a convulsive choke and Sarah realized that she was being strangled to death down there in the dark. Gathering the ends of the rug, she flung it over the man's head, pulling it closer and closer, so that he could scarcely breathe. Instinctively he eased his grip on the girl, struggled to free himself.

"Scream!" muttered Sarah, furiously. "Scream, you little fool!"

Kay Christie seemed to recover her wits. She shrieked, bloodcurdling cries that split the calm night. The cars ahead moved on—on. The men inside them might have thought it no more than an owl hunting through the night. Sarah, struggling with the infuriated man, let out a roar that would have delighted Crook, who was a living exponent of the maxim that if a thing is worth doing it is worth doing well. Kay Christie, leaning over the pair, caught the wheel. The car staggered drunkenly into the middle of the road. Sarah screamed again.

"Murder!" The bitter cry split the tranquil night. There was a jolting noise and a vehicle came to a standstill. Voices rose.

"What on earth . . . ?"

A second voice, scornful and bored, said clearly, "Blasted tarts getting tight. That's what the chaps get drowned for, bringing petrol to take blasted tarts on the bend."

"Take care!" shouted Sarah, making her voice heard above the struggling, the ferocious objurgations, the sound of motor engines. "He's armed." She spoke to the girl. "Feel in his pockets —quick!"

She could not much longer restrain her captive, and she had wit enough to realize that once his fingers closed over the gun he carried even the military convoy might be too late to save them.

It was no easy task to find the pocket of a fiercely contorted man being smothered in a rug, in the confines of a small car, but Kay did it. She found the weapon and slammed it through the wind-screen.

Sarah found herself thinking, "So it wasn't unbreakable glass after all!"

Then everything seemed to happen at once. Men were round the car, someone was asking questions, Kay was speaking with the tears pouring down her face, Winter had struggled free and was saying, "You damned fools! Getting drunk and . . ." Even now he made an effort to save the situation.

"What is this?" demanded a military policeman. "A free-for-all?"

"Murder," said Sarah succinctly.

The policeman said, "Oh, yes? Where? In the car?"

"In a place called Myrtle Cottage near Whipley Cross. Oh, and another at the House of Commons."

"You have been having a night of it," commented the policeman admiringly.

Another voice broke in. "Blimey!" it said. "Praps this is the car they told us to look out for. What's the number?"

"ARCS. 425," said Sarah quickly.

"Here, d'you make a profession of this?" demanded the policeman.

"And it'll be no thanks to you if there isn't another murder in about five seconds," interrupted Sarah. She caught Winter's wrist as his hand flew to his pocket. "Do you know who you've got here?"

"We'll attend to all that," said the police, becoming immensely competent. "We had word to look out for this car."

Sarah thought a minute. "Mr. Crook?" she enquired.

"You know him?"

"I found both the bodies in his company," explained Sarah, rather ambiguously.

219

"Finding bodies is Mr. Crook's idea of a Bank Holiday," said the policeman.

"And you might," said Sarah who, as a political secretary, was accustomed to sorting grain and chaff and keeping a steady hand on the clerical reins, "get in touch with Stoneford two-four, while you're about it. Unless, of course, you've contacted them already."

The car doors were open now and they were all out in the road.

"Who's Stoneford two-four?" asked the authority.

Sarah turned to Kay. "It was Raoul, wasn't it?"

Kay nodded. She was still too much shaken by her narrow escape from a horrible death to be surprised at Sarah's appearance on the scene.

"Yes. But I don't know the address of the house or where it is. They took me by night."

"You'd only just arrived, hadn't you? You were at Myrtle Cottage."

"Yes," said Kay meekly.

"You'd better get her under cover as soon as you can," said Sarah. "She's had a bad time."

"You'd better come with us," said the policeman to Winter.

He didn't put up any fight. Perhaps he had his own way out and was waiting for a chance to use it. He didn't seem to have any feeling about Sarah either. He was oblivious to personalities. It wouldn't have haunted his sleep if he'd killed Kay and disposed of the body. He wouldn't have cared if he'd had to add Sarah to the funeral pyre. He was mad, of course, as all fanatics are mad. You couldn't even admire his courage. He seemed too little human for so warm a quality.

Sarah and Kay got back into the car, and a man in uniform took the wheel. Sarah felt vaguely disappointed to experience no sense of exultation, no relief even, and certainly none of the nobility you come to expect after hearing other people's deeds of prowess. She was mainly aware that her hair was tumbled, there was a ladder in one stocking and her hands wanted washing. She realized, too, when she began to sort impressions in her own mind, that no one was in the least likely to believe her fantastic tale. It wouldn't even be accepted in the House of Commons. But then she remembered that Crook would back her up and her apprehension vanished like dew in sunlight. He might look like a large healthy pig wearing a brown suit, you could be scornful of his English and wonder how it was no one had ever broken him of wearing that unspeakable brown billycock, but there was no doubt about it, you felt the Allies had more chance of winning the war quickly when he came in. He bred confidence, because he was himself incapable of defeat. He wasn't Billy Brown of London Town, and he wouldn't have felt flattered if anyone had suggested that he might be, but the improbable became worthy of consideration and the fantastic became credible as soon as you mentioned his name. She couldn't help wishing he could be in Parliament for just one session.

She grinned to herself. "Nice if we could put him in charge of one of the Ministries, for choice the one whose middle name is Not-this-war, partner" she thought. "Just for six months. Only six months."

It did seem a pity, when Mr. Bevin was calling up all available man-power, that he should overlook such a potential source of national wealth as Mr. Arthur Crook.

Kay here interrupted her musings by fainting, slumping down beside her, heavier than you would think so slight a creature could be. Sarah, who had retained her hold on Squanderbug bag all this while, found smelling-salts and applied them, but felt on the whole it was as well that the girl should remain unconscious. Her thoughts couldn't be either pleasant or amusing.

Then she gave herself up to admiration of Mr. Crook. How he had discovered the number of the car she didn't know, but it was typical, not merely that he should put a message through to the authorities, but that a military convoy should choose to take the road that would intercept the criminals—even typical, she reflected, with a wry smile, that he should have Sarah Bennett in his pocket to lend a hand at the critical moment.

She thought sleepily, "Crook for Confidence" and then mysteriously her eyes closed and she drowsed off. Nature, she reflected as consciousness left her, was more unpredictable than even Mr. Crook.

Chapter XIX

"WHEN SHE OPENED her eyes the next morning to the walls of the unfamiliar room she could not at first remember where she was; and when recollection returned to her it seemed as though the happenings of the past night were no more than some appalling dream."

Sarah had often read such words as these in what Crook inelegantly called the bughouse literature beloved of women, and had wondered if all heroines were as addle-headed as they would lead you to suppose. In any case, if that was true it was one more screw in the coffin of any suggestion that she belonged to that class. Certainly the room was unfamiliar, but that was normal enough, seeing that she was in the local lock-up, where a sympathetic policeman had found her a stretcher for what remained of the night, but she hadn't any doubts at all about what had happened. She remembered the awakening as the car stopped, the difficulty of persuading Kay, who had just recovered consciousness, to get out, the powerfulness of the drink a policeman had provided from the medical stores, her blessed sense of comfort at the thought that someone else had taken over command and she could sleep. You'd think that leadership and responsibility were as much to be envied as the possession of the Victoria Cross, but when you'd been the leader and had the responsibility you knew better. Most writers of adventure stories probably lived in West Kensington or in the more amiable Cathedral towns. She heard a familiar voice outside the door.

"No blooming hurry," it said. There was no mistaking those buoyant Cockney tones. "These young women may be able to take this sort of thing in their stride, but the ones who're getting' on. . . ."

"Do come in, Mr. Crook," called Sarah, and the door opened and he marched in. He looked as fresh as the morning, shaved as a newmown lawn and polished as an exhibition apple.

"And so you are," he said heartily, "gettin' on, I mean. Gettin' on a bit too fast for the police. It's my belief," he beamed at her, "that most policemen are descended from funeral mutes and not descended very far at that. They like to take things at five miles an hour. It takes civilians like you and me to get things goin'."

"I was never more pleased to see anyone," returned Sarah, reflecting that somehow circumstances always seemed to be on Mr. Crook's side. She hadn't had a wash and brush up, and she knew too little about poilce station ethics to know whether she could ask for such facilities. "I think I ought to ring up Mr. Stout."

"Have a heart," protested Crook, feeling for the watch he didn't have. "It's not much after eight. Besides, he may be in chokey for all you know."

"For not getting murdered? The prisons are going to be pretty full at that rate." But she agreed that he probably wouldn't be conscious in the Parliamentary sense of the word at this time of day. Then she asked after Kay.

"Give her time. She'll get over it. They'll all get over it, except the ones who're dated for the little shed—and of course those they've accounted for already."

"Maggie Robinson?"

"And Tom and Mr. Darell and a few more. Still, they've run their course and finished their fight. Thanks to you," he added casually.

"I only carried on," murmured Sarah.

"Neat work getting that 'phone number. The police—God bless 'em!—would never have discovered that rats' nest."

"It was Raoul?"

"And the rest. Oh, it was all very neatly done. Nursing-home for nervous cases. Doctors, nurses, all the bundle. Most of 'em with fake passports, practically all of 'em not born in England.

223

Of course, now and again even in the best-run nursing-home patients die. In a home for nerves it's even possible for a patient to commit suicide—you know, fall out of a window or something of that sort."

"Don't you have to get a licence for a ursing-home?" asked Sarah.

"I've told you all along, sugar, we were up against chaps with brains. That's where the authorities were at a disadvantage. You understand."

He grinned and impulsively Sarah grinned back. But she sobered again a minute later.

"It was a good idea."

"It was a damn good idea. It's been runnin' for some time. Still, the next person who wants to get into that nursin'-home will find it's been commandeered by the military. There are a few things about a war. Everythin' belongs to the military these days—your house, your wife, your money. . . . It don't suit the Powers-that-Be that too much should get into the newspapers, though Members of Parliament mightn't understand that. It's much easier to have the house taken over—less talk. You know. It was a shock to Raoul, too. He didn't expect the police in the small hours. Got him red-handed."

"Just like the pictures," exploded Sarah.

"Not quite like the pictures. They'd have been caught by a chap in uniform and a lovely girl if it had been the pictures. You and me, sugar, we don't fit the bill."

"I ought to say Thank You," murmured Sarah. "You saved my life, didn't you? Both our lives, come to that."

Crook waved a gracious paw. "Just part of the Arthur Crook service," he said. "Not but how you wouldn't have made out yourself anyway. Nice bit of work getting that chap. He and Raoul between them had rigged a very nice case against Lindsay."

"Nice bit of work getting the number of the car," suggested Sarah. "So that's why Raoul wanted the £400."

"That wasn't difficult, not once I knew who it belonged to. They were like two cross-talk comedians. And I knew that the minute I set eyes on that fellow's ugly mug in the cottage."

"What happened at the cottage?" asked Sarah.

Crook at once looked conspiratorial. He was loving this. Death—violent death—didn't seem to bother him. He took it all in his stride.

"I went in at the back and found our beauties there. Very put out they were about the body, very put out indeed. Of course, they knew something was wrong when they found Maggie was dead."

"Did they go on thinking she had telephoned?" asked Sarah.

"They couldn't be sure. The blonde was against it. 'It's a trick,' she said. 'Any minute the police'll come sailing out of the sideboard.' 'We should worry,' said the other chap, 'seeing we've only just arrived.' 'Very pretty,' said Maudie, 'but if you've got an alibi for the rest of the night, I haven't. That flummoxed him a bit. He said they must get on to Raoul, and since it was obvious he'd come back from London, there was only one place where he could be. That's where I strained my eardrums but it didn't get me anywhere. She said, 'Yes, we must let him know, but he won't be there yet.' Then she spoke of the girl. 'I wonder who found out she was here,' she said. Winter suggested Maggie might have sold the pass, or threatened to. She had her head on her shoulders had young Mrs. Robinson. She could have put up a very pretty story about never guessing Raoul and Co. had it in for Tom, and now she'd found out and Hell hath no fury and all the rest of it. I imagine Raoul found her too expensive even for his purse."

"I suppose," said Sarah slowly, "you knew all the time she was the Bearded Lady?"

"Caught sight of her ears. The beard didn't cover the lobes, y'see, and I could see they'd been pierced. Mind you, that only told me it was a woman, but—she'd put herself on the wrong side of the fence with me before that. I told you about it."

"Yes," said Sarah. "Was it a surprise to you to find Winter was involved?"

"I wasn't sure," Crook acknowledged. "Still, he'd made one slip. When I was looking for the girl he said she'd told him she was going to the house in Hampstead, a sudden S.O.S., and that's why she couldn't meet him as arranged. But I happened to know that she never thought of goin' to the place until she realized she was bein' followed and got the wind up. So how did Winter know? I couldn't find more than one answer to that, and if you can find another I—I'll eat my hat."

"I suppose you mean the spy, the man who was tracking her, let Winter—or Raoul—know at the same time as he warned them you were coming down."

Crook was a little disappointed, but he concealed it manfully and drove on to his next point.

"Just so. It was a pity for Winter he made that slip. If only these chaps would remember some of the things they learnt at mother's knee—the tongue is a little member but it is set on fire of hell—they'd be a lot more careful and they'd get into a lot less trouble."

"You were bound to get him in the end," Sarah pointed out, placidly.

Crook experienced a spasm of sympathy for the absent Mr. Stout, but, more long-sighted than the Member, he forbore to argue.

"Comin' back to our muttons," he said, "our bright pair talked it over, and it was agreed that Winter should go hell-for-leather for Raoul's hideaway, and, if he got a chance, get a phone message through to say he was coming. They didn't dare try from the cottage, because the police might check up on the calls. There's no automatic system at Whipley Cross."

"And in any case, the odds are he wouldn't have reached his destination by that time," contributed Sarah.

"You know all the answers," agreed Mr. Crook. "I didn't want to be found on the premises—not by Maudie—so I just acted like Brer Rabbit. I lay low and said nuffin. She went up-stairs to the room where the girl had been. Wanted to get rid of all traces of her, see. She'd promised to do that before Winter went. She was unscrewin' the shutters when I heard the police car arrive and I went down to meet them. I don't say they were pleased to see me—not an emotional lot, the police, as you may have noticed—but I will hand it to them they didn't waste much time. One of them just walked up the stairs and asked the lady very nicely what she thought she was doing. Well, even you. . . ." His red-brown eyes glared at the intrepid Sarah, "might have found it difficult to answer that one."

"One of the question that don't need an answer," Sarah agreed. "Did she say anything?"

"Nothing I'd like to repeat," said Mr. Crook modestly. "Anyhow they took her away and then I told them to find out the number of Winter's car and send out a message."

"Do tell me something," said Sarah. "Did you know I should be in it?"

"Well, you weren't in mine, and you weren't waitin', with notebook and pencil, to take down the story in shorthand, so I knew you were with Winter or somewhere in the ditch. And we couldn't find you in the ditch, so I guessed you were in the car. What I couldn't be so sure about was whether you were likely to be any use backin' up my story." And he sketched an unmistakable gesture across his throat. "Ear to ear" he amplified. "Though, as a matter of fact, the jugular vein ain't where most people seem to think. I've know chaps. . . ." He fell into a momentary reverie. "Gobbets of gore," he said suddenly, "and all because they never went to a First Aid Class and learnt something about anatomy."

"Why did they keep Kay Christie at the cottage?" Sarah wanted to know, showing a deplorable lack of interest in Mr. Crook's bloodthirsty reminiscences. "Why didn't they take her to the nursing-home at once? Wouldn't it have been safer?"

"You know what they say—three people can't keep a secret —and there were a lot more than three at Stoneford. Besides, they could keep her quiet all right—they have ways you wouldn't guess—and there wasn't a hope of that iron-faced woman breaking down. She's the kind would watch you on the rack and adjust the screws for the fun of the thing. There was always that someone at the Home who might suddenly become a bit human—and Raoul wasn't taking any more chances than he had to."

"She hadn't talked, had she? Did he mean to go on till. . . ?"

"Oh, he was counting on breaking her in time. He knew all the answers, remember."

"And why," continued Sarah, tabulating her questions neatly, "could you be so sure that Maggie Robinson had been to London this evening?"

"Think a minute," Crook counseled her. "What time was she murdered? She was still warm when we found her. And it was one o'clock in the morning, but Maggie Robinson was fully dressed! Well, I ask you. If someone wakes you by chucking gravel at your window you slip on a dressing-gown and maybe one of those lace caps and bows ladies wear—if they do wear them still—but you don't stop and put all your clothes on, down to shoes and stockings, just to be murdered. After all, they don't go in for much night life here. Well, what's there to stay up for? The pubs. shut about ten. Even the Bird in Hand shuts at eleven."

"I wonder why he killed her—because I suppose you're sure it was Raoul?"

"Another thing," continued Crook, "her room wasn't even blacked-out. That showed she wasn't here this evening. Hullo, here come the police. Don't let them rattle you, sugar, and remember, your legal adviser's on the premises if you want to call on him. Well, what's worrying you?"

"I'd like to ring up Mr. Stout," said Sarah. "He won't know where I am."

"That won't do him any harm for once. Let him get on with his own letters."

"He won't have collected them," explained Miss Bennett, patiently. "He never does. And there's a meeting of the All England Democrats this afternoon, and he promised to attend just to prove he doesn't see eye to eye with them."

The policeman said that when she'd made her statement she might ring the gentleman up on the police 'phone.

"Be sure to remind him to fasten his suspenders, won't you?" added Mr. Crook kindly. "If you don't, he might get his picture in the papers yet."

The authorities took down Sarah's statement without batting an eyelid. To watch the stolid face of the man who interrogated her you might suppose this sort of thing happened every day of the week. She asked, a little apprehensively, if she'd have to give evidence at the trial, and the policeman said it all depended. He said, "Take my tip and don't go opening your mouth too wide to these newspaper chaps. What they'd make of a few plain facts 'ud surprise Lord Woolton."

Then Sarah put through her call to Mr. Stout, who said peevishly, "What on earth happened to you last night? I looked everywhere. . . ."

Sarah said apologetically she'd been with Mr. Crook.

Mr. Stout's silence said it wasn't Mr. Crook who'd bought her ticket, and asked where she was speaking from. When Sarah told him he said virtuously, "Well. I'll be damned! I suppose I ought to have warned you, though. But I thought you'd size Crook up for yourself." Again his voice said more than his words. You don't pay a secretary a handsome salary to go out night-hawking with a chap like a bookie's tout while your employer's being harried and hunted by the police force, it said.

"I can't help feeling it's a pity they didn't get the right chap last night," said Mr. Crook on the way to town. Sarah had reduced Mr. Stout's speech to shorthand but Crook read it all right.

"You mean instead of Mr. Darell? Oh, no!"

She didn't put the thought into words, but she felt it would have been a reflection on her efficiency as a secretary if he had been murdered under her eyes, as it were.

"You might have taken his place," explained Mr. Crook. "They want a few live wires in the House."

"I'm hardly qualified," returned Miss Bennett primly.

Crook closed one eye. "You're telling me, girlie. Matter of fact, if all the old buffers who're in at present are Trade Union politicians, then I'm all for a bit of unskilled labor. I've sometimes thought," he went on chattily, "that when I'm past earnin' a living, I might stand for some nice quiet constituency myself. Something ultra-respectable, where they'll feel it's quite a feather in their cap to have a chap like me."

"What time do you think we shall get to London?" asked Sarah. "Mr. Stout's got a constituent coming to see him at eleven. A very hard case for deferment of call-up. The man's a butcher, and if his claim's rejected all the people in his neighborhood will have to go an extra three miles for their meat." Her brow creased. In an ideal world Ministry of Food authorities would have to qualify for their positions by standing in carrot queues, going far afield with baskets and bits of newspaper to plead humbly for offal and cats' heads, and make appetizing dishes out of the various peelings and parings so warmly recommended as "tasty supper fare" by the B.B.C. and the advertisement columns of the newspapers. It was a little odd that when Ministers gave official dinners they never went to British Restaurants or Help Yourself Bars in teashops; but reflection told her that they wouldn't think that fair. The cheap eating-places are wanted by the small fry with inconsiderable incomes, like Member's secretaries and temporary Government servants. Naturally, the Big Bugs have to go to the Grand Court and The Gladiators. If they didn't the proprietors might have to go into munition factories.

Crook looked at her and then looked away. It wasn't any good. She was like all women—fickle, unstable, full of vanity, light upon the weights. It was a good thing he hadn't made her any sort of offer. You could never trust a jane. Never.

The car sped on towards London.

Chapter XX

IT HAS BEEN said that Mr. Darell was quite unknown in life. Even to the majority of his constituents he was less than a name. Since his maiden speech he had never attempted to impress his views on his colleagues or the country generally. His papers—he had two—were never asked to spare valuable space reporting a bit of snappy back-answering at Question time, initiated by their political representative. If he did manage to get a question past the Clerk at the Table on to the paper the answer always came back:

> I would refer my hon. Friend to the reply I gave to the Member for West Molesley on the 14th of last month.
> I regret that I can see no grounds for altering my decision.

And he wasn't quick enough or optimistic enough to ask a Supplementary on the spur of the moment. No one appeared to know if he was married or what he had done besides make his meek appearances in the House. Indeed, for all his leonine appearance he was the sort of man you can pass on the stairs and swear you've seen no one.

But after his death people woke for the first time to a realization of his previous existence.

Mr. Stout dared the world of clichés by remarking that nothing so became his life as the leaving of it.

"And he's done himself a damn good turn by leaving it," he would add indignantly.

For Mr. Stout was having a bad time. He was inundated

231

by correspondence. Women from every part of the country wrote offering to be his secretary; a few proposed matrimony; and more, who couldn't by any stretch of imagination feel themselves suitable either as secretary or wife—either on account of a complete lack of qualifications or some tiresome obstacle like a husband—asked for his autograph. They sent dreadful little books with Autographs stamped in gold on wadded green and red and blue covers; or they sent post-cards, stamped and addressed to themselves—and there are very few people with sufficient courage to throw away an unused stamp or to employ it for a purpose other than that for which it was intended. Mr. Stout laid in a stock of small cards and Sarah spent an afternoon with a Quotation Dictionary finding suitable sentiments that she copied as well as she could in what constituents would believe to be Mr. Stout's own hand. Mr. Stout said it was perfectly all right. Lord Tennyson's wife had done the same.

The pleasantest letters, he found, were those that praised him extravagantly for his prowess. These he answered himself. (He threw all his matrimonial offers into the baskets and passed on the would-be secretaries to the Central Conservative Office.) Like Byron he woke to find himself famous. People even tried to move into his constituency, so that they could have him for their Member, regardless of the fact (a) that his was a forbidden area and (b) that even if it hadn't been you had to pay as much for a bird's-nest there as you would for a suite in a London hotel, because of the airfield. Sweethearts and wives packed all the available space and paid whatever was demanded. He was even cheered when he walked into the Chamber, a compliment hitherto reserved for the Prime Minister.

Oh, no two questions about it. He was having jam morning, noon and night. After Raoul and Winter and their confederates —mostly men in mufti who had been smuggled into the airfield in the guise of civilian mechanics—had been executed, and Lindsay and Kay Christie announced their engagement, his picture appeared in the paper alongside theirs, with a caption "M.P. Unites Lovers." Even hard-headed business men, who were accustomed to refer rudely to the House of Commons as the Headquarters of the Gas Company, were impressed by a chap who could persuade someone else to impersonate him at a party and get murdered in his stead. A useful sort of fellow to have on Boards, they decided. He was asked to speak on the B.B.C., write for his local parish magazine, preside at a Wings for Victory Campaign in a rival constituency, become a Vice-President of the All-England Purity League and contribute to a symposium in that notorious magazine, *Gentlemen for Choice* whose editor was collecting opinion from notable bachelors, entitled, "The Lure of the Single Bed."

When Sarah heard that she observed crisply, "Evidently not much choice." Mr. Stout wasn't pleased. You'd might have thought she'd be glad to share his reflected glory. After all, she was his secretary. And when he told her that a world-famous photographer had offered him a free sitting, she looked positively thunderous. Just as well, he reflected, that there wasn't any milk about.

"It might please my constituents," he said in the voice of a man who lives for no grander purpose. "You know, an affair like this is an absolute eye-opener. One doesn't realize in the least just what voters do expect of their Members, not in the ordinary way, I mean. It takes a thing like this. . . ."

Sarah gaped, looking more like Sir Wilbur than anyone would have thought possible. If Mr. Stout could represent Malvoisin for five years and still not realize what constituents expect of their representative the proper place for him was what Mr. Crook inelegantly styled the bughouse. Mr. Stout rampaged through the morning's post that was as full of bouquets as a debutante's first night.

"Very heartening," he observed.

Sarah said it must be.

"One of these days I suppose they'll learn their idol's got feet of clay," said Mr. Stout, rather swept out of his depths by a lady who seemed to think him a combination of Sir Galahad, George, Lord Byron and the Archangel Gabriel.

Sarah reflected sourly it wouldn't be so bad if only they weren't such large feet. She herself hadn't come out of this as well as you might have supposed. In fact, she was about the only person whom everybody overlooked. The main difference the affair had made to her was that she worked longer hours than ever because Mr. Stout, a true parliamentarian, insisted on every one of his letters being answered individually. And those letters were the joke of the Members' Post Office. When Sarah called for them in the morning the man behind the counter would ask if she'd brought the pram and say he'd got a nice rug-strap at home he could let her have. Sarah eyed the blue and gray and white and manilla and patched-up envelopes with loathing. No one, she reflected grimly, offered her auditions on the B.B.C., free stalls for theatres or a place on the National Book Council. Crook, who could have told her that's the way things are, meaning that M.P.s, whatever their age and figure, are news and spinsters of over forty are not, was too busy proving, for the benefit of a new and highly recommended client, that though five beans normally make five there are occasions when they can make six, seven or even four and a half, to remember the existence of Miss Sarah Bennett.

And then, suddenly, even Mr. Stout had had enough. Jam is delicious, particularly the more refined variety, but there comes a moment when the stomach sickens. So it was with Mr. Stout when a lady wrote gravely suggesting that it would show a nice feeling on his part to don a crape band for the unfortunate Mr. Darell.

"A charming idea," said Sarah.

"A damned bit of hypocrisy, you mean," declaimed Mr. Stout. "I don't mourn his death. I mourn it less than anybody. I wake every morning so damn' glad they got the wrong chap I could sing all the way to the House, only the taxi-driver might think I was dotty. If I wear anything at all it ought to be a rose or some symbol of rejoicing. You know, this is beginning to get ridiculous. I must go and see some Shaw. What's on?"

Sarah told him "Pygmalion" at the Artists and "Mrs. Warren's Profession" at the Duchess of Kews. Mr. Stout plumped for the Artists.

While he was away two elderly unmarried sisters came with their autograph albums and looked at Sarah with disapproval when they heard Mr. Stout wasn't available.

"I'm his secretary," Sarah explained.

"Oh, yes," said the elder sister. "Wonderful to have such an exciting life at your age."

Sarah felt she ought to apologize for having come back alive from the field of Waterloo.

"It shows the films aren't true to life, because only young beautiful girls have romances on the films," said the other.

"Romances?" murmured Sarah.

"Working for Mr. Stout," said the first. "There's no doubt about it, this war's been a godsend to the middle-aged woman."

"One wonders," said the second, "how they'll settle down again when it's over?"

Sarah offered to fetch two of Mr. Stout's autographed cards, and gave them "Some chicken, some neck" and "Love me little, love me long." She went back to the mail and presently the policeman in the lobby called her up again to see a young man who scowled at the sight of her and said it was Mr. Stout he wanted.

Sarah said patiently, "I'm his secretary" and the young man said, "Well, it was about the Robinson affair," and Sarah said she knew something about it, had indeed been involved in it. The young man said carelessly, "Yes, I read your part. But it was Mr. Stout my paper wanted. You see, he had the lion's share of the doings, hadn't he?"

Sarah repeated slowly, "The lion's share?"

"Yes. I mean, he got the Minister to take up the case to start with. That was the first step. Then he got this chap, Crook, to take over. That was the second step, and the best bit of publicity he could have worked if he'd thought for a month. He was nearly murdered at the pageant, too, whereas you went off when the police turned up. You don't understand about a story," he added, earnestly. "It don't so much matter what you do so long as you're in the limelight when you do it. And the limelight's on the House of Commons, not on a cottage no one's ever heard of. Oh, yes, he did the lion's share of the job and of course he'll get the lion's share of whatever's going."

He didn't stay long. He said he'd come back presently. Sarah stood watching him, her lips moving.

"Bad as all that?" asked the facetious policeman on the door.
Sarah came to. "I was only thinking," she said, "how clever
lions are!"

2.

Sarah was replying to a gentleman who demanded indignantly in four pages why a country in debt to its ears should be
expected to pay a Member of Parliament six hundred pounds a
year in order to give that gentleman a chance of posturing in
the limelight, when Mr. Stout returned.

"Is this the England of Nelson, of Pitt, of Rudyard Kip-
ling?" demanded the enraged correspondent, to which the only
reply appeared to be Yes. Sarah was saying it in two paragraphs
when the Member in question burst in.

"That new fellow who's playing the Professor," he said.
"The women in the audience were wild about him, but a wart-
hog could have given him points on manners. Incredible the
sort of men women fall for. Anyone been in?"

Sarah told him about the elderly ladies and the young man.

Mr. Stout, whose sense of proportion had been restored by
a visit to his favorite dramatist, said, "I must say they needn't
all take it for granted it was jam for you. *You* had a rotten
time."

"I'd much rather it had been me than you, though," said
Sarah quickly. So she would. Without being specially conceited
she couldn't help knowing she'd made a much better show of it
than Mr. Stout would have done. "Besides," she added rather
maliciously, remembering the young man's diatribe on lions,
"you're valuable. I. . . ."

"Oh, you're valuable, too," said Mr. Stout hurriedly.

Sarah looked surprised. "Am I?"

"Of course. Didn't you know?"

Sarah shook her head. "You never gave me any idea. . . ."
Her eyes were suddenly like a gazelle's.

Mr. Stout's heart turned over. She couldn't, oh, she couldn't,
think he meant that. And yet—what else could she mean? Not
that it was possible, of course. All the same, there flashed across
his mind a vision of his mother the previous Sunday, saying,

"Nothing you can do for Miss Bennett will ever repay her for the risks she ran on your account." He'd said hardily, "I daresay she enjoyed it," and apparently she had, though not for the reasons he'd supposed. He was suddenly furiously angry. He employed a secretary to help him over stiles and out of corners, and here she was creating a worse predicament than any constituent would dare to do, and he couldn't say as he usually did, "You can deal with that one."

"You mean," he stammered, "you thought—you think—you thought—that I. . . ."

"Of course I thought of you," said Sarah. So she had, and how annoyed he'd be that she wasn't there to take down a statement for his papers, and see that it got off by the first available post. He was a single-minded man was the Member for Malvoisin.

"Oh, I can't," Mr. Stout told himself. "No one could expect it of me. I didn't ask the wretched woman to risk her life or her reputation which people tell us, probably falsely, is dearer than life." Still, the fact remained that if she hadn't, the adventure would have ended quite differently and not nearly so much to his credit.

"But I'm like Queen Elizabeth," he assured his conscience. "She said if she married anyone except her realm she'd been committing adultery or words to that effect. And I'm wedded to my constituency, which comes to the same thing." But looking at Sarah, so trim, so cool, he knew he couldn't use a word like that, however desperate his plight.

"When I first went to train at Mrs. Hulton," continued his secretary, "she told us that the essence of a good secretary was to be available in all connections at all times."

"I don't think she could quite have meant that," hazarded the luckless Mr. Stout. "You know what I am," he went on, the words saying themselves as it were, "no memory, can't spell, can't even tell the time according to my mother. . . ." (Only there are some things you can't forget unfortunately, no matter how bad your memory is, and wives are among them.) "I'm not much really," added Mr. Stout, utterly losing his head.

"You mustn't say that," said Sarah. He'd never seen her look so kind. If she'd turned into a black mamba at that instant he'd have been grateful, because not the most original cleric in the National Church could have considered uniting him in sacred bonds to a serpent. The only thing you could say was that Sarah was the first woman he'd ever met who could stand up to Lady Catherine.

He drew a deep breath. "It 'ud be jam for my mother if you married me," he said.

That was Sarah's first and only proposal. She knew it. But she didn't want a second. However felicitously phrased it would be anti-climax after that. The Potts and Owl staff, realizing with the abominable intuition of women what was in the wind had shamelessly abandoned even the pretense of work and were holding their breath, waiting for Sarah's reply. One of them stood at the telephone asking for a number that didn't exist. Another looked through one of the concertina files for a letter that had never been written; a third opened one of the windows and babbled something about the sweetest squirrel, though everyone knows squirrels never come to the House of Commons even on deputations. The other two secretaries stayed by their machines, but they had their ears on sticks for developments.

Mr. Stout knew exactly why mice stand still and let cats get them; and why rabbits are fascinated by snakes. He knew he couldn't escape, knew, too, that by tonight he'd regret his weakness most abominably, though not, probably, so much as on the endless succession of nights following the marriage.

He waited tensely. A cat on hot bricks was in clover by comparison. He thought, "She's not going to speak. She'll do something demonstrative. Or expect me to." He felt the sweat break out on his forehead.

The whole room was aware of the situation. Even the atmosphere thickened. The Potts and Owl staff were terrified in case Mr. Potts came in suddenly and spoilt the best afternoon they'd had since the day that two enraged Members started scrapping in the lobby. But Sarah knew her onions. Even Lilian Baylis would have had to admire her sense of timing. Just when it seemed noone could bear it any longer, that a hysterical shriek or giggle would rob the situation of its tremendous drama, she spoke.

238

Her voice rang in her employer's ears like a gong of gold.

"Risk losing the Spinster's Pension when I'm fifty-five?" she asked in incredulous tones. And quoted his favorite dramatist. "Not—bloody—likely."

Mr. Stout kissed her.

〉〉〉 If you've enjoyed this book and would like to discover more great vintage crime and thriller titles, as well as the most exciting crime and thriller authors writing today, visit: 〉〉〉

The Murder Room
Where Criminal Minds Meet

themurderroom.com